"REAL . . . HAIR-RAISING . . . DRAWS ON THIRTY THOUSAND YEARS OF STORYTELLING."—*poet Gary Snyder*

"LESLIE MARMON SILKO IS A BEAUTIFUL WRITER . . . Complexities are unraveled with great feeling and intelligence. The characters are wonderfully precise. So are her evocations of the landscape . . . But *Ceremony*'s greatest distinction lies in its structure . . . combining European and Indian styles of storytelling: realism and character with legend and archetype."—NEWSWEEK

"THIS NOVEL IS A MOVING, IMPORTANT EXPERIENCE!"—HARPER'S MAGAZINE

"A NOVEL OF LOFTY AMBITION . . . GIVES AMPLE WITNESS TO THE POWER OF STORYTELLING . . . I can't remember when I have read the work of a woman who writes with such ease and assurance about the lives of men."—NEW YORK REVIEW OF BOOKS

"AN EXTRAORDINARY NOVEL . . . A REAL AND REMARKABLE TALENT!"
—*N. Scott Momaday*

CEREMONY

Leslie Marmon Silko

A SIGNET BOOK
NEW AMERICAN LIBRARY
TIMES MIRROR

This book
is dedicated
to my grandmothers,
Jessie Goddard Leslie
and
Lillie Stagner Marmon,
and to my sons,
Robert William Chapman
and
Cazimir Silko

Thanks to the Rosewater Foundation-on-Ketchikan Creek, Alaska, for the artist's residence they generously provided. Thanks also to the National Endowment for the Arts and the 1974 Writing Fellowship.

John and Mei-Mei:
My love and my thanks to you
for keeping me going all this time.

Ts'its'tsi'nako, Thought-Woman,
is sitting in her room
and whatever she thinks about
appears.

She thought of her sisters,
Nau'ts'ity'i and I'tcts'ity'i,
and together they created the Universe
this world
and the four worlds below.

Thought-Woman, the spider,
named things and
as she named them
they appeared.

She is sitting in her room
thinking of a story now

I'm telling you the story
she is thinking.

Ceremony

I will tell you something about stories,
    [he said]
They aren't just entertainment.
Don't be fooled.
They are all we have, you see,
    all we have to fight off
      illness and death.

You don't have anything
if you don't have the stories.

Their evil is mighty
but it can't stand up to our stories.
So they try to destroy the stories
let the stories be confused or forgotten.
They would like that
They would be happy
Because we would be defenseless then.

He rubbed his belly.
I keep them here
    [he said]
Here, put your hand on it
See, it is moving.
There is life here
    for the people.

And in the belly of this story
the rituals and the ceremony
    are still growing.

What She Said:

The only cure
I know
is a good ceremony,
that's what she said.

Sunrise.

Tayo didn't sleep well that night. He tossed in the old iron bed, and the coiled springs kept squeaking even after he lay still again, calling up humid dreams of black night and loud voices rolling him over and over again like debris caught in a flood. Tonight the singing had come first, squeaking out of the iron bed, a man singing in Spanish, the melody of a familiar love song, two words again and again, "*Y volveré.*" Sometimes the Japanese voices came first, angry and loud, pushing the song far away, and then he could hear the shift in his dreaming, like a slight afternoon wind changing its direction, coming less and less from the south, moving into the west, and the voices would become Laguna voices, and he could hear Uncle Josiah calling to him, Josiah bringing him the fever medicine when he had been sick a long time ago. But before Josiah could come, the fever voices would drift and whirl and emerge again—Japanese soldiers shouting orders to him, suffocating damp voices that drifted out in the jungle steam, and he heard the women's voices then; they faded in and out until he was frantic because he thought the Laguna words were his mother's, but when he was about to make out the meaning of the words, the voice suddenly broke into a language he could not understand; and it was then that all the voices were drowned by the music—loud, loud music from a big juke box, its flashing red and blue lights pulling the darkness closer.

He lay there early in the morning and watched the high small window above the bed; dark gray gradually became lighter until it cast a white square on the opposite wall at dawn. He watched the room grow brighter then, as the square of light grew steadily warmer, more yellow with the climbing sun. He had not been able to sleep for a long time—for as long as all things had become tied together like colts in single file when he and Josiah had taken them to the mountain, with the halter rope of one colt tied to the tail of the colt ahead of it, and the lead colt's rope tied to the wide horn on Josiah's Mexican saddle. He could still see them now—the creamy sorrel, the bright red bay, and the gray roan—their slick summer coats reflecting the sunlight as it came up from behind the yellow mesas, shining on them, strung out behind Josiah's horse like an old-time pack train. He could get no rest as long as the memories were tangled with the present, tangled up like colored threads from old Grandma's wicker sewing basket when he was a child, and he had carried them outside to play and they had spilled out of his arms into the summer weeds and rolled away in all directions, and then he had hurried to pick them up before Auntie found him. He could feel it inside his skull—the tension of little threads being pulled and how it was with tangled things, things tied together, and as he tried to pull them apart and rewind them into their places, they snagged and tangled even more. So Tayo had to sweat through those nights when thoughts became entangled; he had to sweat to think of something that wasn't unraveled or tied in knots to the past—something that existed by itself, standing alone like a deer. And if he could hold that image of the deer in his mind long enough, his stomach might shiver less and let him sleep for a while. It worked as long as the deer was alone, as long as he could keep it a gray buck on an unrecognized hill; but if he did not hold it tight, it would spin away from him and become the deer he and Rocky had hunted. That memory would unwind into the last day when they had sat together, oiling their rifles in the jungle of some nameless Pacific island. While they used up the last of the oil in Rocky's pack, they talked about the deer that Rocky had hunted, and the corporal next to them shook his head, and kept saying he had dreamed the Japs would get them that day.

The humid air turned into sweat that had run down the corporal's face while he repeated his dream to them. That was the first time Tayo had realized that the man's skin was not much different from his own. The skin. He saw the skin of the corpses again and again, in ditches on either side of the long muddy road—skin that was stretched shiny and dark over bloated hands; even white men were darker after death. There was no difference when they were swollen and covered with flies. That had become the worst thing for Tayo: they looked too familiar even when they were alive. When the sergeant told them to kill all the Japanese soldiers lined up in front of the cave with their hands on their heads, Tayo could not pull the trigger. The fever made him shiver, and the sweat was stinging his eyes and he couldn't see clearly; in that instant he saw Josiah standing there; the face was dark from the sun, and the eyes were squinting as though he were about to smile at Tayo. So Tayo stood there, stiff with nausea, while they fired at the soldiers, and he watched his uncle fall, and he *knew* it was Josiah; and even after Rocky started shaking him by the shoulders and telling him to stop crying, it was *still* Josiah lying there. They forced medicine into Tayo's mouth, and Rocky pushed him toward the corpses and told him to look, look past the blood that was already dark like the jungle mud, with only flecks of bright red still shimmering in it. Rocky made him look at the corpse and said, "Tayo, this is a *Jap*! This is a *Jap* uniform!" And then he rolled the body over with his boot and said, "Look, Tayo, look at the face," and that was when Tayo started screaming because it wasn't a Jap, it was Josiah, eyes shrinking back into the skull and all their shining black light glazed over by death.

The sergeant had called for a medic and somebody rolled up Tayo's sleeve; they told him to sleep, and the next day they all acted as though nothing had happened. They called it battle fatigue, and they said hallucinations were common with malarial fever.

Rocky had reasoned it out with him; it was impossible for the dead man to be Josiah, because Josiah was an old Laguna man, thousands of miles from the Philippine jungles and Japanese armies. "He's probably up on some mesa right now, chopping wood," Rocky said. He smiled and shook Tayo's shoulders. "Hey, I know you're homesick. But, Tayo, we're *supposed* to be here. This is what we're supposed to do."

Tayo nodded, slapped at the insects mechanically and staring straight ahead, past the smothering dampness of the green jungle leaves. He examined the facts and logic again and again, the way Rocky had explained it to him; the facts made what he had seen an impossibility. He felt the shivering then; it began at the tips of his fingers and pulsed into his arms. He shivered because all the facts, all the reasons made no difference any more; he could hear Rocky's words, and he could follow the logic of what Rocky said, but he could not feel anything except a swelling in his belly, a great swollen grief that was pushing into his throat.

He had to keep busy; he had to keep moving so that the sinews connected behind his eyes did not slip loose and spin his eyes to the interior of his skull where the scenes waited for him. He got out of the bed quickly while he could still see the square of yellow sunshine on the wall opposite the bed, and he pulled on his jeans and the scuffed brown boots he had worn before the war, and the red plaid western shirt old Grandma gave him the day he had come home after the war.

The air outside was still cool; it smelled like night dampness, faintly of rain. He washed his face in the steel-cold water of the iron trough by the windmill. The yellow striped cat purred and wrapped herself around his legs while he combed his hair. She ran ahead of him to the goat pen and shoved her head under his left arm when he knelt down to milk the black goat. He poured milk for her in the lid of an old enamel coffeepot, and then he opened the pen and let them run, greedy for the tender green shoots of tumbleweeds pushing through the sand. The kid was almost too big to nurse any more, and it knelt by the doe and hunched down to reach the tits, butting her to make the milk come faster, wiggling its tail violently until the nanny jumped away and turned on the kid, butting it away from her. The process of weaning had gone on like this for weeks, but the nanny was more intent on weeds than the lesson, and when Tayo left them, the kid goat was back at the tits, a little more careful this time.

The sun was climbing then, and it looked small in that empty morning sky. He knew he should eat, but he wasn't hungry any more. He sat down in the kitchen, at the small square table with the remains of a white candle melted to a nub on the lid of a coffee can; he wondered how long the candle had been there, he wondered if Josiah had been the one to light it last. He thought he would cry then, thinking of Josiah and how he had been here and touched all these things, sat in this chair. So he jerked his head away from the candle, and looked at the soot around the base of the coffeepot. He wouldn't waste firewood to heat up yesterday's coffee or maybe it was day-before-yesterday's coffee. He had lost track of the days there.

The drought years had returned again, as they had after the First World War and in the twenties, when he was a child and they had to haul water to the sheep in big wooden barrels in the old wagon. The windmill near the sheep camp had gone dry, so the gray mules pulled the wagon from the springs, moving slowly so that the water would not splash over the rims. He sat close to his uncle then, on the wagon seat, above the bony gray rumps of the mules. After they had dumped water for the sheep, they went to burn the spines from the cholla and prickly pear. They stood back by the wagon and watched the cows walk up to the cactus cautiously, sneezing at the smoldering ashes. The cows were patient while the scorched green pulp cooled, and then they brought out their wide spotted tongues and ate those strange remains because the hills were barren those years and only the cactus could grow.

Now there was no wagon or wooden barrels. One of the gray mules had eaten a poison weed near Acoma, and the other one was blind; it stayed close to the windmill at the ranch, grazing on the yellow rice grass that grew in the blow sand. It walked a skinny trail, winding in blind circles from the grass to the water trough, where it dipped its mouth in the water and let the water dribble out again, rinsing its mouth four or five times a day to make sure the water was still there. The dry air shrank the wooden staves of the barrels; they pulled loose, and now the rusty steel hoops were scattered on the ground behind the corral in the crazy patterns of some flashy Kiowa hoop dancer at the Gallup Ceremonials, throwing his hoops along the ground where he would hook and flip them into the air again and they would skim over his head and shoulders down to his dancing feet, like magic. Tayo stepped inside one that was half buried in the reddish blow sand; he hooked an edge with the toe of his boot, and then he let it slip into the sand again.

The wind had blown since late February and it did not stop after April. They said it had been that way for the past six years while he was gone. And all this time they had watched the sky expectantly for the rainclouds to come. Now it was late May, and when Tayo went to the outhouse he left the door open wide, facing the dry empty hills and the light blue sky. He watched the sky over the distant Black Mountains the way Josiah had many years before, because sometimes when the rain finally came, it was from the southwest.

Jungle rain had no begining or end; it grew like foliage from the sky, branching and arching to the earth, sometimes in solid thickets entangling the islands, and, other times, in tendrils of blue mist curling out of coastal clouds. The jungle breathed an eternal green that fevered men until they dripped sweat the way rubbery jungle leaves dripped the monsoon rain. It was there that Tayo began to understand what Josiah had said. Nothing was all good or all bad either; it all depended. Jungle rain lay suspended in the air, choking their lungs as they marched; it soaked into their boots until the skin on their toes peeled away dead and wounds turned green. This was not the rain he and Josiah had prayed for, this was not the green foliage they sought out in sandy canyons as a sign of a spring. When Tayo prayed on the long muddy road to the prison camp, it was for dry air, dry as a hundred years squeezed out of yellow sand, air to dry out the oozing wounds of Rocky's leg, to let the torn flesh and broken bones breathe, to clear the sweat that filled Rocky's eyes. It was that rain which filled the tire ruts and made the mud so deep that the corporal began to slip and fall with his end of the muddy blanket that held Rocky. Tayo hated this unending rain as if it were the jungle green rain and not the miles of marching or the Japanese grenade that was killing Rocky. He would blame the rain if the Japs saw how the corporal staggered; if they saw how weak Rocky had become, and came to crush his head with the butt of a rifle, then it would be the rain and the green all around that killed him.

Tayo talked to the corporal almost incessantly, walking behind him with his end of the blanket stretcher, telling him that it wasn't much farther now, and all down hill from there. He made a story for all of them, a story to give them strength. The words of the story poured out of his mouth as if they had substance, pebbles and stone extending to hold the corporal up, to keep his knees from buckling, to keep his hands from letting go of the blanket.

The sound of the rain got louder, pounding on the leaves, splashing into the ruts; it splattered on his head, and the sound echoed inside his skull. It streamed down his face and neck like jungle flies with crawling feet. He wanted to turn loose the blanket to wipe the rain away; he wanted to let go for only a moment. But as long as the corporal was still standing, still moving, they had to keep going. Then from somewhere, within the sound of the rain falling, he could hear it approaching like a summer flash flood, the rumble still faint and distant, floodwater boiling down a narrow canyon. He could smell the foaming floodwater, stagnant and ripe with the rotting debris it carried past each village, sucking up their sewage, their waste, the dead animals. He tried to hold it back, but the wind swept down from the green coastal mountains, whipping the rain into gray waves that blinded him. The corporal fell, jerking the ends of the blanket from his hands, and he felt Rocky's foot brush past his own leg. He slid to his knees, trying to find the ends of the blanket again, and he started repeating "Goddamn, goddamn!"; it flooded out of the last warm core in his chest and echoed inside his head. He damned the rain until the words were a chant, and he sang it while he crawled through the mud to find the corporal and get him up before the Japanese saw them. He wanted the words to make a cloudless blue sky, pale with a summer sun pressing across wide and empty horizons. The words gathered inside him and gave him strength. He pulled on the corporal's arm; he lifted him to his knees and all the time he could hear his own voice praying against the rain.

It was summertime
and Iktoa'ak'o'ya-Reed Woman
was always taking a bath.
She spent all day long
sitting in the river
splashing down
the summer rain.

But her sister
Corn Woman
worked hard all day

sweating in the sun
getting sore hands
in the corn field.
Corn Woman got tired of that
she got angry
she scolded
her sister
for bathing all day long.

Iktoa'ak'o'ya-Reed Woman
went away then
she went back
to the original place
down below.

And there was no more rain then.
Everything dried up
all the plants
the corn
the beans
they all dried up
and started blowing away
in the wind.

The people and the animals
were thirsty.
They were starving.

So he had prayed the rain
away, and for the sixth year it was dry; the grass turned
yellow and it did not grow. Wherever he looked, Tayo
could see the consequences of his praying; the gray mule
grew gaunt, and the goat and kid had to wander farther
each day to find weeds or dry shrubs to eat. In the eve-

nings they waited for him, chewing their cuds by the shed door, and the mule stood by the gate with blind marble eyes. He threw them a little dusty hay and sprinkled some cracked corn over it. The nanny crowded the kid away from the corn. The mule whinnied and leaned against the sagging gates; Tayo reached into the coffee can and he held some corn under the quivering lips. When the corn was gone, the mule licked for the salt taste on his hand; the tongue was rough and wet, but it was also warm and precise across his fingers. Tayo looked at the long white hairs growing out of the lips like antennas, and he got the choking in his throat again, and he cried for all of them, and for what he had done.

For a long time he had been white smoke. He did not realize that until he left the hospital, because white smoke had no consciousness of itself. It faded into the white world of their bed sheets and walls; it was sucked away by the words of doctors who tried to talk to the invisible scattered smoke. He had seen outlines of gray steel tables, outlines of the food they pushed into his mouth, which was only an outline too, like all the outlines he saw. They saw his outline but they did not realize it was hollow inside. He walked down floors that smelled of old wax and disinfectant, watching the outlines of his feet; as he walked, the days and seasons disappeared into a twilight at the corner of his eyes, a twilight he could catch only with a sudden motion, jerking his head to one side for a glimpse of green leaves pressed against the bars on the window. He inhabited a gray winter fog on a distant elk mountain where hunters are lost indefinitely and their own bones mark the boundaries.

He stood outside the train depot in Los Angeles and felt the sunshine; he saw palm trees, the edges of their branches turning yellow, dead gray fronds scaling off, scattered over the ground, and at that moment his body had density again and the world was visible and he realized why he was there and he remembered Rocky and he started to cry. The red Spanish tile on the depot roof got blurry, but he did not move or wipe away the tears, because it had been a long time since he had cried for anyone. The smoke had been dense; visions and memories of the past did not penetrate there, and he had drifted in colors of smoke, where there was no pain, only pale, pale gray of the north wall by his bed. Their medicine drained memory out of his thin arms and replaced it with a twilight cloud behind his eyes. It was not possible to cry on the remote and foggy mountain. If they had not dressed him and led him to the car, he would still be there, drifting along the north wall, invisible in the gray twilight.

The new doctor asked him if he had ever been visible, and Tayo spoke to him softly and said that he was sorry but nobody was allowed to speak to an invisible one. But the new doctor persisted; he came each day, and his questions dissolved the edges of the fog, and his voice sounded louder every time he came. The sun was dissolving the fog, and one day Tayo heard a voice answering the doctor. The voice was saying, "He can't talk to you. He is invisible. His words are formed with an invisible tongue, they have no sound."

He reached into his mouth and felt his own tongue; it was dry and dead, the carcass of a tiny rodent.

"It is easy to remain invisible here, isn't it, Tayo?"

"It was, until you came. It was all white, all the color of the smoke, the fog."

"I am sending you home, Tayo; tomorrow you'll go on the train."

"He can't go. He cries all the time. Sometimes he vomits when he cries."

"Why does he cry, Tayo?"

"He cries because they are dead and everything is dying."

He could see the doctor clearly then, the dark thick hair growing on the backs of the doctor's hands as they reached out at him.

"Go ahead, Tayo, you can cry."

He wanted to scream at the doctor then, but the words choked him and he coughed up his own tears and tasted their salt in his mouth. He smelled the disinfectant then, the urine and the vomit, and he gagged. He raised his head from the sink in the corner of the room; he gripped both sides and he looked up at the doctor.

"Goddamn you," he said softly, "look what you have done."

There was a cardboard name tag on the handle of the suitcase he carried; he could feel it with the tips of his fingers. His name was on the tag and his serial number too. It had been a long time since he had thought about having a name.

The man at the ticket window told him it would be twenty-five minutes before the train left on track four; he pointed out the big doors to the tracks and told Tayo he could wait out there. Tayo felt weak, and the longer he walked the more his legs felt as though they might become invisible again; then the top part of his body would topple, and when his head was level with the ground he would be lost in smoke again, in the fog again. He breathed the air outside the doors and it smelled like trains, diesel oil, and creosote ties under the steel track. He leaned against the depot wall then; he was sweating, and sounds were becoming outlines again, vague and hollow in his ears, and he knew he was going to become invisible right there. It was too late to ask for help, and he waited to die the way smoke dies, drifting away in currents of air, twisting in thin swirls, fading until it exists no more. His last thought was how generous they had become, sending him to the L.A. depot alone, finally allowing him to die.

He lay on the concrete listening to the voices that surrounded him, voices that were either soft or distant. They spoke to him in English, and when he did not answer, there was a discussion and he heard the Japanese words vividly. He wasn't sure where he was any more, maybe back in the jungles again; he felt a sick sweat shiver over him like the shadow of the angel Auntie talked about. He fought to come to the surface, and he expected a rifle barrel to be shoved into his face when he opened his eyes. It was all worse than he had ever dreamed: to have drifted all those months in white smoke, only to wake up again in the prison camp. But he did not want to be invisible when he died, so he pulled himself loose, one last time.

The Japanese women were holding small children by the hands, and they were surrounded by bundles and suitcases. One of them was standing over him.

"Are you sick?" she asked.

He tried to answer her, but his throat made a coughing, gagging sound. He looked at her and tried to focus in on the others.

"We called for help," she said, bending over slightly, the hem of her flower-print dress swaying below her knees. A white man in a train uniform came. He looked at Tayo, and then he looked at the women and children.

"What happened to him?"

They shook their heads, and the woman said, "We saw him fall down as we were coming from our train." She moved away then, back to the group. She reached down and picked up a shopping bag in each hand; she looked at Tayo one more time. He raised himself up on one arm and watched them go; he felt a current of air from the movement of their skirts and feet and shopping bags. A child stared back at him, holding a hand but walking twisted around so that he could see Tayo. The little boy was wearing an Army hat that was too big for him, and when he saw Tayo looking he smiled; then the child disappeared through the wide depot doors.

The depot man helped him get up; he checked the tag on the suitcase.

"Should I call the Veterans' Hospital?"

Tayo shook his head; he was beginning to shiver all over.

"Those people," he said, pointing in the direction the women and children had gone, "I thought they locked them up."

"Oh, that was some years back. Right after Pearl Harbor. But now they've turned them all loose again. Sent them home. I don't guess you could keep up with news very well in the hospital."

"No." His voice sounded faint to him.

"You going to be all right now?"

He nodded and looked down the tracks. The depot man glanced at a gold pocket watch and walked away.

The swelling was pushing against his throat, and he leaned against the brick wall and vomited into the big garbage can. The smell of his own vomit and the rotting garbage filled his head, and he retched until his stomach heaved in frantic dry spasms. He could still see the face of the little boy, looking back at him, smiling, and he tried to vomit that image from his head because it was Rocky's smiling face from a long time before, when they were little kids together. He couldn't vomit any more, and the little face was still there, so he cried at how the world had come undone, how thousands of miles, high ocean waves and green jungles could not hold people in their place. Years and months had become weak, and people could push against them and wander back and forth in time. Maybe it had always been this way and he was only seeing it for the first time.

He sat on the bed with his back against the whitewashed wall and watched tiny crystals in the gypsum plaster as they glittered in the stream of sun from the window. He relaxed now that the goats were loose and the yellow cat had her milk. As the sun went higher and left the eastern sky, the square of sunshine on the wall grew larger and diffuse, and the bright yellow color of early morning was gone. The tiny crystals disappeared gradually, the way stars did at dawn.

He knew at some point the sunlight on the wall would

collapse into his thoughts like pale gray cobwebs, clinging to all things within him, and then his stomach would begin to convulse, and he would have to hold himself with both hands to try to hold back the tremor that grew inside. He went outside before it happened.

The wind was practicing with small gusts of hot air that fluttered the leaves on the elm tree in the yard. The wind was warming up for the afternoon, and within a few hours the sky over the valley would be dense with red dust, and along the ground the wind would catch waves of reddish sand and make them race across the dry red clay flats. The sky was hazy blue and it looked far away and uncertain, but he could remember times when he and Rocky had climbed Bone Mesa, high above the valley southwest of Mesita, and he had felt that the sky was near and that he could have touched it. He believed then that touching the sky had to do with where you were standing and how the clouds were that day. He had believed that on certain nights, when the moon rose full and wide as a corner of the sky, a person standing on the high sandstone cliff of that mesa could reach the moon. Distances and days existed in themselves then; they all had a story. They were not barriers. If a person wanted to get to the moon, there was a way; it all depended on whether you knew the directions—exactly which way to go and what to do to get there; it depended on whether you knew the story of how others before you had gone. He had believed in the stories for a long time, until the teachers at Indian school taught him not to believe in that kind of "nonsense." But they had been wrong. Josiah had been there, in the jungle; he had come. Tayo had watched him die, and he had done nothing to save him.

Tayo was sitting under the elm tree in the shade when Harley came riding up on the black burro. The burro was veering hard to the right, attempting to turn around and go in the opposite direction; Harley had the rope reins of the hackamore pulled all the way to the left, so that the burro's head was twisted around to the north, but the

19

burro's legs and body moved sideways and drifed toward the east. Harley had to stop the burro every few hundred yards to correct their direction. He swatted the burro across the rump with a black horsehair quirt, the kind the old Mexicans used to braid; dust from the burro's hide flew up around Harley. Harley saw Tayo, and he tried to guide the burro to the tree, but it ignored the direction its head was aimed and walked sideways to the water trough and stopped. It stood there with its head up and a haughty look in its eyes; it waited unil Harley was under the elm tree before it tasted the water.

"That burro sure hates you, Harley."

Harley laughed. "Nobody ever rode it before, except maybe some of the kids when my dad had it over at Casa Blanca."

"Does it buck?"

"It tries, but I think I'm too heavy for it. It doesn't jump very high." Harley was big and stocky. "My legs almost touch the ground anyway."

Tayo smiled again. His mouth felt stiff at the corners. Harley had been at Wake Island with Leroy Valdez and Emo. They had all come back with Purple Hearts, but it didn't seem as if the war had changed Harley; he was still a little fat, and he still made them laugh, joking and clowning.

"Hey! You don't happen to have a beer, do you?"

Tayo shook his head. "There's some coffee on the stove."

"No, they say coffee is bad for you." He laughed, and Tayo smiled because Harley didn't use to like beer at all, and maybe this was something that was different about him now, after the war. He drank a lot of beer now. But Tayo could remember that time in the eighth grade when they had followed old Benny to see where he kept his wine. They watched him weave unsteadily through the salt bush down to the river willows and tamarics, growing along the river, all the while clutching his brown shopping bag close to his chest. They watched him take one last taste of the wine and push the cork in tight before he put it back in the bag, then carefully dig into the sandy riverbank, pushing white sand around the bag tenderly. They crouched with their chins on the sand and fallen willow leaves, peeking through the willows at him as he took a last look, as if to memorize the hiding place, and then walked crookedly up the hill, away from the river. They got to their feet then, and when Benny disappeared over the hill, they ran to the hiding place, where the river flowed into a quiet pool. Rocky and Tayo took the bottle of wine because there was only one bottle of beer.

"Okay for you, Harley," Rocky said, "beer tastes awful."

"Aw, you don't know. You never tasted any," Harley answered, trying to pry off the bottle cap with the short blade of his pocket knife.

"He's right, Harley. Josiah let us taste some one time."

The wine was sweet and sticky, a little like cough syrup, but they drank it anyway because they had to if they wanted to get drunk. Harley finally got the beer open, and he was anxious to catch up with them so he took a big swallow. He made a terrible face, wrinkling up his nose and rolling his eyes. He spent the rest of the afternoon spitting into the river, and they had to keep laughing because he kept saying, "Ugh! Awful! It tastes like poison!" And then he would spit again and try to wipe the inside of his mouth on the sleeve of his shirt.

Harley squatted down beside Tayo. He traced little figures in the dirt by his feet. Tayo closed his eyes and leaned back against the bottom of the tree; he flexed his feet out in front of him. They were quiet for awhile. The wind was getting stronger; it made a whirling sound as it came around the southwest corner of the ranch house. A piece of old tin on the roof of the shed began to rattle. Tayo felt as if he could sleep, and maybe make up for the bad night before. There was a peaceful silence beneath the sounds of the wind; it was a silence with no

21

trace of people. It was the silence of hard dry clay and old juniper wood bleached white.

But Harley was restless; Tayo could feel it. Harley kept wiping away the outlines he drew in the dirt and starting over again, angry that he couldn't draw them the way he wanted them. Tayo brought his knees up in front of him and concentrated on staying awake. Harley grinned at him.

"We got it easy, huh? All the livestock down at Montaño and nothing for us war heroes to do but lay around and sleep all day." He reached over and poked Tayo gently in the ribs when he said "war heroes."

"I tried to go down there and help out, you know, when they first decided to move all the cattle and sheep down there. That was when you were still sick." Harley shook his head. "Really, man, I tried to help. I told my old man, 'Hey, let me do it. I promise I won't mess up. Honest.' " Harley was drawing an intricate pattern in the dirt, moving his forefinger without pausing then.

"But you know what happened, so they don't want me down there any more. They told me I could look after the ranch out here. Like you." Harley looked up quickly to see Tayo's face.

"You know what I mean, Tayo," he said quickly, "you were really sick when you got back, and there isn't a damn thing wrong with me."

Tayo nodded, but he was thinking about what happened while Harley was at the Montaño herding sheep, and he wasn't sure if Harley was right.

The Montaño had not been as hard hit by the drought, so people with cattle and sheep moved them from areas of the reservation which had no grass or water to the Montaño, where they would keep them until the rains came, or for as long as the grass held out. Harley had gone to herd sheep for his family. They pitched a small square camp tent for him and brought him supplies and fresh things to eat every two or three days. He had a sheep dog to help him and a horse to ride all day long behind the grazing animals. His family was happy that he wanted to do this, because it had taken Harley a while to settle down after he got home from the war. He had done a lot of drinking and raising hell with Emo and some of the other veterans.

But after a week down there, Harley left the sheep grazing, with only the sheep dog to watch them, and he rode the horse over to the highway. When they found the horse, it was still standing there, tied to the fence, only somebody had come along and stolen the saddle off it. Harley was gone, and a couple of days later he wrote from the jail in Los Lunas. By the time they got down to the Montaño, the sheep were scattered all over the hills. At the camp they found the sheep dog dead, killed and torn to pieces by the wild animals that had killed thirty head of sheep.

"It was too bad about the dog and those sheep," Tayo said.

But Harley laughed; he shook his head and laughed very loudly. "They weren't worth anything anyway. So skinny and tough the coyotes had to kill half of them just to make one meal." He laughed again.

Tayo felt something stir along his spine; there was something in Harley's laugh he had never heard before. Somehow Harley didn't seem to feel anything at all, and he masked it with smart talk and laughter. Harley stood up then, but Tayo couldn't tell if it was because he didn't want to talk about the sheep or if he was only getting stiff from squatting so long.

"I'd give just about anything for a cold beer," he said, looking around the place, at the house, the shed, and the corrals.

"They didn't leave you the truck, did they? I don't even see Josiah's wagon."

"It's under the shed by the corral. But there's nothing to pull it anyway."

"What about that gray mule?"

"It's blind."

"Boy, they sure fixed you up good. I guess they don't want you wandering around either."

Tayo knew he was referring to that time at the Dixie Tavern when he had almost killed Emo. They were even now. Tayo had asked about the sheep that were killed while Harley was gone, and Harley brought up the fight.

"I wanted to be alone. This is a good place for it."

"Yeah, well not me. My old lady got out her Phillips 66 road map, and she looked at it all night until she found the place on the reservation that was the farthest away from any bars. I might be there right now, living on top of some mesa, if my father hadn't talked her into sending me to the ranch." Harley looked toward the southwest, in the direction of the ranch. "Shit, I think it *is* the farthest place anyway."

Tayo shrugged his shoulders. They were twenty-five or thirty miles from the bars on the other side of the reservation boundary line. People called it "going up the line," and the bars were built one after the other alongside 66, beginning at Budville and extending six or seven miles past San Fidel to the Whiting Brothers' station near McCartys.

"They can't stop me, so I don't know why they even try. Like the time they left me out there and they forgot to drain the gas out of the tractor. I hot-wired it and drove it all the way to San Fidel. I could have gotten back too, but I ran out of gas near Paraje." Harley laughed. His eyes were shining. It had been a victory for him; he had outsmarted all of them—his parents, his older brothers, everyone who worked to keep him away from beer and out of trouble.

"But this is the first time I've ridden a burro up the line, Tayo, and"—he paused to rub his ass—"I think it will be the last time." He walked over and kicked the sole of Tayo's boot. "Come on. Get up. Don't die here under this tree. Let's go, man."

Tayo shook his head and threw his arms up in front of him, pretending to push the idea away.

"Hey, come on. We can set some kind of world's record—you know, longest donkey ride ever made for a cold beer or something like that. An Indian world's record." When Harley talked like that, things that had happened, the dead sheep, the bar fight, even jail—all seemed very remote. Harley held out his hand, and Tayo grabbed hold of it; he pulled himself to his feet.

Tayo went inside to get his wallet. When he came out, he saw Harley by the windmill; the wind had blown the brim of his hat against his forehead, but he had the gray mule and he was pulling the bridle over the long gray ears.

The mule was getting bony; its hip bones looked sharp enough to push through the gray hide, the way bones tear through a carcass. Drought years shrank the hide tighter to the bones; ewes dropped weak lambs and cows had no calves in the spring. If it didn't start raining soon, all the livestock would have to be sold, like in the thirties, when buyers came from Albuquerque and Gallup and bought the cattle and sheep for almost nothing. But selling was better than watching them die when the grass was gone and there was no more cactus to burn for them. Emo liked to point to the restless dusty wind and the cloudless skies, to the bony horses chewing on fence posts beside the highway; Emo liked to say, "Look what is here for us. Look. Here's the Indians' mother earth! Old dried-up thing!" Tayo's anger made his hands shake. Emo was wrong. All wrong.

The wind whipped the mule's thin tail between its hind legs as Harley gave the reins to Tayo. "Don't you have a saddle?" Harley asked. Tayo shook his head. "How about an old saddle blanket? That mule's backbone will strike you in a vital place." They laughed, and Harley disappeared inside the old garage, and Tayo could hear noise of empty tubs, oil cans, and links of chain moved around; Harley came out shaking the dust from four gunny sacks, letting the wind pull at them like kites. He was grinning. Tayo stood watching all this time, and except for smiling or laughing or speaking when Harley spoke to him, he wasn't doing anything. He was standing with the wind at his back, like that mule, and he felt he could stand there indefinitely, maybe forever, like a fence post or a tree. It took a great deal of energy to be a human being, and the more the wind blew and the sun moved southwest, the less energy Tayo had. Harley was patient; he stood by the mule's head while Tayo jumped belly first onto the mule's back and swung a leg over; Harley held the gunny sacks in place until Tayo was on. Tayo felt like a little kid; he felt eight again, and Josiah was boosting him onto the back of Siow's pinto.

Harley tied a lead rope on the mule's bridle, but the gray mule followed the burro without any trouble, holding its head alert, and its jackrabbit ears forward, nostrils flaring wide, testing for imagined dangers ahead. Tayo didn't even bother to hold the reins; he knotted them the way Josiah had shown him when he was a little kid, so that the reins stayed together on the horse's neck. That way the horse couldn't jerk them from his hands, and he couldn't accidentally drop one. When you were so little that you couldn't reach the stirrups without climbing up on a fence or big rock, these details were important.

The wind was blowing from the southwest, and it pushed against Tayo's right shoulder. The noise of the wind was too loud for conversation, so Tayo closed his eyes. He relaxed his thighs and let his feet dangle; he slouched forward over the mule's bony shoulders. He was tired of fighting off the dreams and the voices; he was tired of guarding himself against places and things which evoked the memories. He let himself go with the motion of the mule, swaying forward and backward with each stride, feeling the rise and fall of the mule's breathing under his legs. Above the wind, sometimes he could hear Harley cussing out the burro, telling it what he would do if he had a gun.

The gusting winds had turned the sky dusty red. After two or three hours Harley pulled his hat low over his eyes to keep it on; and he dozed off, with both arms out in front of him, holding the donkey's neck, propping him up. The burro must have been able to feel the change in Harley's grip on its neck when Harley dozed off because it would begin to drift, gradually, from the right side of the road to the middle hump of sand and weeds, where it lowered its head quickly to reach a mouthful of weeds but always kept moving, trying to keep Harley from noticing any change. It got to the left side of the road that way and walked along steadily, only long enough to fool Harley, then the burro left the road entirely and completed the wide turn it had been engineering for almost half an hour. Tayo watched the burro's deliberate moves, but its stubbornness made it predictable, and every fifteen minutes Harley jerked the burro's head sharply to the right, flicked its flanks with the horsehair quirt, and put them back on course again. So they traveled in wide arcs, moving gradually to the north. Tayo thought about animals then, horses and mules, and the way they drifted with the wind. Josiah said that only humans had to endure anything, because only humans resisted what they saw outside themselves. Animals did not resist. But they persisted, because they became part of the wind. "Inside, Tayo, inside the belly of the wind." So they moved with the snow, became part of the snowstorm which drifted up against the trees and fences. And when they died, frozen solid against a fence, with the snow drifted around their heads? "Ah, Tayo," Josiah said, "the wind convinced them they were the ice." He wished Josiah were there, not forever like he had been wishing, but just long enough so Tayo could tell him how he'd been feeling lately, how he'd almost been convinced he was brittle red clay, slipping away with the wind, a little more each day.

The wind didn't blow as hard up there as it did on the clay flats. Harley stopped at the top of the hill and took a piss. The burro chewed the dry tufts of grass as close to the gray shale as it could and strained against the reins to reach another sparse clump of grass. But the mule stood alert, its milky staring eyes wide open. They were the same—the mule and old Grandma, she sitting in the corner of the room in the wintertime by the potbelly stove, or the summertime on an apple crate under the elm tree; she was as blind as the gray mule and just as persistent. She never hesitated to tell them that Rocky had promised to buy her a kerosene stove with his Army pay, even after Tayo came home from the hospital and she knew the sound of Rocky's name made him cry.

"Don't cry, Tayo, don't cry. You know he wanted me to have it. And he didn't want you to cry." So finally Auntie took forty dollars of the insurance money and sent Robert to town, and he brought home an old heater with an automatic thermostat, so that once it was lighted, all it needed was a barrel of fuel oil on the wooden rack outside. She ordered that kind because she didn't want to impose on any of them to look after her stove for her. Last year, on the coldest day of the winter, when San José creek froze solid and Auntie had gone to the store and old Grandma was all alone, the fire in the wood stove went out. This story always made Auntie stop whatever she was doing then, to say, "Mama, the coals were still warm when we got home," and old Grandma always pretended she didn't hear this, and she continued on about the things Rocky was going to do for her. They all mourned Rocky that way, by slipping, lapsing into the plans he had for college and for his football career. It didn't take Tayo long to see the accident of time and space: Rocky was the one who was alive, buying Grandma her heater with the round dial on the front; Rocky was there in the college game scores on the sports page of the *Albuquerque Journal*. It was him, Tayo, who had died, but somehow there had been a mistake with the corpses, and somehow his was still unburied.

He started to cry, and when Harley looked back at

him he did not wipe the tears away or pretend it was the dust and wind in his eyes. He was suddenly hollow; his fingers loosened and fell from the reins, slippery with sweat. The force of gravity seemed to surge up at him and pull him down. He hung with both arms to the mule's neck, but he was caught and being dragged away. Rolling end over end in a flash flood in a big arroyo. After his hands slipped loose, his knees hit muddy ruts and there was screaming and the sound of bone crushing, hollow white skull bone beaten to bayonet edges by the jungle rain. The flood water was the color of the earth, of their skin, of the blood, his blood dried brown in the bandages.

Harley helped him up; he brushed the sand and weeds from Tayo's shirt and handed him his hat. He walked with him to the shade at the foot of the mesa. He hobbled the mule and tied a long rope to the burro and let them graze on the thin, bluish green leaves of salt bushes growing at the entrance to the canyon. The sand felt cool. He squeezed it in both fists until it made little rivulets between his fingers. Harley sat down beside him and wiped his face on the sleeve of his shirt.

"Sunstroke. They always warned me about it, Tayo. We should've stopped to rest sooner." He looked at Tayo closely. "Are you okay?"

Tayo nodded. He wanted to make a joke about himself, say something like "Sunstroke hell, the wind blew me off," but he didn't have energy to move his lips, to even form the words. Beyond the shade everything shimmered in waves of heat and the wind. The cliffs across the little wash, the junipers growing among the big orange boulders, and the hazy pink sky were bright colors of a dream, and the longer Tayo stared at them, the more he knew he was going to be sick. So he scratched a hole in the dry sand beside him, and when the glare of that light finally blinded him, he turned to his right side and vomited into the hole.

29

When he got off the train at New Laguna, his legs were shaky and the sleeves of his coat smelled like puke, although he had tried to rinse out the coat in the washroom sink on the train. He didn't want them to know how sick he had been, how all night he had leaned against the metal wall in the men's room, feeling the layers of muscle in his belly growing thinner, until the heaving was finally a ripple and then a quiver.

But Auntie stared at him the way she always had, reaching inside him with her eyes, calling up the past as if it were his future too, as if things would always be the same for him. They both knew then she would keep him and take care of him all the months he would lie in a bed too weak to walk. This time she would keep him because he was all she had left. Many years ago she had taken him to conceal the shame of her younger sister. Now she stood over the bed and looked at him, and if he opened his eyes, he knew he would see her probing for new shame, the anticipation of what she might find swelling inside her. What would it be this time? She remembered what that old fool Josiah had done; it wasn't any different from Little Sister and that white man. She had fiercely protected them from the gossip in the village. But she never let them forget what she had endured, all because of what they had done. That's why Tayo knew she wouldn't send him away to a veterans' hospital.

He lay with his face in the pillow. She had always watched him more closely than Rocky, because Rocky had been her own son and it had been her duty to raise him. Those who measured life by counting the crosses would not count her sacrifices for Rocky the way they counted her sacrifices for her dead sister's half-breed child. When Rocky died he became unassailable forever in his frame on top of her bureau; his death gave her new advantages with the people: she had given so much. But advantages wear out; she needed a new struggle, another opportunity to show those who might gossip that she had still another unfortunate burden which proved that, above all else, she was a Christian woman. That was how it would be; he figured it out the first afternoon he was home.

At the end of the first week, she came into the room and pulled the sheets and blankets from all the beds, and he realized then she changed the beds as if Josiah and Rocky still slept there, tucking the dark wool blankets around the corners of the clean sheets, stuffing the pillows into starched white pillowcases she had ironed the day before. Finally he heard her step close to his bed and lift the lid on the slop jar to see if it needed to be emptied.

"How are you feeling?"

He knew she wanted him to get out of the bed while she changed the sheets. He sat up and swung his legs around to the floor. He got up unsteadily and moved toward the chair at the foot of the bed, but she took his arm and guided him to Rocky's bed. He wanted to pull out of her reach and go to the chair, but he was swaying with nausea. She pushed him into the bed and brought the slop jar. He pulled his knees up to his belly and writhed in the bed, fighting back the gagging. He felt the old mattress then, where all the years of Rocky's life had made contours and niches that Tayo's bones did not fit: like plump satin-covered upholstery inside a coffin, molding itself around a corpse to hold it forever. He called for help, and he drew his legs and arms stiffly to his sides and arched his back away from the mattress. His heart was pounding louder than his calls for help; he could hear old Grandma answering him, but Auntie did not come. Finally she came in from the porch. The sleeves of her dress were rolled up, her hands were damp and smelled like bleach. She pulled him from the bed, her face tight with anger.

He pointed at the windows. "The light makes me vomit."

She pulled down the shades, and he knew she was staring at him, almost as if she could see the outline of his lie in the dim light. But his advantage was the Army doctors who told her and Robert that the cause of battle fatigue was a mystery, even to them. He felt better in the dark because he could not see the beds, where the blankets followed smooth concave outlines; he could not see the photographs in the frames on the bureau. In the dark he could cry for all the dreams that Rocky had as he stared out of his graduation picture; he could cry for Josiah and the spotted cattle, all scattered now, all lost, sucked away in the dissolution that had taken everything from him. Old Grandma sat by her stove, comfortable with darkness too. He knew she listened to him cry; he knew she listened to the clang of the enamel lid of the slop jar as he removed it and leaned over to vomit.

In the beginning old Grandma and Robert stayed away from him, except to say "Good morning" or "Good night"; the sickness and his crying overwhelmed them. Auntie had taken charge of him. In low clear tones that Tayo could hear, she warned them to be careful to make no mention of Rocky or Josiah. Tayo could see what she was trying to do.

When he heard Robert come in from a trip to the ranch, he sat up on the bed and called him.

"The bay mare had her colt. A horse colt. Sorrel with a blaze. Sort of crooked down his face, like this." Robert spoke slowly and softly, indicating the marking on the colt's forehead by outlining it with a finger on his own face.

Tayo realized then that as long as Josiah and Rocky had been alive, he had never known Robert except as a quiet man in the house that belonged to old Grandma and Auntie. When Auntie and old Grandma and Josiah used to argue over how many lambs should be sold, or when Auntie and old Grandma scolded Josiah for the scandal of his Mexican girl friend, Robert sat quietly. He had cultivated this deafness for as many years as he had been married to Auntie. His face was calm; he was patient with them because he had nothing to say. The sheep, the horses, and the fields—everything belonged to them, including the good family name. Now Robert had all the things that Josiah had been responsible for. He looked tired.

"I helped my brother-in-law with the fields. But they don't expect me to do very much now. They know I'm pretty busy over here."

"When I get better, I can help you."

Robert smiled and nodded. "That would be nice," he said softly, "but don't hurry. You take it easy. Get well." He stood up. He was a short, slight man with a dark angular face. He put his hand on Tayo's arm. "I'm glad you are home, Tayo," he said. "I sure am glad."

He woke up crying. He had dreamed Josiah had been hugging him close the way he had when Tayo was a child, and in the dream he smelled Josiah's smell—horses, woodsmoke, and sweat—the smell he had forgotten until the dream; and he was overcome with all the love there was. He cried because he had to wake up to what was left: the dim room, empty beds, and a March dust storm rattling the tin on the roof. He lay there with the feeling that there was no place left for him; he would find no peace in that house where the silence and the emptiness echoed the loss. He wanted to go back to the hospital. Right away. He had to get back where he could merge with the walls and the ceiling, shimmering white, remote from everything. He sat up and pushed off the blankets; he was sweating. He looked at old Grandma sitting in her place beside the stove; he couldn't tell if she was sleeping or if she was only listening to the wind with her eyes closed. His voice was shaking; he called her. He wanted to tell her they had to take him back to the hospital. He watched her get up slowly, with old bones that were stems of thin glass she shuffled across the linoleum in her cloth slippers, moving cautiously as if she did not trust memory to take her to his bed. She sat down on the edge of the bed and she reached out for him. She held his head in her lap and she cried with him, saying "A'moo'oh, a'moo'ohh" over and over again.

"I've been thinking," she said, wiping her eyes on the edge of her apron, "all this time, while I was sitting in my chair. Those white doctors haven't helped you at all. Maybe we had better send for someone else."

When Auntie got back from the store, old Grandma told her, "That boy needs a medicine man. Otherwise, he will have to go away. Look at him." Auntie was standing with a bag full of groceries in her arms. She set the bag down on the table and took off her coat and bandanna; she looked at Tayo. She had a way she looked when she saw trouble; she frowned, getting her answer ready for the old lady.

"Oh, I don't know, Mama. You know how they are. You know what people will say if we ask for a medicine man to help him. Someone will say it's not right. They'll say, 'Don't do it. He's not full blood anyway.'" She hung up her coat and draped the scarf on top of it.

"It will start all over again. All that gossip about Josiah and about Little Sister. Girls around here have babies by white men all the time now, and nobody says anything. Men run around with Mexicans and even worse, and nothing is ever said. But just let it happen with our family—" Old Grandma interrupted her the way she always did whenever Auntie got started on that subject.

"He's my grandson. If I send for old Ku'oosh, he'll come. Let them talk if they want to. Why do you care what they say? Let them talk. By planting time they'll forget." Old Grandma stood up straight when she said this and stared at Auntie with milky cataract eyes.

"You know what the Army doctor said: 'No Indian medicine.' Old Ku'oosh will bring his bag of weeds and dust. The doctor won't like it." But her tone of voice was one of temporary defeat, and she was already thinking ahead to some possible satisfaction later on, when something went wrong and it could be traced back to this decision. Like the night she tried to tell them not to keep the little boy for Sis any more; by then she was even running around with colored men, and she was always drunk. She came that night to leave the little boy with them. They could have refused then. They could have told her then not to come around any more. But they didn't listen to her then either; later on though, they saw, and she used to say to them, "See, I tried to tell you." But they didn't care. Her brother, Josiah, and her mother. They didn't care what the people were saying about their family, or that the village officers had a meeting one time and talked about running Sis off the reservation for good.

Old Grandma pulled the chair from the foot of the bed, and the old man sat down. He nodded at Tayo but didn't say anything; Tayo didn't understand what he was waiting for until he saw old Grandma wearing her coat and wool scarf, waiting while Auntie put on her coat. They left, and old Ku'oosh waited until the voices of the women could no longer be heard before he moved the chair closer to the bed. He smelled like mutton tallow and mountain sagebrush. He spoke softly, using the old dialect full of sentences that were involuted with explanations of their own origins, as if nothing the old man said were his own but all had been said before and he was only there to repeat it. Tayo had to strain to catch the meaning, dense with place names he had never heard. His language was childish, interspersed with English words, and he could feel shame tightening in his throat; but then he heard the old man describe the cave, a deep lava cave northeast of Laguna where bats flew out on summer evenings. He pushed himself up against the pillows and felt the iron bed frame against his back. He knew this cave. The rattlesnakes liked to lie there in the early spring, when the days were still cool and the sun warmed the black lava rock first; the snakes went there to restore life to themselves. The old man gestured to the northeast, and Tayo turned his head that way and remembered the wide round hole, so deep that even lying on his belly beside Rocky, he had never been able to see bottom. He remembered the small rocks they had nudged over the edge and how they had listened for some sound when the rocks hit bottom. But the cave was deeper than the sound. Auntie told them she would whip them if they didn't stay away from that place, because there were snakes around there and they might fall in. But they went anyway, on summer nights after supper, when the crickets smelled the coolness and started singing. They were careful of the snakes that came out hunting after sundown, and they sneaked up to the cave very quietly and waited for the bats to fly out. He nodded to the old man because he knew this place. People said back in the old days they took the scalps and threw them down there. Tayo knew what the old man had come for.

Ku'oosh continued slowly, in a soft chanting voice, saying, "Maybe you don't know some of these things," vaguely acknowledging the distant circumstance of an absent white father. He called Josiah by his Indian name and said, "If he had known then maybe he could have told you before you went to the white people's big war." He hesitated then and looked at Tayo's eyes.

"But you know, grandson, this world is fragile."

The word he chose to express "fragile" was filled with the intricacies of a continuing process, and with a strength inherent in spider webs woven across paths through sand hills where early in the morning the sun becomes entangled in each filament of web. It took a long time to explain the fragility and intricacy because no word exists alone, and the reason for choosing each word had to be explained with a story about why it must be said this certain way. That was the responsibility that went with being human, old Ku'oosh said, the story behind each word must be told so there could be no mistake in the meaning of what had been said; and this demanded great patience and love. More than an hour went by before Ku'oosh asked him.

"You were with the others," he said, "the ones who went to the white people's war?"

Tayo nodded.

"There is something they have sent me to ask you. Something maybe you need, now that you are home."

Tayo was listening to the wind outside; late in the afternoon it would begin to die down.

"You understand, don't you? It is important to all of us. Not only for your sake, but for this fragile world."

He didn't know how to explain what had happened. He did not know how to tell him that he had not killed any enemy or that he did not think that he had. But that he had done things far worse, and the effects were everywhere in the cloudless sky, on the dry brown hills, shrinking skin and hide taut over sharp bone. The old man was waiting for him to answer.

Tayo reached down for the slop jar and pulled it closer.

"I'm sick," he said, turning away from the old man to vomit. "I'm sick, but I never killed any enemy. I never even touched them." He was shivering and sweating when he sat up.

"Maybe you could help me anyway. Do something for me, the way you did for the others who came back. Because what if I didn't know I killed one?"

But the old man shook his head slowly and made a low humming sound in his throat. In the old way of warfare, you couldn't kill another human being in battle without knowing it, without seeing the result, because even a wounded deer that got up and ran again left great clots of lung blood or spilled guts on the ground.

37

That way the hunter knew it would die. Human beings were no different. But the old man would not have believed white warfare—killing across great distances without knowing who or how many had died. It was all too alien to comprehend, the mortars and big guns; and even if he could have taken the old man to see the target areas, even if he could have led him through the fallen jungle trees and muddy craters of torn earth to show him the dead, the old man would not have believed anything so monstrous. Ku'oosh would have looked at the dismembered corpses and the atomic heat-flash outlines, where human bodies had evaporated, and the old man would have said something close and terrible had killed these people. Not even oldtime witches killed like that.

The way
I heard it
was
in the old days
long time ago
they had this
Scalp Society
for warriors
who killed
or touched
dead enemies.

They had things
they must do
otherwise
K'oo'ko would haunt their dreams
with her great fangs and
everything would be endangered.
Maybe the rain wouldn't come

or the deer would go away.
That's why
they had things
they must do

The flute and dancing
blue cornmeal and
hair-washing.

All these things
they had to do.

                               The room was almost dark.
Tayo wondered where Auntie and old Grandma had
been all this time. The old man put his sack on his lap
and began to feel around inside it with both hands. He
brought out a bundle of dry green stalks and a small
paper bag full of blue cornmeal. He laid the bundle of
Indian tea in Tayo's lap. He stood up then and set the
bag of cornmeal on the chair.

"There are some things we can't cure like we used
to," he said, "not since the white people came. The
others who had the Scalp Ceremony, some of them are not
better either."

He pulled the blue wool cap over his ears. "I'm
afraid of what will happen to all of us if you and the
others don't get well," he said.

Old man Ku'oosh left that day, and as soon as he
had closed the door Tayo rolled over on his belly and
knocked the stalks of Indian tea on the floor. He pressed
his face into the pillow and pushed his head hard against
the bed frame. He cried, trying to release the great
pressure that was swelling inside his chest, but he got no
relief from crying any more. The pain was solid and
constant as the beating of his own heart. The old man

only made him certain of something he had feared all along, something in the old stories. It took only one person to tear away the delicate strands of the web, spilling the rays of sun into the sand, and the fragile world would be injured. Once there had been a man who cursed the rain clouds, a man of monstrous dreams. Tayo screamed, and curled his body against the pain.

Auntie woke him up and gave him a cup of Indian tea brewed dark as coffee. It was late and they had already eaten supper. Robert was sitting at the kitchen table saddle-soaping a bridle. Old Grandma was dozing beside her stove. The tea was mild, tasting like the air after a rainstorm, when all the grass and plants smell green and earth is damp. She brought him a bowl of blue cornmeal mush. He shook his head when he looked at it, but she sat down on the chair by the bed and fed him spoonful by spoonful. He looked at her while she fed him; he knew she had asked Ku'oosh not to mention the visit, except to the old men. He knew she was afraid people would find out he was crazy. The cornmeal mush tasted sweet; his stomach did not cramp around it like it did with other food. She took the empty bowl and cup away. He slid down under the blankets and waited for the nausea to come. If this didn't work, then he knew he would die. He let himself go limp; he did not brace himself against the nausea. He didn't care any more if it came; he didn't care any more if he died.

He was sitting in the sun outside the screen door when they came driving into the yard. He had been looking at the apple tree by the woodshed, trying to see the tiny green fruits that would grow all summer until they became apples. He had been thinking about how easy it was to stay alive now that he didn't care about being alive any more. The tiny apples hung on that way; they didn't seem to fall, even in strong wind. He could eat regular food. He seldom vomited any more. Some nights he even slept all night without the dreams.

He went with them in the old Ford coupé. He laid his head back on the dusty seat and felt the sun getting hot on his shoulders and neck. He didn't listen to them while they laughed and talked about how Emo bought the car. He didn't hear where they said they were going. He didn't care.

It was already getting hot, and it was still springtime. The sky was empty. The sun was too hot and it made the color of the sky too pale blue. He was the last one through the screen door at Dixie Tavern.

Harley pushed a bottle of beer in front of him. Harley said something to Tayo, and the others all laughed. These good times were courtesy of the U.S. Government and the Second World War. Cash from disability checks earned with shrapnel in the neck at Wake Island or shell shock on Iwo Jima; rewards for surviving the Bataan Death March.

"Hey, Tayo, you cash your check yet?"

Tayo pushed a ten dollar bill across the table. "More beer," he said.

Emo was getting drunk on whiskey; his face was flushed and his forehead sweaty. Tayo watched Harley and Leroy flip quarters to see who was buying the next round, and he swallowed the beer in big mouthfuls like medicine. He could feel something loosening up inside. He had heard Auntie talk about the veterans—drunk all the time, she said. But he knew why. It was something the old people could not understand. Liquor was medicine for the anger that made them hurt, for the pain of the loss, medicine for tight bellies and choked-up throats. He was beginning to feel a comfortable place inside himself, close to his own beating heart, near his own warm belly; he crawled inside and watched the storm swirling on the outside and he was safe there; the winds of rage could not touch him.

They were all drunk now, and they wanted him to talk to them; they wanted him to tell stories with them.

Someone kept patting him on the back. He reached for another bottle of beer.

White women never looked at me until I put on that uniform, and then by God I was a U.S. Marine and they came crowding around. All during the war they'd say to me, "Hey soldier, you sure are handsome. All that black thick hair." "Dance with me," the blond girl said. You know Los Angeles was the biggest city I ever saw. All those streets and tall buildings. Lights at night everywhere. I never saw so many bars and juke boxes—all the people coming from everywhere, dancing and laughing. They never asked me if I was Indian; sold me as much beer as I could drink. I was a big spender then. Had my military pay. Double starch in my uniform and my boots shining so good. I mean those white women fought over me. Yeah, they did really! I went home with a blonde one time. She had a big '38 Buick. Good car. She let me drive it all the way.

Hey, whose turn to buy?

The first day at Oakland he and Rocky walked down the street together and a big Chrysler stopped in the street and an old white woman rolled down the window and said, "God bless you, God bless you," but it was the uniform, not them, she blessed.

"Come on, Tayo! They didn't keep you on latrine duty the whole war, did they? You talk now!"

"Yeah! Come on!"

Someone jerked the bottle out of his hand. His hand was cold and wet; he clenched it into a fist. They were

42

outside him, in the distance; his own voice sounded far away too.

"America! America!" he sang, "God shed his grace on thee." He stopped and pulled a beer away from Harley.

"One time there were these Indians, see. They put on uniforms, cut their hair. They went off to a big war. They had a real good time too. Bars served them booze, old white ladies on the street smiled at them. At Indians, remember that, because that's all they were. Indians. These Indians fucked white women, they had as much as they wanted too. They were MacArthur's boys; white whores took their money same as anyone. These Indians got treated the same as anyone: Wake Island, Iwo Jima. They got the same medals for bravery, the same flag over the coffin." Tayo stopped. He realized the others weren't laughing and talking any more. They were listening to him, and they weren't smiling. He took another beer from Harley's hand and swallowed until the bottle was empty. Harley yelled, "Hey, Mannie!" to the bartender. "Plug in the juke box for us!" But Tayo yelled, "No! No. I didn't finish this story yet. See these dumb Indians thought these good times would last. They didn't ever want to give up the cold beer and the blond cunt. Hell no! They were America the Beautiful too, this was the land of the free just like teachers said in school They had the uniform and they didn't look different no more. They got respect." He could feel the words coming out faster and faster, the momentum building inside him like the words were all going to explode and he wanted to finish before it happened.

"I'm half-breed. I'll be the first to say it. I'll speak for both sides. First time you walked down the street in Gallup or Albuquerque, you knew. Don't lie. You knew right away. The war was over, the uniform was gone. All of a sudden that man at the store waits on you last, makes you wait until all the white people bought what they wanted. And the white lady at the bus depot, she's real careful now not to touch your hand when she counts out your change. You watch it slide across the counter at you, and you know. Goddamn it! You stupid sonofabitches! You know!"

The bartender came over. He was a fat Mexican from Cubero who was losing his hair. He looked at them nervously. Harley and Leroy were holding Tayo's arms gently. They said something to the bartender and he went away. The juke box lit up, and Hank Williams started singing. Tayo got quiet. He looked across at Emo, and he saw how much Emo hated him. Because he had spoiled it for them. They spent all their checks trying to get back the good times, and a skinny light-skinned bastard had ruined it. That's what Emo was thinking. Here they were, trying to bring back that old feeling, that feeling they belonged to America the way they felt during the war. They blamed themselves for losing the new feeling; they never talked about it, but they blamed themselves just like they blamed themselves for losing the land the white people took. They never thought to blame white people for any of it; they wanted white people for their friends. They never saw that it was the white people who gave them that feeling and it was white people who took it away again when the war was over.

Belonging was drinking and laughing with the platoon, dancing with blond women, buying drinks for buddies born in Cleveland, Ohio. Tayo knew what they had been trying to do. They repeated the stories about good times in Oakland and San Diego; they repeated them like long medicine chants, the beer bottles pounding on the counter tops like drums. Another round, and Harley tells his story about two blondes in bed with him. They forget Tayo's story. They give him another beer. Two bottles in front of him now. They go on with it, with their good old times. Tayo starts crying. They think maybe he's crying about what the Japs did to Rocky

44

because they are to that part of the ritual where they damn those yellow Jap bastards.

Someone pats Tayo on the back. Harley wants to comfort him. They don't know he is crying for them. They don't know that he doesn't hate the Japanese, not even the Japanese soldiers who were grim-faced watching Tayo and the corporal stumble with the stretcher.

The short one had stopped and looked at Rocky in the blanket; he called the tall one over. The tall one looked like a Navajo guy from Fort Defiance that Tayo had known at Indian School. They looked tired too, those Japanese soldiers. Like they wanted this march to be over too. That tall one, he even shook his head like Willie Begay did: two abrupt movements, almost too quick to see, and then he pulled the corporal to his feet. But when Tayo tried to give the corporal his end of the blanket again, the tall soldier pushed Tayo away, not hard, but the way a small child would be pushed away by an older brother. It was then Tayo got confused, and he called this tall Jap soldier Willie Begay; "You remember him, Willie, he's my brother, best football player Albuquerque Indian School ever had."

The tall soldier looked at him curiously. He pushed Tayo out of the way, into the ditch running full of muddy water. He pulled the blanket over Rocky as if he were already dead, and then he jabbed the rifle butt into the muddy blanket. Tayo never heard the sound, because he was screaming. Later on, he regretted that he had not listened, because it became an uncertainty, loose inside his head, wandering into his imagination, so that any hollow crushing sound he heard—children smashing gourds along the irrigation ditch or a truck tire running over a piece of dry wood—any of these sounds took him back to that moment. Screaming, with mud in his mouth and in his eyes, screaming until the others dragged him away before the Japs killed him too. He fought them, trying to lie down in the ditch beside the blanket already partially buried in the mud. He had never planned to go any farther than Rocky went. They tried to help him. The corporal who had helped carry Rocky for so long put his arm around Tayo and kept him on his feet. "Easy, easy, it's okay. Don't cry. Your brother was already dead. I heard them say it. Jap talk for dead. He was already gone anyway. There was nothing anyone could do."

At the prison camp, behind the barbed wire enclosed in many more layers of barbed wire, Tayo thought he saw the tall soldier come each day to stand beside the guard at the south fence and stare for a long time in his direction. But the soldier was too far away, and the fever was too severe for Tayo to be sure of anything he had seen.

"How's your sunstroke?" Harley said when he saw that Tayo was awake. Harley had a handful of wild grapes not much bigger than blueberries; he reached over and gave Tayo some. The leaves were small and dark green. Tayo looked up at the big orange sandrock where the wild grape vine grew out of the sand and climbed along a fissure in the face of the boulder. Harley picked some more. He ate them in big mouthfuls, chewing the seeds because most of the grape was seed anyway. Tayo could not bite down on the seeds. Once he had loved to feel them break between his teeth, but not any more. The sound of crushing made him sick. He got up and walked the sandy trail to the spring. He didn't want to hear Harley crush the seeds.

The canyon was the way he always remembered it; the beeweed plants made the air smell heavy and sweet like wild honey, and the bumblebees were buzzing around waxy yucca flowers. The leaves of the cottonwood trees that crowded the canyon caught reflections of the afternoon sun, hundreds of tiny mirrors flashing. He blinked his eyes and looked away to the shade below the cliffs where the rabbit brush was green and yellow daisies were blooming. The people said that even in the driest years nobody could ever remember a time when the spring had dried up.

Josiah had told him about the spring while they waited for the water barrels to fill. He had been sitting on the wagon seat, taken from a '23 Chrysler that wrecked near Paraje, and after all those years the springs poked through the faded mouse-fur fabric like devil claws. Tayo used to stand in the big sandstone cave and hold the siphon hose under the water in the shallow pool where the spring water splashed down from the west wall of the cave. The water was always cold, icy cold, even in the summer, and Tayo liked the way it felt when he was sweating and took off his shirt: the splashing water made an icy mist that almost disappeared before it touched him.

"You see," Josiah had said, with the sound of the water trickling out of the hose into the empty wooden barrel, "there are some things worth more than money." He pointed his chin at the springs and around at the narrow canyon. "This is where we come from, see. This sand, this stone, these trees, the vines, all the wildflowers. This earth keeps us going." He took off his hat and wiped his forehead on his shirt. "These dry years you hear some people complaining, you know, about the dust and the wind, and how dry it is. But the wind and the dust, they are part of life too, like the sun and the sky. You don't swear at them. It's people, see. They're the ones. The old people used to say that droughts happen when people forget, when people misbehave."

Tayo knelt on the edge of the pool and let the dampness soak into the knees of his jeans. He closed his eyes and swallowed the water slowly. He tasted the deep heart-rock of the earth, where the water came from, and he thought maybe this wasn't the end after all.

47

One time
Old Woman K'yo's
son came in
from Reedleaf town
up north.
His name was Pa'caya'nyi
and he didn't know who his father was.

He asked the people
"You people want to learn some magic?"
and the people said
"Yes, we can always use some."

Ma'see'wi and Ou'yu'ye'wi
the twin brothers
were caring for the
mother corn altar,
but they got interested
in this magic too.

"What kind of medicine man
are you,
anyway?" they asked him.
"A Ck'o'yo medicine man,"
he said.

"Tonight we'll see
if you really have magical power," they told him.

So that night
Pa'caya'nyi
came with his mountain lion.
He undressed
he painted his body
the whorls of flesh
the soles of his feet
the palms of his hands
the top of his head.

He wore feathers
on each side of his head.

He made an altar
with cactus spines
and purple locoweed flowers.
He lighted four cactus torches
at each corner.
He made the mountain lion lie
down in front and
then he was ready for his magic.

He struck the middle of the north wall
He took a piece of flint and
he struck the middle of the north wall.
Water poured out of the wall
and flowed down
toward the south.

He said "What does that look like?
Is that magic power?"
He struck the middle of the west wall
and from the east wall
a bear came out.
"What do you call this?"
he said again.

"Yes, it looks like magic all right,"
Ma'see'wi said.
So it was finished
and Ma'see'wi and Ou'yu'ye'wi
and all the people were fooled by
that Ck'o'yo medicine man,
Pa'caya'nyi.

From that time on
they were
so busy
playing around with that

Ck'o'yo magic
they neglected the mother corn altar.

They thought they didn't have to worry
about anything
They thought this magic
could give life to plants
and animals.
They didn't know it was all just a trick.

Our mother
Nau'ts'ity'i
was very angry
over this
over the way
all of them
even Ma'see'wi and Ou'yu'ye'wi
fooled around with this
magic.

"I've had enough of that,"
she said,
"If they like that magic so much
let them live off it."

So she took
the plants and grass from them.
No baby animals were born.
She took the
rainclouds with her.

           Harley's burro went faster
after they left the spring, and the gray mule had to walk
faster to keep slack in the rope. The sun was moving
toward the west; Tayo squinted, trying to find some

clouds on the west horizon. He wished then they had taught him more about the clouds and the sky, about the way the priests called the storm clouds to bring the rain. Tayo watched the sun for a long time, and at the Acoma road they stopped and he watched it disappear behind the hills in the west.

Harley was looking down the road with his head turned slightly to the side, listening to something.

"I think I hear a car. Yeah. Okay, Tayo." Harley's voice was excited. "If they stop for us, let's leave the burro and the mule here. There's a windmill over there. We can come back and get them later on." Harley was already untying the rope around the burro's neck to use for a hobble. Tayo could see the outline of a car coming from Acoma; it had an umbrella of road dust above it. Harley stood on the side of the road and started waving his arms to flag it down.

"Tuesday nights are slow," the bartender said. Harley finished his second beer and joked with the bartender about how far they had come just for a cold beer. Tayo held onto the beer bottle, feeling moisture condense on his fingers. The bar didn't change; whatever the color of the walls, they were always dirty, dark grime of stale beer and cigarette smoke; it always smelled the same too, a lingering odor of urine and vomit. Even the light bulb above the pool table shined dim soiled light. He was glad he noticed it now, before he drank the beer. He had seen the color of that light once before, but he had never been sure if it was the light or the beer he was drinking. He drank the beer slowly and waited to feel it spread from his belly, warming him all over. He finished the bottle and leaned back in the chair. He wanted to remember Rocky's face again, and to think of them together.

Rocky was standing in a small clearing surrounded by thickets of scrub oak. It was still early in the fall and only a few of the coppery yellow leaves had fallen from the oaks. Tayo had to strain to see the deer in the tall yellow grass. He crossed a narrow dry gulley, and then he could see the antlers. He approached the deer slowly It had fallen on its right side with its forelegs tucked under its belly; the hind legs were curled under to the left as if it were still sleeping in the grass. The eyes were still liquid and golden brown, staring at dark mountain dirt and dry oak leaves tangled in the grass.

When he was a little child he always wanted to pet a deer, and he daydreamed that a deer would let him come close and touch its nose. He knelt and touched the nose; it was softer than pussy willows, and cattails, and still warm as a breath. The bright blood in the nostrils was still wet. He touched the big mule-size ears, and they were still warm. He knew it would not last long; the eyes would begin to cloud and turn glassy green, then gray, sinking back in the skull. The nose would harden, and the ears would get stiff. But for that moment it was so beautiful that he could only stand and feel the presence of the deer; he knew what they said about deer was true.

Rocky was honing his knife; he tested the blade on a thread hanging from the sleeve of his jacket. The sun was settling down in the southwest sky above the twin peaks. It would be dark in an hour or so. Rocky rolled the carcass belly up and spread open the hind legs. When Tayo saw he was getting started, he looked at the eyes again; he took off his jacket and covered the deer's head.

"Why did you do that?" asked Rocky, motioning at the jacket with the blade of his knife. Long gray hairs were matted into the blood on the blade. Tayo didn't say anything, because they both knew why. The people said you should do that before you gutted the deer. Out of respect. But Rocky was funny about those things. He was an A-student and all-state in football and track. He had to win; he said he was always going to win. So he

52

listened to his teachers, and he listened to the coach. They were proud of him. They told him, "Nothing can stop you now except one thing: don't let the people at home hold you back." Rocky understood what he had to do to win in the white outside world. After their first year at boarding school in Albuquerque, Tayo saw how Rocky deliberately avoided the old-time ways. Old Grandma shook her head at him, but he called it superstition, and he opened his textbooks to show her. But Auntie never scolded him, and she never let Robert or Josiah talk to him either. She wanted him to be a success. She could see what white people wanted in an Indian, and she believed this way was his only chance. She saw it as her only chance too, after all the village gossip about their family. When Rocky was a success, no one would dare to say anything against them any more.

Rocky slit the throat. Blood spilled over the grass and into the dirt; it splashed on his boots. He didn't believe in drinking the warm blood as some hunters did. Tayo held a hind leg; it was beginning to get stiff. Rocky cut off the musk glands and testicles. He slit the belly open carefully, to avoid spilling the contents of the stomach. The body heat made steam in the cold air. The sun was down, and the twilight chill sucked the last of the deer's life away—the eyes were dull and sunken; it was gone. Josiah and Robert came then and unloaded their rifles and leaned them against a scrub oak. They went to the deer and lifted the jacket. They knelt down and took pinches of cornmeal from Josiah's leather pouch. They sprinkled the cornmeal on the nose and fed the deer's spirit. They had to show their love and respect, their appreciation; otherwise, the deer would be offended, and they would not come to die for them the following year.

Rocky turned away from them and poured water from the canteen over his bloody hands. He was embarrassed at what they did. He knew when they took the deer home, it would be laid out on a Navajo blanket, and Old Grandma would put a string of turquoise around its neck and put silver and turquoise rings around the tips of the antlers. Josiah would prepare a little bowl of cornmeal and place it by the deer's head so that anyone who went near could leave some on the nose. Rocky tried to tell them that keeping the carcass on the floor in a warm room was bad for the meat. He wanted to hang the deer in the woodshed, where the meat would stay cold and cure properly. But he knew how they were. All the people, even the Catholics who went to mass every Sunday, followed the ritual of the deer. So he didn't say anything about it, but he avoided the room where they laid the deer.

They marked the place with Tayo's T-shirt spread across the top of some scrub oaks. It was getting dark when they started hiking back to the truck. Tayo wrapped the liver and heart in the clean cheesecloth Josiah carried with him. An early winter moon was rising in front of them, and a chill wind came with it, penetrating feet and hands. Tayo held the bundle tighter. He felt humbled by the size of the full moon, by the chill wind that swept wide across the foothills of the mountain. They said the deer gave itself to them because it loved them, and he could feel the love as the fading heat of the deer's body warmed his hands.

Harley slid another bottle of Coors across the table to him and said, "Hey, man, we didn't come here to stare at the walls. We can do that anytime. We need some music." He walked over to the juke box. "Something to get us happy right now." Harley was a little nervous; he remembered the time Tayo went crazy in the bar and almost killed Emo. He remembered how Tayo had sat staring at the wall, not saying anything all afternoon while the rest of them had been laughing and drinking beer and telling Army stories. Harley told the others not to bother him, but they were drunk and they kept after him. Finally, Tayo jumped up and broke a beer bottle against the table; and before they could stop him, he shoved the jagged glass into Emo's belly.

Tayo smiled and looked over at Harley. "I won't push any broken bottle into your belly, Harley. Your belly's too big anyway."

Harley laughed. "You sure scared us that time, man. Skinny as you are, it took three guys to pull you off him."

"You know what they say, Harley, 'Crazy people are extra strong.' "

Harley shook his head, he was serious. "No, Tayo, you weren't crazy. You were just drunk."

They all had different explanations for the attack. Emo claimed they never got along, not since grade school when they had rock fights in the school yard; he said Tayo had wanted to get even with him for a long time.

They all had explanations; the police, the doctors at the psychiatric ward, even Auntie and old Grandma; they blamed liquor and they blamed the war.

"Reports note that since the Second World War a pattern of drinking and violence, not previously seen before, is emerging among Indian veterans." But Tayo shook his head when the doctor finished reading the report. "No?" the doctor said in a loud voice.

"It's more than that. I can feel it. It's been going on for a long time."

"What do you think it is?"

"I don't know what it is, but I can feel it all around me."

"Is that why you tried to kill Emo?"

"Emo was asking for it."

The wind stirred the dust.
The people were starving.
"She's angry with us,"
        the people said.
"Maybe because of that

55

Ck'o'yo magic
we were fooling with.
We better send someone
to ask our forgiveness."

They noticed hummingbird
was fat and shiny
he had plenty to eat.
They asked how come he
looked so good.

He said
Down below
Three worlds below this one
everything is
green
all the plants are growing
the flowers are blooming.
I go down there
and eat.

"You were real lucky, man.
Real lucky. You could've gone to jail. But they just sent
you to the hospital again. If it had been me, I probably
still been sitting in jail." Harley's words were becoming
disjointed and he was accenting the words at the beginning and swallowing the ending sounds until it didn't
sound like English any more. He had another beer and
then he was rambling on to himself in Laguna.

Emo rattled the Bull Durham
sack. He bounced it in the palm of one hand and then

the other; he took another swallow of whiskey. He had to have two or three swallows of whiskey before he'd talk; he took out the little cloth sack when he was ready.

"You know," he said, slurring the words, "us Indians deserve something better than this goddamn dried-up country around here. Blowing away, every day." He laughed at the rhyme he made. The other guy laughed too because Emo was mean when he was drinking.

"What we need is what they got. I'll take San Diego." He laughed, and they all laughed loudly. He threw the bag up in the air and caught it, confident of his audience. He didn't see Tayo sitting back in the corner, leaning back in the chair with his eyes closed. He didn't know that Tayo was clenching all his muscles against their voices; he didn't know that Tayo was sweating, trying to fight off the nausea that surged at him whenever he heard the rattle in the little bag.

"We fought their war for them."

"Yeah, that's right."

"Yeah, we did."

"But they've got *everything*. And we don't got shit, do we? Huh?"

They all shouted "Hell no" loudly, and they drank the beer faster, and Emo raised the bottle, not bothering to pour the whiskey into the little glass any more.

"They took our land, they took everything! So let's get our hands on white women!" They cheered. Harley and Leroy were grinning and slapping each other on the back. Harley looked over at Tayo, who was reading the label on the beer bottle. (COORS BEER brewed from pure Rocky Mountain spring water. Adolph Coors, Co., Golden, Colorado.) He looked at the picture of the cascading spring on the bottle. He didn't know of any springs that big anywhere. Did they ever have droughts in Colorado? Maybe Emo was wrong: maybe white people didn't have everything. Only Indians had droughts. He finished off the beer; Harley was watching him and gave him another one. He couldn't hear the rattling in the little bag any more, but he could still see Emo playing with it. He was thirsty. Deep down, somewhere behind his belly, near his heart. He drank the beer as if it were the tumbling ice-cold stream in the mountain canyon on the beer label. He kept drinking it, and Harley kept shoving the bottles across the table at him. Attention shifted from Emo to Tayo.

"Hey, look at him!"

"No wonder he doesn't say nothing. How many does that make?" Harley counted the empty bottles. He said something, but it was difficult for Tayo to hear clearly; their voices sounded dim and far away.

He got up and weaved his way between the chairs and tables to the toilet at the back of the room. The yellow stained walls were at the far end of the long tunnel between him and the world. He reached out across this distance to try to steady himself against the walls. He looked down at the stream of urine; it wasn't yellow but clear like water. He imagined then that if a man could bring the drought, he could also return the water, out of his own belly, out of his own body. He strained the muscles of his belly and forced it out.

He pushed down on the handle of the toilet, but it didn't flush; the lid of the toilet tank was leaning against the wall and the floor was covered with dirty water. It was soaking through his boots. The sensation was sudden and terrifying; he could not get out of the room, and he was afraid he would fall into the stinking dirty water and have to crawl through it, like before, with jungle clouds raining down filthy water that smelled ripe with death. He lunged at the door; he landed on his hands and knees in the dark outside the toilet. The dreams did not wait any more for night; they came out anytime.

When he got back to the table he saw that Emo's glasses were sitting crookedly on his puffy face. Emo watched him walk across the room to the table.

"There he is. He thinks he's something all right. Because he's part white. Don't you, half-breed?" Tayo stopped in front of them. He saw all their faces clustered around Emo's fat, sweaty head; he thought of dogs standing over something dead, crowded close together. He couldn't make out Harley or Leroy or Pinkie; all he could see was Emo's sullen face. He stood there in front of them for a long time until his eyes lost focus. Someone touched his arm.

"Come on, Tayo, sit down with us," Leroy said. He put his mouth close to Tayo's ear. "Emo didn't mean nothing. He's just drunk, that's all."

Tayo sat down. He knew Emo meant what he said; Emo had hated him since the time they had been in grade school together, and the only reason for this hate was that Tayo was part white. But Tayo was used to it by now. Since he could remember, he had known Auntie's shame for what his mother had done, and Auntie's shame for him. He remembered how the white men who were building the new highway through Laguna had pointed at him. They had elbowed each other and winked. He never forgot that, and finally, years later, he understood what it was about white men and Indian women: the disgrace of Indian women who went with them. And during the war Tayo learned about white women and Indian men.

We went into this bar on 4th Ave., see,
me and O'Shay, this crazy Irishman.
We had a few drinks, then I saw
these two white women
sitting all alone.
One was kind of fat
She had dark hair.
But this other one, man,
She had big tits and
real blond hair.
I said to him
"Hey buddy, that's the one I want.
Over there."

He said, "Go get 'em, Chief."
He was my best drinking buddy, that guy
He'd watch me
see how good I'd score with each one.
"I'm Italian tonight."
"Oh a Wop!" He laughed
and hollered so loud
both of those girls were watching us then.
I smiled at
both of them, see, so they'd
both think I was friendly.
But I gave my "special look"
to the blonde. So she'd know, see.
That's how I'd do it.
Then I went up to the bar and
I told the bartender I wanted
two more of whatever the ladies over there was
drinking, and I went over.
They took the
drinks and the fat one asked me
to sit down.
I sat down close to the blonde
and told them my name.
I used Mattuci's name that night—this Wop
in our unit.

The fat girl had a car.
I sat in the middle, grabbing titties
with both hands
all the way to Long Beach.
Next day my buddy
was dying to know.
He kept asking
all morning
"Well? Well?"
I told him
"Well, I scored
all right."

"Which one, which one?"
"Not one," I said
"Both of them!"
"Well, I'll be goddamned!"
he said
"all in the same bed?"
"Yes, sir, this In'di'n
was grabbin' white pussy
all night!"
"Shit, Chief,
that's some reputation
you're making for Mattuci!"
"Goddamn," I said
"Maybe next time
I'll send him a bill!"

Pinkie was holding his belly, laughing so hard. Leroy and Harley were slapping each other on the backs, laughing real loud.

"Hey, Emo, that's a good one!"

"Hey, tell the one about the time that guy told on you."

"Which guy?"

"When you were balling that little redhead and what's his name—the Irishman? . . ."

"Yeah, he knocked on the door. You know, the Irishman knocked on the door and yelled, 'Hey, Geronimo!'"

"Oh. Yeah. That time." Emo's forehead was covered with little balls of sweat. He wiped them off with the back of his hand. He was looking at Tayo.

"Come on, Emo, tell it."

"I don't feel like it." The corners of his mouth looked sullen.

"It's so damn funny! That white guy yells, 'Hey Geronimo!' and the white woman hears him and says, 'Who's that?' He says, 'A drunk Irishman.' She says, 'No, who's that Geronimo?' You have a titty in your mouth so you don't answer. She says, 'That's an Indian, isn't it?' She yells back at him, 'This guy's an Indian?' He says, 'Yeah—his name is Geronimo.' She starts screaming and faints."

"Passed out."

"Well, anyway, she fainted or passed out." Leroy and Pinkie finished the story and went for more beer. There was something about the story Emo didn't like. Tayo was watching him; he didn't turn his eyes away when Emo looked back at him. They sat staring at each other across the big round table. Tayo remembered fighting tomcats then, the frozen pose, arched bodies coiled, only the tails twitching with their anger, until one or the other made a move and they went rolling around in the dirt.

"You don't like my stories, do you? Not good enough for you, huh? You think you're hot shit, like your cousin. Big football star. Big hero." Emo pointed a finger at the empties in front of Tayo. "One thing you can do is drink like an Indian, can't you? Maybe you aren't no better than the rest of us, huh?"

Tayo thought of Rocky then, and he was proud that Emo was so envious. The beer kept him loose inside. Emo's words never touched him. The beer stroked a place deep under his heart and put all the feeling to sleep.

Then Emo took out the little bag again. He fumbled with the yellow pull-strings and opened it. He poured the human teeth out on the table. He looked over at Tayo and laughed out loud. He pushed them into circles and rows like unstrung beads; he scooped them into his hand and shook them like dice. They were his war souvenirs, the teeth he had knocked out of the corpse of a Japanese soldier. The night progressed according to that ritual: from cursing the barren dry land the white man had left them, to talking about San Diego and the cities where the white women were still waiting for them to come back to give them another taste of what white women never got enough of. But in the end, they always came around to it.

"We were the best. U.S. Army. We butchered every Jap we found. No Jap bastard was fit to take prisoner. We had all kinds of ways to get information out of them before they died. Cut off this, cut off these." Emo was grinning and hunched over, staring at the teeth.

"Make them talk fast, die slow." He laughed. Pinkie and Harley laughed with him, at his joke. Leroy came over for more money; Tayo threw him a twenty dollar bill. He was getting tense. He needed more beer to keep him loose inside and to make his stomach feel better. He swallowed some more. Every word Emo said pulled the knot in his belly tighter.

"I went after the officers. These teeth, they were from a Jap colonel. Yeah."

Tayo could hear it in his voice when he talked about the killing—how Emo grew from each killing. Emo fed off each man he killed, and the higher the rank of the dead man, the higher it made Emo.

"We blew them all to hell. We should've dropped bombs on all the rest and blown them off the face of the earth."

He went into the old man's field to look at the melons, all round and full of slippery sinews of wet seeds. He raised his foot carefully and brought his boot down hard on the center of the melon. It made a popping sound. Seeds and wet pulp squirted out from the broken rind; they glistened with juice. He kicked the pieces and scattered them around the corn plants. He pulled one from its stem and held it in his hands. The skin was shiny and smooth, veined and mottled like green turquoise; he felt the shape. The symmetry of the oval pleased him; he raised it high over his head and smashed it against the ground. He made certain they were all gone. He looked back, down the long row. Tiny black ants were scurrying over the shattered melons; the flies were rubbing

their feet on fragments of pulp and rind. He trampled
the ants with his boots, and he kicked dirt over the seeds
and pulp. He watched flies buzz in circles above the
burial places.

Emo had liked what they showed him: big mortar shells
that blew tanks and big trucks to pieces; jagged steel
flakes that exploded from the grenades; the way the flame
thrower melted a rifle into a shapeless lump. He understood them right away; he knew what they wanted. He
was the best, they told him; some men didn't like to feel
the quiver of the man they were killing; some men got
sick when they smelled the blood. But he was the best;
he was one of them. The best. United States Army.

Something was different about
the beer this time; it swelled through his blood and made
all the muscles loose and warm, but it was also loosening
something deeper inside which clenched the anger and
held it in place. He could feel it happening. Like two days
of snow piled deep on the branches of a big pine tree the
morning of the second day, when the sun came out and
crystal by crystal penetrated the snow, melting it away
from the pine needles until a single gust of mountain
wind and suddenly all the snow came tumbling down.
    Emo played with the teeth; he pretended to put them
in his own mouth at funny angles. Everyone was laughing. The teeth sucked up the light, and darkness closed
around Tayo with an ambush of voices in English and
Japanese. He clenched his hands around the bottle until
he felt a sharp snap. It was too late then. It tore loose.
The little Japanese boy was smiling in the L.A. depot;
darkness came like night fog and someone was bending
over a small body.

Tayo jumped up from the table, panting; the sweat ran down his face like tears.

"Killer!" he screamed. "Killer!"

The others were quiet, but Emo started laughing. His voice echoed around the room.

"You drink like an Indian, and you're crazy like one too—but you aren't shit, white trash. You love Japs the way your mother loved to screw white men."

Emo's shirt had dark circles of sweat under each arm. Tayo watched his belly and the way the shirt stuck to it with sweat; he watched the belly quiver when Emo laughed at him. He moved suddenly, with speed which was effortless and floating like a mountain lion. He got stronger with every jerk that Emo made, and he felt that he would get well if he killed him. But they wouldn't let him do it; they grabbed his arms and pulled his hands out of Emo's belly. He saw their mouths open, yelling, but he didn't hear them, and the snow tumbled over him. The silence was dense; the darkness was cold.

When the cops came, he was still gripping the broken bottle in his hand, and watching his own blood flow between the fingers of his fist and drip on the Mexican's oiled wood floor. He stood still; only his brain was moving. The haze from the beer was gone, like heat and dust washed out of the sky by a summer rain. He should have hated Emo; he should have hated the Jap soldiers who killed Rocky. The space to carry hate was located deep inside, below his lungs and behind his belly; but it was empty. He watched while they knelt over Emo and then loaded him into the ambulance. His hand didn't hurt either; the blood felt like warm water trickling down his fingers. He didn't feel anything.

The cops made him show them the hand. They wrapped it tight with a big roll of gauze and handcuffed him. He dozed in the back seat of the police car all the way to Albuquerque; he knew what his eyes had seen, and what his ears had heard; he knew what he felt in his belly and up and down his backbone. But he wasn't sure any more what to believe or whom he could trust. He wasn't sure.

       The Army recruiter had taped posters of tanks and marching soldiers around the edge of a folding table. The Government car was parked next to the post office under the flagpole, and he had set up the table next to the car, trying to find shelter from the wind. But the posters were flapping and twisting around, and the brittle edges of the paper were beginning to split and tear. There was a chill in the wind during the last days the sun occupied a summer place in the sky—and something relentless in the way the wind drove the sand and dust ahead of it. The recruiter was sitting on his folding chair, but he had to keep both hands on his pamphlets to keep them from scattering. He had been waiting for more people to show up before he began his speech, but Rocky and Tayo and old man Jeff were the only people out in the wind that afternoon.

"Anyone can fight for America," he began, giving special emphasis to "America," "even you boys. In a time of need, anyone can fight for her." A big gust of sand swirled around them; Rocky turned his back to it and Tayo covered his face with his hands; old man Jeff went inside the post office. The recruiter paused to rearrange the pamphlets and check the damage the wind had done to the posters. He looked disgusted then, as though he were almost ready to leave. But he went on with his speech.

"Now I know you boys love America as much as we do, but this is your big chance to *show* it!" He stood up then, as he had rehearsed, and looked them in the eye sincerely. He handed them color pamphlets with a man in a khaki uniform and gold braid on the cover; in the background, behind the figure in the uniform, there was a gold eagle with its wings spread across an American flag.

Rocky read each page of the pamphlet carefully. He looked up at Tayo and his face was serious and proud. Tayo knew right then what Rocky wanted to do. The wind blew harder; a gust caught the pamphlets and swirled them off the card table. They scattered like dry leaves across the ground. The recruiter ran after them with his arms out in front of him as if he were chasing turkeys. Rocky helped him pick them up, and he nodded sharply for Tayo to help too. Rocky talked to the recruiter about the training programs while they shook sand out of the brochures and folded them up again.

"I want to be a pilot." He paused and looked at the recruiter. "You can fly all over the world that way, can't you?"

The recruiter was packing the leaflets into a cardboard box; he didn't look up. "Sure, sure," he said, "you enlist now and you'll be eligible for everything—pilot training —everything." He folded the legs under the little table and slammed down the lid of the car's trunk. He glanced at his big chrome wristwatch.

"You men want to sign up?"

Rocky looked at Tayo as if he wanted to ask him something. It was strange to see that expression on his face, because Rocky had always known what he was doing, without asking anyone.

"And my brother," Rocky said, nodding at Tayo. "If we both sign up, can we stay together?"

It was the first time in all the years that Tayo had lived with him that Rocky ever called him "brother." Auntie had always been careful that Rocky didn't call Tayo "brother," and when other people mistakenly called them brothers, she was quick to correct the error.

"They're not brothers," she'd say, "that's Laura's boy. You know the one." She had a way of saying it, a tone of voice which bitterly told the story, and the disgrace she and the family had suffered. The things Laura had done weren't easily forgotten by the people, but she could maintain a distance between Rocky, who was her pride, and this other, unwanted child. If nobody else ever knew about this distance, she and Tayo did.

He was four years old the night his mother left him there. He didn't remember much: only that she had come after dark and wrapped him in a man's coat—it smelled like a man—and that there were men in the car with them: and she held him all the way, kept him bundled tight and close to her, and he had dozed and listened, half dreaming their laughter and the sound of a cork squeaking in and out of a bottle. He could not remember if she had fed him, but when they got to Laguna that night, he wasn't hungry and he refused the bread Uncle Josiah offered him. He clung to her because when she left him, he knew she would be gone for a long time. She kissed him on the forehead with whiskey breath, and then pushed him gently into Josiah's arms as she backed out the door. He cried and fought Josiah, trying to follow her, but his uncle held him firmly and told him not to cry because he had a brother now: Rocky would be his brother, and he could stay with them until Christmas. Rocky had been staring at him, but with the mention of Christmas he started crying and kicking the leg of the table. There were tears all over his face and his nose was running.

"Go away," he screamed, "you're not my brother. I don't want no brother!" Tayo covered his ears with his hands and buried his face against Josiah's leg, crying because he knew: this time she wasn't coming back for him. Josiah pulled out his red bandanna handkerchief and wiped Tayo's nose and eyes. He looked at Rocky sternly and then took both of the little boys by the hand. They walked into the back room together, and Josiah showed him the bed that he and Rocky would share for so many years.

When old Grandma and Auntie came home that night from the bingo game at church, Tayo and Rocky were already in bed. Tayo could tell by the sound of his breathing that Rocky was already asleep. But he lay there in the dark and listened to voices in the kitchen, voices of Josiah and Auntie and the faint voice of old Grandma. He never knew what they said that night, because the voices merged into a hum, like night insects around a lamp; but he thought he could hear Auntie raise her voice and the sound of pots and pans slamming together on the stove. And years later he learned she did that whenever she was angry.

It was a private understanding between the two of them. When Josiah or old Grandma or Robert was there, the agreement was suspended, and she pretended to treat him the same as she treated Rocky, but they both knew it was only temporary. When she was alone with the boys, she kept Rocky close to her; while she kneaded the bread, she gave Rocky little pieces of dough to play with; while she darned socks, she gave him scraps of cloth and a needle and thread to play with. She was careful that Rocky did not share these things with Tayo, that they kept a distance between themselves and him. But she would not let Tayo go outside or play in another room alone. She wanted him close enough to feel excuded, to be aware of the distance between them. The two little boys accepted the distance, but Rocky was never cruel to Tayo. He seemed to know that the narrow silence was reserved only for times when the three of them were alone together. They sensed the difference in her when old Grandma or Josiah was present, and they adjusted without hesitation, keeping their secret.

But after they started school, the edges of the distance softened, and Auntie seldom had the boys to herself any more. They were gone most of the day, and old Grandma was totally blind by then and always there, sitting close to her stove. Rocky was more anxious than Tayo to stay away from the house, to stay after school for sports or to play with friends. It was Rocky who withdrew from her, although only she and Tayo realized it. He did it naturally, like a rabbit leaping away from a shadow suddenly above him.

Tayo and Auntie understood each other very well. Years later Tayo wondered if anyone, even old Grandma or Josiah, ever understood her as well as he did. He learned to listen to the undertones of her voice. Robert and Josiah evaded her; they were deaf to those undertones. In her blindness and old age, old Grandma stubbornly ignored her and heard only what she wanted to hear. Rocky had his own way, with his after-school sports and his girl friends. Only Tayo could hear it, like fingernails scratching against bare rock, her terror at being trapped in one of the oldest ways.

An old sensitivity had descended in her, surviving thousands of years from the oldest times, when the people shared a single clan name and they told each other who they were; they recounted the actions and words each of their clan had taken, and would take; from before they were born and long after they died, the people shared the same consciousness. The people had known, with the simple certainty of the world they saw, how everything should be.

But the fifth world had become entangled with European names: the names of the rivers, the hills, the names of the animals and plants—all of creation suddenly had two names: an Indian name and a white name. Christianity separated the people from themselves; it tried to crush the single clan name, encouraging each person to stand alone, because Jesus Christ would save only the individual soul; Jesus Christ was not like the Mother who loved and cared for them as her children, as her family.

The sensitivity remained: the ability to feel what the others were feeling in the belly and chest; words were not necessary, but the messages the people felt were confused now. When Little Sister had started drinking wine and riding in cars with white men and Mexicans, the people could not define their feeling about her. The Catholic priest shook his finger at the drunkenness and lust, but the people felt something deeper: they were losing her, they were losing part of themselves. The older sister had to act; she had to act for the people, to get this young girl back.

It might have been possible if the girl had not been ashamed of herself. Shamed by what they taught her in school about the deplorable ways of the Indian people; holy missionary white people who wanted only good for the Indians, white people who dedicated their lives to helping the Indians, these people urged her to break away from her home. She was excited to see that despite the fact she was an Indian, the white men smiled at her from their cars as she walked from the bus stop in Albuquerque back to the Indian School. She smiled and waved; she looked at her own reflection in windows of houses she passed; her dress, her lipstick, her hair—it was all done perfectly, the way the home-ec teacher taught them, exactly like the white girls.

But after she had been with them, she could feel the truth in their fists and in their greedy feeble love-making; but it was a truth which she had no English words for. She hated the people at home when white people talked about their peculiarities; but she always hated herself more because she still thought about them, because she knew their pain at what she was doing with her life. The feelings of shame, at her own people and at the white people, grew inside her, side by side like monstrous twins that would have to be left in the hills to die. The people wanted her back. Her older sister must bring her back. For the people, it was that simple, and when they failed, the humiliation fell on all of them; what happened to the girl did not happen to her alone, it happened to all of them.

They focused the anger on the girl and her family, knowing from many years of this conflict that the anger could not be contained by a single person or family, but that it must leak out and soak into the ground under the entire village.

So Auntie had tried desperately to reconcile the family with the people; the old instinct had always been to gather the feelings and opinions that were scattered through the village, to gather them like willow twigs and tie them into a single prayer bundle that would bring peace to all of them. But now the feelings were twisted, tangled roots, and all the names for the source of this growth were buried under English words, out of reach. And there would be no peace and the people would have no rest until the entanglement had been unwound to the source.

He could anticipate her mood by watching her face. She had a special look she gave him when she wanted to talk to him alone. He never forgot the strange excitement he felt when she looked at him that way, and called him aside.

"Nobody will ever tell you this," she said, "but you must hear it so you will understand why things are this way." She was referring to the distance she kept between him and herself. "Your uncle and grandma don't know this story. I couldn't tell them because it would hurt them so much." She swallowed hard to clear the pain from her throat, and his own throat hurt too, because without him there would have not been so much shame and disgrace for the family.

"Poor old Grandma. It would hurt her so much if she ever heard this story." She looked at Tayo and picked a thread off the bottom of her apron. Her mouth was small and tight when she talked to him alone. He sat on a gunny sack full of the corn that Robert and Josiah had dried last year, and when he shifted his weight even slightly, he could hear the hard kernels move. The room was always cool, even in the summertime, and it smelled like the dried apples in flour sacks hanging above them from the rafters. That day he could smell the pale, almost blue clay the old women used for plastering the walls.

"One morning," she said, "before you were born, I got up to go outside, right before sunrise. I knew she had been out all night because I never heard her come in. Anyway, I thought I would walk down toward the river. I just had a feeling, you know. I stood on that sandrock, above the big curve in the river, and there she was, coming down the trail on the other side." She looked at him closely. "I am only telling you this because she was your mother, and you have to understand." She cleared her throat. "Right as the sun came up, she walked under that big cottonwood tree, and I could see her clearly: she had no clothes on. Nothing. She was completely naked except for her high-heel shoes. She dropped her purse under that tree. Later on some kids found it there and brought it back. It was empty except for a lipstick." Tayo swallowed and took a breath.

"Auntie," he said softly, "what did she look like before I was born?"

She reached behind the pantry curtains and began to rearrange the jars of peaches and apricots on the shelves, and he knew she was finished talking to him. He closed the storeroom door behind him and went to the back room and sat on the bed. He sat for a long time and thought about his mother. There had been a picture of her once, and he had carried the tin frame to bed with him at night, and whispered to it. But one evening, when he carried it with him, there were visitors in the kitchen, and she grabbed it away from him. He cried for it and Josiah came to comfort him; he asked Tayo why he was crying, but just as he was ashamed to tell Josiah about the understanding between him and Auntie, he also could not tell him about the picture; he loved Josiah too much to admit the shame. So he held onto Josiah tightly, and pressed his face into the flannel shirt and smelled woodsmoke and sheep's wool and sweat. He even forgot about

the picture except sometimes when he tried to remember
how she looked. Then he wished Auntie would give
it back to him to keep on top of Josiah's dresser. But
he could never bring himself to ask her. The day in
the storeroom, when he asked how his mother had
looked before he was born, was the closest he'd ever
come to mentioning the picture.

"So that's where our mother went.
How can we get down there?"

Hummingbird looked at all the
skinny people.
He felt sorry for them.
He said, "You need a messenger.
Listen, I'll tell you
what to do":

Bring a beautiful pottery jar
painted with parrots and big
flowers.
Mix black mountain dirt
some sweet corn flour
and a little water.

Cover the jar with a
new buckskin
and say this over the jar
and sing this softly
above the jar:
After four days
you will be alive
After four days
you will be alive
After four days
you will be alive
After four days
you will be alive

The Army recruiter looked closely at Tayo's light brown skin and his hazel eyes.

"You guys are brothers?"

Rocky nodded coolly.

"If you say so," the recruiter said. It was beginning to get dark and he wanted to get back to Albuquerque.

Tayo signed his name after Rocky. He felt light on his feet, happy that he would be with Rocky, traveling the world in the Army, together, as brothers. Rocky patted him on the back, smiling too.

"We can do real good, Tayo. Go all over the world. See different places and different people. Look at that guy, the recruiter. He's got his own Government car to drive, too."

But when he saw the house and Josiah's pickup parked in the yard, he remembered. The understanding had always been that Rocky would be the one to leave home, go to college or join the Army. But someone had to stay and help out with the garden and sheep camp. He had made a promise to Josiah to help with the Mexican cattle. He stopped. Rocky asked him what was wrong.

"I can't go," he said. "I told Josiah I'd stay and help him."

"Him and Robert can get along."

"No," Tayo said, feeling the hollow spread from his stomach to his chest, his heart echoing in his ears. "No."

Rocky walked on without him; Tayo stood there watching the darkness descend. He was familiar with that hollow feeling. He remembered it from the nights after they had buried his mother, when he stuffed the bed covers around his stomach and close to his heart, hugging the blankets into the empty space of loss, regret for things which could not be changed.

"Let him go," Josiah said, "you can't keep him forever."

Auntie let the lid on the frying pan clatter on top of the stove.

"Rocky is different," she kept saying, "but this one, he's supposed to stay here."

"Let him go," old Grandma said. "They can look after each other, and bring each other home again."

Rocky dunked his tortilla in the chili beans and kept chewing; he didn't care what they said. He was already thinking of the years ahead and the new places and people that were waiting for him in the future he had lived for since he first began to believe in the word "someday" the way white people do.

"I'll bring him back safe," Tayo said softly to her the night before they left. "You don't have to worry." She looked up from her Bible, and he could see that she was waiting for something to happen; but he knew that she always hoped, that she always expected it to happen to him, not to Rocky.

Part of the five hundred dollar deal was that Ulibarri would deliver the cattle. Tayo helped Josiah separate the best ones from the rest of the herd. Josiah had borrowed Ulibarri's big palomino horse, the one Ulibarri claimed was a brother to the champion cutting horse at the State Fair. Whenever Josiah cut a cow away from the rest of the herd, Tayo swung the gate open wide and stepped back to let it run into the holding pen. Josiah cut out twenty cows; he looked for the youngest and strongest ones. They didn't want Ulibarri to try anything funny, like substituting a crippled cow for a sound one or sending one with runny eyes; so before they left, they walked around the pen slowly, memorizing each cow—the shape of the long curved horns, the patterns of the brown spots on their ivory hides, their size and weight. The last thing Josiah did was lean out the window of the truck and tell Ulibarri, "Don't starve them to death."

All the way home from Magdalena, Josiah pulled at the short hairs in the little mustache he wore drooping down at the corners of his mouth, always at odds with his mouth because Josiah was always smiling. He looked over at Tayo and grinned.

"I'm thinking about those cattle, Tayo. See, things work out funny sometimes. Cattle prices are way down now because of the dry spell. Everybody is afraid to buy. But see, this gives us the chance. Otherwise, we probably never would get into the cattle business."

The sun was shining in the back window of the truck, and Tayo had the window rolled down and his arm hanging out, feeling the air rush past. He felt proud when Joaish talked about cattle business. He was ready to work hard with his uncle. They had already discussed it. He was graduating in a month, and then he would work with Josiah and Robert. They would breed these cattle, special cattle, not the weak, soft Herefords that grew thin and died from eating thistle and burned-off cactus during the drought. The cattle Ulibarri sold them were exactly what they had been thinking about. These cattle were descendants of generations of desert cattle, born in dry sand and scrubby mesquite, where they hunted water the way desert antelope did.

"Cattle are like any living thing. If you separate them from the land for too long, keep them in barns and corrals, they lose something. Their stomachs get to where they can only eat rolled oats and dry alfalfa. When you turn them loose again, they go running all over. They are scared because the land is unfamiliar, and they are lost. They don't stop being scared either, even when they look quiet and they quit running. Scared animals die off easily." They were driving down the gravel road, going east from Magdalena to catch the highway near Socorro. Tayo was used to him talking like that, going over his ideas and plans out loud, and then asking Tayo what he thought.

"See, I'm not going to make the mistake other guys

made, buying those Hereford, white-face cattle. If it's going to be a drought these next few years, then we need some special breed of cattle." He had a stack of books on the floor beside his bed, with his reading glasses sitting on top. Every night, for a few minutes after he got in bed, he'd read about cattle breeding in the books the extension agent had loaned to him. Scientific cattle breeding was very complicated, he said, and he used to wait until Rocky and Tayo were doing their homework on the kitchen table, and then he would come in from the back room, with his glasses on, carrying a book.

"Read this," he would tell Rocky, "and see if you think it's saying the same thing I think it says." When Rocky finished it, Josiah pushed the book in front of Tayo and pointed at the passage. Then he'd say, "Well?" And the boys would tell him what they got out of it. "That's what I thought too," Josiah would say, "but it seemed like such a stupid idea I wasn't sure if I was understanding it right." The problem was the books were written by white people who did not think about drought or winter blizzards or dry thistles, which the cattle had to live with. When Tayo saw Ulibarri's cattle, he thought of the diagram of the ideal beef cow which had been in the back of one of the books, and these cattle were everything that the ideal cow was not. They were tall and had long thin legs like deer; their heads were long and angular, with heavy bone across the eyes supporting wide sharp horns which curved out over the shoulders. Their eyes were big and wild.

"I guess we will have to get along without these books," he said. "We'll have to do things our own way. Maybe we'll even write our own book, *Cattle Raising on Indian Land*, or how to raise cattle that don't eat grass or drink water."

Tayo and Robert laughed with him, but Rocky was quiet. He looked up from his books.

"Those books are written by scientists. They know everything there is to know about beef cattle. That's the trouble with the way the people around here have always done things—they never knew what they were doing." He went back to reading his book. He did not hesitate to speak like that, to his father and his uncle, because the subject was books and scientific knowledge—those things that Rocky had learned to believe in.

Tayo was suddenly sad because what Rocky said was true. What did they know about raising cattle? They weren't scientists. Auntie had been listening but she did not seem to notice Rocky's disrespect. She valued Rocky's growing understanding of the outside world, of the books, of everything of importance and power. He was becoming what she had always wanted: someone who could not only make sense of the outside world but become part of it. She did not like the cattle business and she was pleased to have a scientific reason for the way she felt. This cattle deal was bound to be no good, because Ulibarri was a cousin to that whore. She was almost certain it was that woman who had been talking to Josiah, telling him things which were not true, things which did not agree with the scientific books that the BIA extension man had loaned them. But it was his money, and if that's what he wanted to do with twenty years of money he saved up, then let him make a fool of himself.

"I think it was some kind of trick," she told Rocky and Tayo one evening, when old Grandma was snoring in her chair. Auntie glanced over at her to be sure she was asleep before she said it. "That dirty Mexican woman did it so Ulibarri could get rid of those worthless cattle. They gypped him. They made an old fool out of him."

Rocky did not hear her; he was reading a sports magazine. But Tayo had heard; he always listened to her, and now his stomach felt tense; he was afraid maybe she was right, because he already knew she was right about some things.

"One thing after another all the time." She looked at Tayo, and he turned away and stared at old Grandma.

Her mouth hung open a little when she slept, and occasionally he could hear a snoring sound.

"Well," she said with a big sigh, "it will give them something else to laugh about."

Rocky didn't say anything; but when he turned the page he looked up at her as though he were tired of the sound of her voice. Tayo knew that what village people thought didn't matter to Rocky any more. He was already planning where he would go after high school; he was already talking about the places he would live, and the reservation wasn't one of them.

Auntie got out her black church shoes and wiped them carefully with a clean damp cloth, putting her finger inside the cloth and cleaning around each of the eyelets where the laces were strung; she examined them closely by the lamp on the table to make sure that any dust or spots of dirt left from last Sunday had been removed. She had gone to church alone, for as long as Tayo could remember; although she told him that she prayed they would be baptized, she never asked any of them, not even Rocky, to go with her. Later on, Tayo wondered if she liked it that way, going to church by herself, where she could show the people that she was a devout Christian and not immoral or pagan like the rest of the family. When it came to saving her own soul, she wanted to be careful that there were no mistakes.

Old Grandma woke up. She asked Auntie what she was doing. She asked Tayo and then Rocky. Auntie had to speak to Rocky because he didn't hear old Grandma the first time when she asked him what he was doing. Then old Grandma straightened up in her chair.

"Church," she said, wiping her eyes with a Kleenex from her apron pocket. "Ah Thelma, do you have to go there again?"

They unloaded the cows one by one, looking them over carefully. The cattle seemed thinner than the week before in Magdalena, but as Josiah said, you couldn't expect Ulibarri to feed someone else's stock. Tayo swung open the big gate to the cattle chute and Robert opened the door on the truck. They bolted down the ramp nimbly, and as each cow saw the open gate ahead, she lowered her head and snorted, racing out the opening. They kept running, and they didn't stop to look back at the big truck or the corrals until they were a quarter mile away. They bunched up, wary and skittish; when the last cow had run into the little herd, they stood for a moment, staring at the windmills and corrals and at the men beside the truck. Then they took off, heading south in a steady, traveling gait. Tayo watched them disappear over the horizon, their ivory hides shining, speckled brown like a butterfly's wing.

"They are really beautiful, aren't they?" Josiah said.

Tayo nodded. The truck driver slammed the door and started the diesel engine. Robert joined them.

"Well?" Josiah said.

"Well, how far will they run?" Robert was smiling. "I haven't seen anything so fast since the horse races at the State Fair."

They had unloaded them on the Sedillo Grant because the grass was still good down there. Josiah wanted to give them a good start because they would be calving later on. But a week later, when they went to check on the cattle, they didn't find them around the windmill where they had unloaded them. Ordinary cattle would have stayed near the water unless there had been rain or many other places for water. Josiah stopped the truck and got out; he pulled his leather work gloves from his hip pocket and put them on. Tayo untied the horses and opened the gate on the stock rack. He backed the big sorrel out first.

They rode south with the sun climbing up in the east, making the sky bright, almost blinding. There were no clouds and the air still smelled cool. He wanted to remember the morning, bright and clear as the leaves on the little green plants which grew low and close to the sandy ground. It had the clarity of the sky after a summer rainstorm, when the dust was washed away, and the colors of the hills and the shadows of the mesas had an intensity which made everything he saw accessible, as if he could touch all of it, even the little green rabbit weed growing close to the sand, its tiny leaves clustered like stars.

He looked over at Josiah. He was blowing little puffs of smoke from a thin cigarette he had rolled; he looked very satisfied too, as if he were satisfied with everything that morning, even that his cattle had wandered away. He was thinking about something. Probably the cattle. They'd left the windmill, so they would have to travel until they found more water. Herefords would not look for water. When a windmill broke down or a pool went dry, Tayo had seen them standing and waiting patiently for the truck or wagon loaded with water, or for riders to herd them to water. If nobody came and there was no snow or rain, then they died there, still waiting. But these Mexican cattle were different. Josiah grinned at Tayo and nodded. Tayo smiled and nodded back at him.

When they got to the Sedillo fence, they dismounted and walked along a thirty-foot section where the tracks crisscrossed and the cattle had milled around before they broke through the fence. There were tufts of hair snagged in the barbs of wire, and in some places a strand of wire had been pulled loose from a fence pole and was hanging slack like old clothesline.

"Well, I guess we have to expect this too," he said, pulling some of the hairs loose from the wire and letting them blow away in the wind.

"What if they just keep going, you know, crossing fences all the way back to Mexico?"

"They try that the first two or three days after you move them, but they'll settle down. We can handle them, Tayo."

The Mexican cattle settled down and moved more slowly, but they still had little regard for fences. They watered and grazed at the Cañoncito windmill for a few days before they started traveling again. It was simple to keep track of them because they were always moving south. By the end of May they were all the way to the flats by Fernando's place; but they still ran if the men on horseback tried to get close; and if they were pushed into a corner where fences intersected, they lunged through the wire without hesitation and trotted away to a safe distance, where they stood in a semicircle to watch the horsemen.

They had not bothered to brand the cattle because they had a bill of sale which acknowledged their Mexican brands. But when they saw how the cattle kept moving, Josiah got worried and decided to brand them in case they got off reservation land. So in the middle of June, Tayo and Rocky and Robert went to help Josiah with his cows. It took almost the entire day to round them up because they were so wild. As Robert said, it was okay as long as they were in flat open country with only a few places to water; they could be found then. But he would hate to see them get up into the hills in the thick junipers and piñons where they could hide. "You'll never get them then, except with a thirty-thirty," Robert said, and Josiah nodded. There were three calves born where they corralled them, and two of the cows looked as if they would calve within a few days. The little calves reminded Tayo of new shoes, bright white with light brown speckles, silky and untouched by mud and sand. It was difficult to see how these calves would grow according to Josiah's theories. They were the same color as their mothers and they had the same wild eyes. But Robert had to admit that the calves were stocky through the shoulder and hip, showing at least some trace of the fine registered Hereford bull that Ulibarri had insisted and sworn was their sire. They still ran like antelope in the big corral, bawling to escape the men with ropes. But Josiah said they would grow up heavy and covered with meat like Herefords, but tough too, like the Mexican cows, able to withstand hard winters and many dry years. That was his plan.

It was a good day when they branded them. Big fluffy clouds that were high on the west horizon in the morning were dark blue and low by the afternoon, and a sudden rain shower came and washed down the dust of the corral and the sweat from the work. The cows already had big Mexican brands on their sides, extending across their ribs, a brand so big you could see it for a half mile, Josiah said. And Robert nodded, and added, "That's about as close as you can get to them anyway." The brand wasn't like American brands, which were initials or letters or even numbers; it looked like a big butterfly with its wings outstretched, or two loops of rope tied together in the center. They added Auntie's brand, a rafter 4, on the left shoulder of the cows and calves, and let them go. They galloped away, kicking up red clay dust; they were still going south.

Josiah went to see her the day after the cattle were delivered. He talked to Tayo in a low confidential tone and told him not to let Auntie or old Grandma find out. They were outside at the woodpile, each with an arm full of kindling, but he whispered to Tayo as if Auntie were only a few feet away from them. He straightened up and glanced over Tayo's head at the sun, which was was almost down, and spoke in a more natural tone.

84

"Anyway," he said casually, "I am only going up there to thank her again for letting me in on a good deal." He changed his shirt and put on a stiff new pair of Levis and wiped off his fifty dollar boots with the towel that was still damp from drying his arms and face. He told Tayo to get the sharp scissors out of Auntie's sewing basket, and he trimmed the hairs in his thin mustache. Tayo followed him outside into the cool dim evening. Josiah looked at his own reflection in the truck window, stroking the hairs of his mustache into place. He made Tayo promise to tell Auntie and Grandma that he had gone to Paguate on business. Tayo nodded, but he figured they already knew where Josiah was going anyway.

She was sitting in the shade on her wicker chair; her eyes were closed and her face was relaxed. He liked to look at the way her light brown skin had wrinkled at the corners of her eyes and her mouth, from too much laughing she liked to say. She knew he was standing there because the stairs up to the second floor porch were loose and squeaked. "Sit down," she said, without opening her eyes, "enjoy the springtime with me." He liked the way she talked. There was something in her eyes too. He saw it the first time when she had said, "I've seen you before many times, and I always remembered you." Josiah could not remember ever seeing her before, but there was something in her hazel brown eyes that made him believe her. He sat on the straight-back chair beside her and looked over at the big cottonwood that grew next to the porch, its branches sweeping and wide, hiding a portion of the northeast sky.

On the fourth day
something buzzed around
inside the jar.

They lifted the buckskin
and a big green fly
with yellow feelers on his head
flew out of the jar.

"Fly will go with me," Hummingbird said.
"We'll go see
what she wants."

They flew to the fourth world
below.
Down there
was another kind of daylight
everything was blooming
and growing
everything was so beautiful.

        The hot weather and the fact
that Lalo had always bootlegged beer to the Lagunas and
Acomas brought him there one day when she was sitting
in the shade of the porch outside the bar. She spoke first,
asking if he had a cigarette paper. Josiah was surprised
that a Mexican woman had spoken to him, and he gave
her the paper without looking at her face. He stared at the
sack of Bull Durham in her lap and watched the way she

rolled the cigarette without spilling any tobacco. He was suddenly aware that she was watching him, and he mumbled something about it being a hot day, and then left with his paper sack full of cold beer. But the rest of the afternoon, and that night too, he had an uncomfortable feeling that he had forgotten or lost something at Lalo's. After supper he went out to make sure his work gloves were on the seat of the truck. He reached into his pocket and counted the money to make sure Lalo had given him the right change. He didn't sleep well that night either, and even while he dreamed he was still aware of this feeling, that something had been left behind. So the next day he went back to Cubero. It wasn't until he drove past the Cubero store and found himself looking to see if she was sitting on the porch that he realized his heart was beating like a boy's, and it was too late. He knew then what it was he had left behind.

She looked up and smiled as if she had been waiting for him. She got up from her chair as he came up the steps and gestured at the bright sun and cloudless sky. "It's too hot down here," she said, walking to the stairs at the end of the long porch. He didn't say anything; he just followed her up the spiral stairs.

"Some things I don't remember too well," she said, "names of the places, names of the people, or even their faces. These small towns like El Paso and Socorro were full of people passing through the way I was. I danced. That was all that was important."

She got up from the bed and disappeared through the curtains across the doorway. Josiah heard her cranking the Victrola; the needle scratched over the flamenco music. She brought out the shoes from a trunk under the bed. They had been wrapped carefully in white tissue paper: shiny black leather with high square heels. She hitched the blue silk dress higher on her wide hips and held the edges of the fabric in both hands as she arched her back and tossed her head. At first, all he was aware of were the heels of the shoes beating rapidly against the floor, and he wondered if Lalo and the afternoon customers in the bar downstairs could hear it. But as the music gathered speed, he forgot about how she made the room shake, because the spinning and tossing of her body and the momentum of the music had gathered him close, and he found himself breathing hard and sweating when the Victrola finally ran down.

She sat back down on the bed beside him and wiped the shoes on the hem of the blue dress before she wrapped them up again and put them back in the trunk. "They called me the Night Swan," she said. "I remember every time I have danced."

                      If she had not been so young, she would have realized that he was nothing, that the power she was feeling had always been inside her, growing, pushing to the surface, only its season coinciding with her new lover. But she was young and she had never felt the power of the dance so strongly before, and she wanted to keep it; she wanted it with a great ferocity which she mistook for passion for this man. She was certain about him; he could not get enough of her. He would lie beside her under the blanket and his eyes would be fevered even after he was limp and incapable of taking any more from her. She kept him there for as long as she could, searching out the boundary, the end to the power of the feeling. She wanted to prowl those warm close places until she discovered the end because at that time she had not yet seen that the horizon was an illusion and the plains extended infinitely; and up until that final evening, she had found no limit.

She knew it before he spoke. His eyes were still feverish as he spoke and his fingers quivered like the legs of a dreaming dog; at that moment he wanted her more than he had ever wanted her. And it was for that she would not forgive him. She could have accepted it if he had told her that her light brown belly no longer excited him. She would have sensed it herself and told him to go. But he was quitting because his desire for her had uncovered something which had been hiding inside him, something with wings that could fly, escape the gravity of the Church, the town, his mother, his wife. So he wanted to kill it: to crush the skull into the feathers and snap the bones of the wings.

"Whore! Witch! Look at what you made me do to my family and my wife."

"You came breathlessly," she answered in a steady voice, "but you will always prefer the lie. You will repeat it to your wife; you will repeat it at confession. You damn your own soul better than I ever could."

He grabbed her shoulders; his mouth was twisted open and the breath was hot and short; but it was his own body, not hers, which shook. Then his hands went limp and fell with their own weight from her shoulders.

"We will run you out of town," he said. "People listen to me. I'm somebody in this town."

That night she danced he was already a dead man, a living dead man who sucked life from the living, desiring and hating it even as he took it. The ecstasy he found in her had illuminated the dead tissues and outlined the hollow of his spirit. She danced, spinning her body, pulling her thighs and hips into tight sudden motions, bending, sweeping, veering, and lunging—whirling until she was the bull and at the same time the killer, holding out her full skirts like a cape.

The men sitting around tables at the edge of the dance floor pushed themselves away, some stumbling over chairs, spilling their beer in a panic that pounded in their chests like her heels against the floor. The bartender left a towel stuffed in a glass he had been wiping. But they watched; pressing close to one another, shivering in the farthest corner of the bar, they watched her; and when the guitar player finally laid his instrument on the floor and held his head between his hands, she danced on.

"I knew nothing of minutes or hours. There were changes I could feel; the boards of the dance floor began to flex and glisten. The creaking of the wood became a moan and a cry; my balance was precarious as if the floor were no longer level. And then I could feel something breaking under my feet, the heels of my dancing shoes sinking into something crushed dark until the balance and smoothness were restored once again to the dance floor." She looked up at Josiah and pulled at a blue thread hanging from the sleeve of her dress.

"His wife came into the bar screaming. The damp cold of the snowstorm wind followed her through the door she had thrown open wide. Memory is strange. I don't remember her face or her name, but I remember her feet. There was new snow on her bare feet where she had run from her house to the cantina; they were pale and small on the dark oiled-wood floor. I watched the snow melt into little streams between her toes while she accused me."

She paused and rolled herself another thin cigarette. "There had been some kind of accident with his horses late that night," she said as she lighted it, inhaling deep and shaking her head slowly. "His screaming woke her up. She ran into the snow like that—nightgown and bare feet—and found him in the corral. His own horses had trampled him. That was all." Her hazel eyes were shining; she smiled at Josiah. "Who listens to the stories wives tell?" She squeezed his arm. "But all that was a long time ago—I don't even remember how many years ago that happened in Las Cruces." She poured him more beer in a thick pottery cup with yellow flowers painted around it. "I'm a grandmother now. My daughter in

Los Angeles has two beautiful little daughters. And when I dance now, I dance for them."

She moved closer to him on the bed. "One day I got up and walked down the main street of Socorro. The wind was blowing dust down the little side streets and I felt like I was the only one living there any more. The drought was drying out the land, stealing away the river, so that even the cottonwoods and tamarics along the banks were drying up. I had a feeling then—something inside me beginning to shrink thin and dry like old newspapers gone yellow in the bottom of a trunk. I rode the bus this far. I saw the mountain, and I liked the view from here." She nodded in the direction of the mountain, Tse-pi'na, the woman veiled in clouds.

She shook her head slowly and emptied the last of the beer into her cup. "Old age," she said, laughing, "the first sign of old age is all this talking when we could be doing something else. . . ." She winked at him and Josiah pulled her close, promising himself he would never ask her what it was about the mountain that caused her to stop there.

At first the Cubero people were upset about the Night Swan's choice of a retirement place. Lalo was sullen when anyone asked, and he said it was his wife who had rented her the rooms above the bar. He always added that they were old and dusty and no one else would live up there because the juke box played loud and drunks yelled and stomped up and down the long porch downstairs. Of course only that kind of woman, used to that kind of life, would tolerate such things. After she moved in, people said the steps on the spiral staircase at the end of the porch were never dusty any more; but that was only rumor, and there were conflicting stories about where she got her money. But the facts remained: she was an old cantina dancer with eyes like a cat. The women watched the bright blue door on the second-story porch, and they imagined unspeakable scenes between the Night Swan and their husbands or sons. When Josiah started coming to see her, and his blue GMC truck was parked there every evening until midnight, the Cubero women relaxed. They could even laugh a little.

"She's so old and wrinkled," they whispered, "all worn out. Only some old Indian would want her anyway." But still they watched every evening to make sure his truck was there, as if they knew the sensation in the groin of their husbands each time the men passed Lalo's and saw the bright blue door.

"That's what all the rumors say," Auntie hissed at Tayo in the storeroom where she had cornered him. "I was the last one to know what my own brother has been doing. Why didn't you tell me?"

"Because I didn't know for sure."

"Liars and fools," she said, rearranging the Mason jars full of peaches on the shelf, pushing them hard against each other until he thought the glass might break.

"I've spent all my life defending this family, but nobody ever stops to think what the people will say or that Father Kenneth will call me aside after mass to speak with me." She straightened herself as tall as she could, because she was short and heavyset. Her eyes were full of accusations.

"It doesn't bother me," she said, assuming a lighter tone of voice, "but this hurts old Grandma so much." Her words were shaky. "Our family, old Grandma's family, was so highly regarded at one time. She is used to being respected by people." She stopped pushing the Mason jars around and began dusting off the table where the old shopping bags were folded and stacked.

"Young people don't understand how important it is. To be able to walk through the village without worrying or wondering what the people are whispering about you." She wiped tears from the corners of her eyes with the

92

hem of her apron and walked out of the storeroom. She slammed the door behind her fiercely.

Tayo always wondered how she knew that people were whispering about her as she walked out of the church; he wondered too if Auntie was lying or if she really didn't realize that old Grandma didn't care what anyone said. She liked to sit by her stove and gossip about the people who were talking about their family.

"I know a better one than that about her! That woman shouldn't dare be talking about us. What about the time they found her rolling around in the weeds with that deaf man from Encinal? What about that? Everyone remembers it!" She pounded her cane on the floor in triumph. The story was all that counted. If she had a better one about them, then it didn't matter what they said.

"I've been thinking," the Night Swan said to Josiah, one evening when they were sitting in her room. She was sitting on the edge of the bed looking into the mirror, and he was sitting on the old blue armchair in the corner. "All these years you've done the same things," she said. He smiled and shrugged his shoulders. "That's how I've lived so long. Up until now." She laughed at his reference to her. "My cousin Ulibarri in Magdalena wrote," she said, "he's selling some Mexican cattle very cheap. They are off the desert, in Sonora, and he said he thought someone up this way might want to buy them." "I don't know," Josiah said, "last time there was a drought, we had to sell everything, even the sheep and goats." "I don't know anything about cattle," she said, "but he said these had been living off rocks and sand." She laughed, and went out to the kitchen to pour them some coffee. "Why are you looking so serious?" she said as she handed him the cup. "I'm thinking about the cattle business," he said.

By late July Josiah divided his time between the cattle, which were past Flower Mountain then, still heading southwest, and this woman. Josiah didn't mention her much any more, not since Auntie had cornered Tayo in the storeroom. He said it was better this way; Tayo wouldn't have to lie if he didn't know anything. Tayo helped him as he had promised, riding along the fence line between Acoma land and Laguna land. When they found tracks and sagging wires on the fences with bits of light hair caught in the barbs, they rode through the Acoma gate and brought the cows back again.

When they finished with the cattle, there was always the sheep camp. Auntie insisted that they check on the sheepherder because she was certain that he would run off and leave the sheep penned up to slowly die of thirst, or worse yet, that the sheepherder had got drunk and burned up the little sheep-camp house. Even after they had driven over the bumps and washed-out places on the sandy road, and made sure that these things had not happened, she would be satisfied for only two or three days. Then she would be convinced that the sheepherder had lost all the sheep, and that he was too lazy to hunt for them, and the sheep were wandering in the red rocks, where coyotes would pick them off, three and four at a time. Tayo wondered where she got these ideas, because they never happened, but when she talked about them, they sounded possible, not likely, but possible, so they had to go again. At first Tayo thought it was because Auntie never trusted her sheepherders, but later on, he saw that she wanted to keep Josiah busy, too busy to go to Cubero. They had a good man working for them then, an Apache guy from White River, and he was probably the best sheepherder they ever had; but whenever she wanted to persuade Josiah to go check up on things, she would go into a long history of what the Apaches had done to the Pueblo people, dwelling especially on Geronimo. Once Robert heard her as he was leaving for the fields. He winked at Josiah and Tayo, and then with a serious face he said, "I thought the sheepherder's name was Mike, not Geronimo," and walked out the door.

As dry as it was, with the grass getting thin and short, Josiah said it was a good thing to check anyway, especially in case the river started drying up and they'd have to start hauling water to the sheep again, as they had during the dry years before. They took Mike some sugar and flour and a little coffee. He never had much to say to them, but Tayo saw that he was reading some kind of book about auto mechanics. He took good care of the sheep in an offhand way, carrying the book around with him while he herded them; and when the old black mother dog had had pups, he had trained the best two for sheep dogs. Tayo mentioned the book to Josiah, and he shook his head. "Well, he won't be around long then. Too bad. He's a good man." A week later the Apache left for California and they hired their cousin Pinkie again. Auntie was against it because Pinkie had black-out spells, and she said, "The whole herd of sheep could wander onto the tracks and get hit by the Santa Fe Super Chief before Pinkie woke up." They hired him anyway and six sheep disappeared right after that, during a dust storm, Pinkie said, but he had a new harmonica and a blue pearl-button cowboy shirt they'd never seen before.

All that summer, while Josiah and Tayo watched the cattle and the sheep camp, and Robert worked in the fields each day, Rocky read magazines and ran laps at the baseball diamond twice a day. In the afternoons he hitchhiked to Paguate to see his girl friend. Auntie made it clear to everyone that it was all necessary if Rocky were to keep his football scholarship to the university. But Tayo knew that Rocky was already talking about the war and about joining the Army before he got drafted. He would be the first one ever to get a football scholarship, the first one to go with no help from the BIA or anyone. She could hold her head up, she said, because of Rocky. And she looked hard at Josiah when she made the remark, as if to let him know that there were others who prevented her from carrying herself quite so proud.

In the evenings, after they ate, Josiah would wash up, change his clothes, and go out again. Old Grandma was back in her chair beside the stove after all day outside under the elm tree, and she would listen carefully for Josiah to pour water into the tin basin. Then she would say, "Aren't you going to rest, Josiah?" He dried his face and hands slowly, without answering her, because they both knew what she was really asking. When was this affair with this Mexican woman going to end? His hair was gray, but when he combed it and walked out the door, he was smiling and his face wasn't tired or old. After he was gone, Auntie made an inaudible remark from the stove, where she kept her dishpan to keep the dishwater hot. She poured rinse water over the dishes so that they rattled together violently. She wiped them and put them in the cupboard, slamming the doors and dropping the frying pan down hard on top of the stove. This way they all knew she was angry, and all summer long, every night, they listened. Grandma never said anything about it; Tayo didn't know when or how she had learned about it, or if maybe she had known all along. They got onto the habit of leaving before Josiah did, or right afterward. Robert left earlier, with the excuse that he had to chop wood or see how the little apple trees behind the house were doing. Rocky wasn't even there, because he ate most of his evening meals at Paguate with his girl friend's family. Auntie didn't care for that either, but Rocky was her special one, so all she said to him was, "How do you like living at Paguate now?" looking angry as she said it.

Tayo got up to leave after he heard Josiah's truck pull out of the yard. But before he got out the door, Auntie turned around and looked at him; she didn't seem to care if old Grandma heard what she said or not. "I was always happy he didn't get married," she said grimly, "but now, worse things are happening. The way he goes off every night reminds me of our old dog, Pepper. That dog was the same way every time a female dog was in heat. Just like that. I try to tell him to stay with our own kind; but he doesn't listen to me. That woman is after anything she can get now." Old Grandma nodded her head and said, "That's right, that's what will happen." Auntie sat down on the bench by the table, triumphantly. She folded and refolded the damp dishcloth on the table in front of her. Tayo was aware of how dim the room was then with no light except the faint twilight still coming in the windows.

"Remember what happened to that dog?" She seemed to be talking to both of them, although Tayo had never even seen Pepper. Her voice seemed to come from every part of the room. "Pepper got run over on the highway, chasing some she-dog in heat."

He remembered when his mother died. It had been dry then too. The day they buried her the wind blew gusts of sand past the house and rattled the loose tin on the roof. He never forgot that sound and the sand, stinging his face at the graveyard while he stood close to Josiah. He kept his head down, staring at small round pebbles uncovered by the wind. Josiah held his hand as they walked away from the grave-yard. He lifted him into the front seat of the truck and gave him a candy cane left over from Christmas. He told him not to cry any more.

He knew the holy men had their ways during the dry spells. People said they climbed the trails to the mountaintops to look west and southwest and to call the clouds and thunder. They studied the night skies from the mountaintops and listened to the winds at dawn. When they came back down they would tell the people it was time to dance for rain. Josiah never told him much about praying, except that it should be something he felt inside himself. So that last summer, before the war, he got up before dawn and rode the bay mare south to the spring in the narrow canyon. The water oozed out from the dark orange sandstone at the base of the long mesa. He waited for the sun to come over the hills. He tied the mare to a juniper tree at the mouth of the canyon, and walked up the narrow trail, with the cliffs closer on both sides as he walked farther into the canyon. The canyon was full of shadows when he reached the pool. He had picked flowers along the path, flowers with yellow long petals the color of the sunlight. He shook the pollen from them gently and sprinkled it over the water; he laid the blossoms beside the pool and waited. He heard the water, flowing into the pool, drop by drop from the big crack in the side of the cliff. The things he did seemed right, as he imagined with his heart the rituals the cloud priests performed during a drought. Here the dust and heat began to recede; the short grass and stunted corn seemed distant.

The air smelled damp and it was cool even after the sun got high enough to shine into the canyon. The dark orange sandstone formation held springs like this one, all along the base of the sandstone where wind and erosion had cut narrow canyons into the rock. These springs came from deep within the earth, and the people relied upon them even when the sky was barren and the winds were hot and dusty.

The spider came out first. She drank from the edge of the pool, careful to keep the delicate egg sacs on her abdomen out of the water. She retraced her path, leaving faint crisscrossing patterns in the fine yellow sand. He remembered stories about her. She waited in certain locations for people to come to her for help. She alone had known how to outsmart the malicious mountain Ka't'sina who imprisoned the rain clouds in the northwest room of his magical house. Spider Woman had told Sun Man how to win the storm clouds back from the Gambler so they would be free again to bring rain and snow to the people. He knew what white people thought about the stories. In school the science teacher had explained what superstition was, and then held the science textbook up for the class to see the true source of explanations. He had studied those books, and he had no reasons to believe the stories any more. The science books explained the causes and effects. But old Grandma always used to say, "Back in time immemorial, things were different, the animals could talk to human beings and many magical things still happened." He never lost the feeling he had in his chest when she spoke those words, as she did each time she told them stories; and he still felt it was true, despite all they had taught him in school—that long ago things *had* been different, and human beings could understand what the animals said, and once the Gambler had trapped the storm clouds on his mountaintop.

When the shadows were gone, and the cliff rock began to get warm, the frogs came out from their sleeping places in small cracks and niches in the cliff above the pool. They were the color of the moss near the spring, and their backs were spotted the color of wet sand. They moved slowly into the sun, blinking their big eyes. He watched them dive into the pool, one by one, with a graceful quiet sound. They swam across the pool to the sunny edge and sat there looking at him, snapping at the tiny insects that swarmed in the shade and grass around the pool. He smiled. They were the rain's children. He had seen it happen many times after a rainstorm. In dried up ponds and in the dry arroyo sands, even as the rain was still falling, they came popping up through the ground, with wet sand still on their backs. Josiah said they could stay buried in the dry sand for many years, waiting for the rain to come again.

Dragonflies came and hovered over the pool. They were all colors of blue—powdery sky blue, dark night blue, shimmering with almost black iridescent light, and mountain blue. There were stories about the dragonflies too. He turned. Everywhere he looked, he saw a world made of stories, the long ago, time immemorial stories, as old Grandma called them. It was a world alive, always changing and moving; and if you knew where to look, you could see it, sometimes almost imperceptible, like the motion of the stars across the sky.

The horse was dozing under the tree. Her left hind foot was flexed and resting on the toe, the way horses did when they had to stand in one place for a long time. He rode slowly through the groves of dry sunflower stalks left over from better years, and it was then he saw a bright green hummingbird shimmering above the dry sandy ground, flying higher and higher until it was only a bright speck. Then it was gone. But it left something with him; as long as the hummingbird had not abandoned the land, somewhere there were still flowers, and they could all go on.

The next day he watched the clouds gather on the west horizon; by the next morning the sky was full of low dark rain clouds. They loaded the shovels and hoes into the back of the truck and went to the fields. While they waited, they pulled weeds around the chili plants and shoveled dirt around the low places in the rows of corn where the water might be lost. When they stopped to eat the bread and tamales Auntie had packed for them, they could hear a low rumble of thunder in the distance, from the direction of Tse-pi'na, Mount Taylor. The wind came up from the west, smelling cool like wet clay. Then he could see the rain. It was spinning out of the thunderclouds like gray spider webs and tangling against the foothills of the mountain. They joined the other people who had fields there, by the main ditch, and nobody went back to work after lunch. They stood around, smiling and joking, keeping an eye on the clouds overhead while they waited. As the first big drops began to splatter down on the leaves of the corn plants, making loud rattling sounds, Josiah motioned for Tayo to walk to the truck with him. The rain made a steady thumping sound on the cab of the truck. Josiah wrote in the little spiral notebook he carried in his shirt pocket; he tore out the blue-lined page and folded it carefully.

"Can you take this note to her? I told her I would come this afternoon and drive her to Grants, but now with the rain I will be too busy."

Tayo nodded. He could hear his heart beating and he was breathing fast; something was shaking in his belly.

She had watched him all summer, whenever he had gone to Cubero with Josiah. She sat in the wicker rocking chair in the shade on the upstairs porch above the bar, and she stared down at him. She watched him while Josiah was inside buying a six-pack; Tayo tried to avoid her eyes, but she was a patient woman. She watched him steadily, rocking slowly in the chair, waiting for him to sneak a quick glance at her. She smiled down at him until Josiah reached the top of the stairs. Then she smiled at Josiah and said, "You have a fine nephew, Joseó," as she got up from the rocker and followed Josiah inside.

His hands felt slippery on the steering wheel, and he felt as if every curve in the road were slowing him down and he might never reach the place. The sun was hidden by the clouds, and he was not aware any more of the color of the land. As he got closer, he was afraid she wouldn't be there. He shifted down to second gear and crossed the cattle guard by the old graveyard. He was close enough then to feel afraid, so he repeated over and over inside his head that he was only delivering a message, and she might not be there anyway. Raindrops splattered across the windshield like flying bugs hitting head-on. He wanted to turn around. He took his foot off the gas pedal and looked for a place to turn around, but the road was narrow, and on either side the ditches were muddy and flowing with the run-off. Up ahead he could see the big cottonwood tree.

The rain rattled on the rusted tin roof, and rainwater leaked out of the rain gutter and splashed off the porch railing. He walked up the spiral staircase slowly, smelling wet adobe plaster and listening to the rain rattle the waxy green cottonwood leaves growing near the porch. A scratchy Victrola was playing guitars and trumpets; a man sang sad Spanish words. "*Y volvere*" were the only words Tayo could understand. He stood at the screen door and knocked, looking down at Josiah's note. He held it carefully because his hands were sweaty and he didn't want to smear the writing. He wiped his hands on the thighs of his Levis while he waited. Nobody came to the door, but the music was playing loudly. He knocked on the screen door again, this time pounding it so hard that it bounced against the door frame. He waited, breathing hard, and felt the sweat run down his ribs like rainwater. He decided to push the note under the screen door; she would find it. He was kneeling to slide the note under the door when she came. He could smell her before he could even see her; the perfume smelled like the ivory locust blossoms that hung down from the trees in the spring. Her smell drifted out the screen on the air currents from the storm. The doorway at the back of the room had a long white curtain across it, and it swelled open as she came through. He looked at her through the sagging screen that had a fluffy ball of cotton stuck in the middle to scare the flies away. He saw her feet, the open-toe blue satin slippers and her painted toenails. The kimono was blue satin and it wrapped around her closely, outlining her hips and belly. He stood up quickly and felt his face get hot. He held out the note. She smiled, but she did not look at it. She looked at him.

"Come in," she said. She pointed to a blue armchair with dark wooden feet carved like eagle claws. The room smelled like the white clay the people used for whitewash. It was cool. The curtain at the back of the room drifted in a cool stream of air from the window or door behind it. The music came from behind the curtain too; the songs were soft and slow, without voices. Outside the thunder sounded like giant boulders cracking loose from the high cliffs and crashing into narrow canyons. Sometimes the room shook, and the panes of glass in the window behind him rattled. He watched her read the note and wondered what she kept behind the curtains. He could feel something back there, something of her life which he could not explain. The room pulsed with feeling, the feeling flowing with the music and the breeze from the curtains, feeling colored by the blue flowers painted in a border around the walls. He could feel it everywhere, even in the blue sheets that were stretched tightly across the bed. Somewhere, from another room, he heard a clock ticking slowly and distinctly, as if the years, the centuries, were lost in that sound. The rain pounded louder on the tin roof, and she looked up from the note then, at the screen door and the cottonwood tree outside, its leaves beaten flat by the downpour. The kimono was open slightly at the neck and he could see the light brown color of her skin. Her long brown hair was curled and piled on her head in long ringlets, the style of some past time. She did not look old or young to him then; she was like the rain and the wind; age had no relation to her. She got up from the edge of the bed and hooked the screen door. She closed the door and pushed the bolt forward. The music had stopped, and there was only the sound of the storm.

He dreamed it again and again, sinking and rolling with the light blue sheets twisted around his thighs and ankles, and the excitement of wet smells of rain, and their sweat. He wanted to lie like that forever.

She whispered in Spanish and touched him gently, rubbing his back and neck first, then brushing his ear and neck with her lips. She pressed against his chest and belly, and he clenched himself tight until he felt the warmth and softness of her legs and belly. Her sounds were gentle and the storm outside was loud. He could hear the rain rattling the roof and the sound of the old cottonwood tree straining in the wind. He moved his mouth over her face and slowly opened his eyes; she was smiling. He felt her shiver, and when he held her closer, he realized he was shaking too. Something was coiling tight. She breathed harder and he breathed with the same rhythm. She slid beneath him then, like a cat squeezing under a gate. She moved under him, her rhythm merging into the sound of the wind shaking the rafters and the sound of the rain in the tree. And he was lost somewhere, deep beneath the surface of his own body and consciousness, swimming away from all his life before that hour.

She sat with the sheets pulled around her and watched him get dressed. "I have been watching you for a long time," she said. "I saw the color of your eyes."

Tayo did not look at her.

"Mexican eyes," he said, "the other kids used to tease me."

The rain was only a faint sound on the roof, and the sound of the thunder was distant, and moving east. Tayo unbolted the door and opened it; he watched the rainwater pour out the rain gutter over the side of the long porch. "I always wished I had dark eyes like other people. When they look at me they remember things that happened. My mother." His throat felt tight. He had not talked about this before with anyone.

She shook her head slowly. "They are afraid, Tayo. They feel something happening, they can see something happening around them, and it scares them. Indians or Mexicans or whites—most people are afraid of change. They think that if their children have the same color of skin, the same color of eyes, that nothing is changing." She laughed softly. "They are fools. They blame us, the ones who look different. That way they don't have to think about what has happened inside themselves."

She was looking at him intently, and he felt uncomfortable. He walked over to the doorway, aware of the damp earth smell outside. He had one hand on the screen door, ready to leave.

"You don't have to understand what is happening. But remember this day. You will recognize it later. You are part of it now." She was looking up, at the pine vigas that held the roof. She turned her head and smiled at him. "Ah, Tayo," she said softly, and he felt that she cared a great deal about him.

"Good-bye," he said. He pushed the screen door open, into the cool damp air outside. "Good-bye, Tayo. Thank you for bringing the message."

He left Harley holding a bottle of Coors in both hands, talking to himself. He walked west. He could see the peaks of Mount Taylor high above everything, high above the valley. The thin winter snow was already gone from the high peaks, and the sacred mountain was a dusty, dry blue color. He could feel the heat from the ground through his boots, and shimmering waves of heat dance around him from the pavement, making him shaky, as though he were walking in a strong wind. The trucks and cars that went speeding past him made ripples in the heavy blanket of heat, but the air that circulated was only slightly cooler.

The old Mexican man brought him a bowl of *menudo*. They were alone in the little café. Tayo could see through the narrow kitchen to the back door, which was propped open with a chair so that cool air could find its way in and the hot air could leave by the front door, which was also open. On both screen doors the flies sat rubbing their legs together, waiting to get inside. The old man sat on a stool by the front door with a red rubber fly swatter in his right hand, watching them. Occasionally he glanced up at the low plaster ceiling, where a half dozen shiny yellow fly ribbons were hanging like party decorations. The ribbons were speckled with dead flies and a few that made feeble attempts to pull loose. He paid the old man and left, opening the screen door only enough to squeeze out and closing it quickly so that no flies got in. The sun was behind the hills southwest of McCartys by then, and he walked with the long shadows back to the bar to find Harley. He was thinking about the time when he was young and swatting flies in the kitchen with a willow switch because it was fun to chase them, not the serious business that the old Mexican man had made fly killing. Anyway, Josiah had come in from outside and he asked Tayo what he was doing, and Tayo had pointed proudly to a pile of dead flies on the kitchen floor. Josiah looked at them and shook his head.

"But our teacher said so. She said they are bad and carry sickness."

"Well, I didn't go to school much, so I don't know about that but you see, long time ago, way back in the time immemorial, the mother of the people got angry at them for the way they were behaving. For all she cared, they could go to hell—starve to death. The animals disappeared, the plants disappeared, and no rain came for a long time. It was the green-bottle fly who went to her, asking forgiveness for the people. Since that time the people have been grateful for what the fly did for us."

Tayo let the willow switch slide out of his hand. He stared at it on the floor by his feet. "What will happen now?" he asked in a choked voice.

"I think it will be okay," Josiah said, poking at the dead flies with the toe of his boot. "None of them were greenbottle flies—only some of his cousins. People make mistakes. The flies know that. That's how the greenbottle fly first came around anyway. To help the people

106

who had made some m
close. "Next time, just re

But in the jungle he ha
flies that had crawled ov
He had cursed their st
when he could reach the
his hands.

empty except for an
near her face. He
sunset.
The reflec
bright gol
of the lo
long ti
the
ad

Harley wasn't there. The Mexican bartender had gone home, and now the white man who owned the place was behind the bar, dusting off the bottles with a rag. Tayo stood in the door and looked around inside, at the empty tables with crooked legs of different lengths. Someone had swept the floor, and the beer bottles and cigarette butts were piled high in the middle next to the broom leaning against the back of a chair. The stale bar air followed him out the door— smelling like old cigarette smoke and spilled beer. He stood outside facing the south, but all his feelings were focused behind him, northeast, in the direction of Cubero. He turned around. The yellow sandstone outcrop ran parallel to the big arroyo behind the bar. All he had to do was follow it. He walked to Cubero in the twilight, looking up occasionally at the mountain, where the peaks were caught in the sunset. It was warm. Over on the highway he could see headlights and taillights moving east and west, but he felt alone, as if that world were distant from him. No traffic came along the dirt road, and it was quiet except for the crickets in the rocks and a few evening insects buzzing past his face; in the distance dogs were barking. The store in Cubero was closed, and the gas pumps had locks on the handles. Somewhere he smelled chili cooking for supper. The road past the store was

old cow with a broken horn hanging
didn't have to turn around to see the

ion of its colors made the sandstone cliffs
, and then deep red. He sat on the steps
ng porch and looked at the adobe walls for a
me. Years of rain and wind had weathered away
dobe plaster, exposing the symmetry of the brown
obes which were beginning to lose their square shape,
taking on the softer contours of the mesas and hills.

He remembered sitting this way, on these steps with
Rocky, while Josiah went inside Lalo's to get cold beer
and bottles of soda pop for them. Lalo had retired during
the war. He had sold the liquor license and closed the
bar. But it had changed very little. The circular stairs
were still there, at the end of the long porch. They had
been cut from heavy oak planks, and they spiraled around
the massive center timber like the small bones of a spine
held in place by thick wooden pegs. Years of hands on
the railing and feet on the steps had left the wood polished
smooth and bone gray. The big tree was dying. Thick
limbs at its center were brittle and white. One of the
remaining live limbs brushed against the porch railing
at the top of the stairs. He smelled the waxy dark green
leaves, and remembered climbing the big cottonwood
trees along the river and plucking heavy hanging bunches
of cottonwood berries that grew on the female trees
late in the summer. They had carried home arm-
loads of the seed pods, the size of peas, full of fluffy
cotton when they split open. The smell of the crushed
leaves had been exciting then because the cottonwood
berries were ammunition to use against the other boys
from the village, who tucked their shirttails into their
jeans and filled the inside of the shirts with cottonwood
berries until they had pendulous bellies. Then they ran,
laughing and throwing handfuls of the green berries
at one another.

The cottonwood trees had not lost their familiar feeling with him. They had always been there with the people but they were much more than summer shade. After hundreds of years, when the great trees finally got too old and dry, the Ka't'sina carvers from the villages came searching for them to cut pieces of their soft dry wood to carve.

He sat down on the upstairs porch with his back against the adobe wall and closed his eyes. In a world of crickets and wind and cottonwood trees he was almost alive again; he was visible. The green waves of dead faces and the screams of the dying that had echoed in his head were buried. The sickness had receded into a shadow behind him, something he saw only out of the corners of his eyes, over his shoulder.

The place felt good; he leaned back against the wall until its surface pushed against his backbone solidly. He picked up a fragment of fallen plaster and drew dusty white stripes across the backs of his hands, the way ceremonial dancers sometimes did, except they used white clay, and not old plaster. It was soothing to rub the dust over his hands; he rubbed it carefully across his light brown skin, the stark white gypsum dust making a spotted pattern, and then he knew why it was done by the dancers: it connected them to the earth.

He became aware of the place then, of where he was. He had never seen her again after that day. The summer kept them busy, and by early September he and Rocky had enlisted and were gone. They said that she left after Josiah's funeral, and nobody knew where she went, only that she walked to the highway with a suitcase.

The screen door was propped open against the side of the building with a large round sandrock. He expected the door to be locked when he turned the cut-glass knob, but it swung open. The room was empty. His steps inside sounded hollow, like a sandstone cave in the cliffs. The floor was covered with a layer of fine brown dust that had pushed under the door, and between the walls

109

and the window sash; the dust drifted up in little clouds around his feet.

The white curtains were gone, and he could see through the doorway to a small back room. Whatever had been there, the music, the currents of air that had moved so restlessly that day, was gone. He looked for some signs of what had been there, but all that was left was a hole in the ceiling where the stove pipe had been.

He stood in the dim gray light, watching the darkness push between him and the bare room. He breathed deeply, trying to find a trace of the locust-blossom perfune, but all he smelled was the white clay plaster, as timeless as the cliffs where it came from.

He walked all the way to Casa Blanca, listening to the crickets scattered around him like the stars. He climbed the old ladder into the loft of the barn behind Harley's grandpa's house. It was a warm night; he lay down in the old hay and he slept all night without dreams.

Fly started sucking on
sweet things so
Hummingbird had to tell him
to wait:
"Wait until we see our mother."
They found her.
They gave her blue pollen and yellow pollen
they gave her turquoise beads
they gave her prayer sticks.

"I suppose you want something," she said.
"Yes, we want food and storm clouds."
"You get old Buzzard to purify
your town first

110

and then, maybe, I will send you people
food and rain again."

Fly and Hummingbird
flew back up.
They told the town people
that old Buzzard had to purify
the town.

"I'm feeling better," Tayo said, "I've been doing okay.
I can start helping you now." He poured Robert a cup
of coffee and carried it over to the table; his hands
were shaking when he set the cup down. Robert didn't
say anything. He stirred the sugar into the coffee slowly,
silently, as if getting ready to say something. Maybe
there would always be those shadows over his shoulder
and out of the corner of each eye; and in the nights the
dreams and the voices. Maybe there was nothing anyone
could do for him. Robert looked up at him. "The other
day old man Ku'oosh came to the house. He told your
grandma what some of the old men are thinking. They
think you better get help pretty soon."

"But I haven't been in trouble for a long time, not
since that time with Emo."

"I know, but there are other things too."

"Oh." Tayo knew. There were other things. "It isn't
just me, Robert. The other guys, they're still messed up
too. That ceremony didn't help them."

Robert didn't answer. His face was still; Tayo didn't
know the last few minutes if it was anger or sadness
he saw. He got up from the table slowly; all his energy
had drained out of him.

"I'll go," he said softly, "whatever they say."

The old feeling was back again. He wanted to fade
until he was as flat as his own hand looked, flat like
a drawing in the sand which did not speak or move,
waiting for the wind to come swirling along the ground
and blow the lines away. He could hear what Auntie

111

would have to say; he could see her rigid face, her jaws clenched against the things which were being said about him in the village. He would let them take him— whatever they wanted, because they were right. They'd always been right about him.

"The traveling made me tired. But I remember when we drove through Gallup. I saw Navajos in torn old jackets, standing outside the bars. There were Zunis and Hopis there too, even a few Lagunas. All of them slouched down against the dirty walls of the bars along Highway 66, their eyes staring at the ground as if they had forgotten the sun in the sky; or maybe that was the way they dreamed for wine, looking for it somewhere in the mud on the sidewalk. This is us, too, I was thinking to myself. These people crouching outside bars like cold flies stuck to the wall."

They parked the truck by the Trailways bus station and walked across the railroad tracks. It was still early in the morning, and the shadows around the warehouses and buildings were long. The streets were empty, and on a Saturday morning in Gallup, Tayo knew what they would see. From the doorway of a second-hand store he could see feet, toes poking through holes in the socks. Someone sleeping off the night before, but without his boots now, because somebody had taken them to trade for a bottle of cheap wine. The guy had his head against the door; his brown face was peaceful and he was snoring loudly. Tayo smiled. Gallup was that kind of

112

place, interesting, even funny as long as you were just passing through, the way the white tourists did driving down 66, stopping to see the Indian souvenirs. But if you were an Indian, you attended to business and then left, and you were never in that town after dark. That was the warning the old Zunis, and Hopis, and Navajos had about Gallup. The safest way was to avoid bad places after dark.

The best time to see them was at dawn because after the sun came up they would be hiding or sleeping inside shelters of old tin, cardboard, and scrap wood. The shelters were scattered along the banks of the river. Some of them were in the wide arroyo that the creek cut through Gallup, but the others were in the salt-cedar and willow thickets that grew along the stream banks. Twice, or maybe three times a year, the police and the welfare people made a sweep along the river, arresting the men and women for vagrancy and being drunk in public, and taking the children away to the Home. They were on the north side of town anyway, Little Africa, where blacks, Mexicans, and Indians lived; and the only white people over there were Slav storekeepers. They came at Gallup Ceremonial time to clean up before the tourists came to town. They talked about sanitation and safety as they dragged the people to the paddy wagons; in July and August sudden cloudbursts could fill the arroyos with flood water and wash the shelters away.

They had been born in Gallup. They were the ones with light-colored hair or light eyes, bushy hair and thick lips—the ones the women were ashamed to send home for their families to raise. Those who did not die grew up by the river, watching their mothers leave at sundown. They learned to listen in the darkness, to the sounds of footsteps and loud laughing, to voices and sounds of wine; to know when the mother was returning with a man. They learned to stand at a distance and see if she would throw them food—so they would go away to eat and not peek through the holes in the rusting tin, at the man spilling wine on himself as he unbuttoned his pants.

They found their own places to sleep because the men stayed until dawn. Before they knew how to walk, the children learned how to avoid fists and feet.

When she woke up at noon she would call the child to bring her water. The lard pail was almost empty; the water looked rusty. He waited until she crawled to the opening. He watched her throat moving up and down as she drank; he tried to look inside to see if she had brought food, but the sun was high now and the inside of the shelter was in shadow. She dropped the pail when it was empty and crawled back inside. "Muh!" he called to her because he was hungry and he had found no food that morning. The woman with the reddish colored hair, the one who used to feed him, was gone. Her shelter was already torn down, taken away in pieces by others in the arroyo. He had prowled for garbage in the alleys behind the houses, but the older children had already been there. He turned away from the shelter and looked up at the traffic on the bridge. Once he had crawled up there and stood on the bridge, looking down at the shelter, and then around at the street where it crossed the tracks; he could even see downtown. She had taken him with her when he was very small. He remembered the brightness of the sun, the heat, all the smells of cars and food cooking, the noise, and the people. He remembered the inside, the dark, the coolness, and the music. He lay on his belly with his chin on the wooden floor and watched the legs and the shoes under the tables, the legs moving across the floor; some moved slowly, some stumbled. He searched the floor until he found a plastic bar straw, and then he played with piles of cigarette butts he had gathered. When he found chewing gum stuck beneath the tables, he put it in his mouth and tried to keep it, but he always swallowed it. He could not remember when he first knew that cigarettes would make him vomit if he ate them. He played for hours under the tables, quiet, watching for someone to drop a potato-chip bag or a wad of gum. He learned about coins, and searched for them, putting them in his mouth when he found them. Once they had lived somewhere else, a place full of food. He dreamed about that place in the past, and about a red blanket that was warm and moved rhymically like breathing.

He got used to her leaving the bar with men, giving somebody a dollar to buy the boy food while she was out. After he ate, he slept under the tables and waited for her to come back. The first time she did not come back, the man who swept floors found him. He did not cry when the man woke him; he did not cry when the police came and tried to ask him his name. He clutched the last piece of bread in his hand and crouched in the corner; he closed his eyes when they reached for him. After a long time, she came for him. She smelled good when she carried him and she spoke softly. But the last time he remembered the white walls and the rows of cribs. He cried for a long time, standing up in the bed with his chin resting on the top rail. He chewed the paint from the top rail, still crying, but gradually becoming interested in the way the paint peeled off the metal and clung to his front teeth.

When she came for him she smelled different. She smelled like the floors of the room full of cribs, and her long hair had been cut. But she came back for him, and she held him very close.

They stayed in the arroyo after that. The woman with the reddish hair helped them drag twisted pieces of old roof tin from the dump, down the banks of the river to the place the other shacks were, in sight of the bridge. They leaned the tin against the crumbly gray sides of the arroyo. His mother rolled big bricks up from the riverbed to hold the pieces of cardboard in place. It was cold then, and when the sun went down they built small fires from broken crates they found in the alleys and with branches they tore from the tamaric and willow. The willows and tamarics were almost bare then, except for the branches higher than a man could reach. One of the men brought an ax with a broken handle, and the drunks who lived in the arroyo chopped down the tamarics and willows, laughing and passing a bottle around as they took turns with the ax. The only trees they did not cut down were the ones the people used. A strong, stinging smell came from that place. He learned to watch out for shit and in the winter, when it was frozen, he played with it—flipping it around with a willow stick. He did not play with the other children; he ran from them when they approached. They belonged to the woman who stayed under the bridge, with low tin walls to block the west wind. That winter he heard a strange crying sound coming from under the bridge, and he saw the children standing outside the low sides of the shelter, watching. He listened for a long time and watched. The next day it was quiet, and the woman carried a bundle of bloody rags away from the bridge, far away north, toward the hills. Later on he walked the way she had gone, following the arroyo east and then north, where it wound into the pale yellow hills. He found the place near the side of the arroyo where she had buried the rags in the yellow sand. The sand she had dug with her hands was still damp on the mound. He circled the mound and stared at a faded blue rag partially uncovered, quivering in the wind. It was stiff with a reddish brown stain. He left that place and he never went back; and late at night when his mother was gone, he cried because he saw the mound of pale yellow sand in a dream.

Damp yellow sand choking him, filling his nostrils first, and then his eyes as he struggled against it, fought

116

to keep his eyes open to see. Sand rippled and swirled in his dream, enclosing his head, yellow sand and shadows filling his mouth until his body was full and still. He woke up crying in a shallow hole beside the clay bank where his mother had thrown the old quilt.

He slept alone while his mother was with the men—the white men with necks and faces bright red from the summertime, Mexican men who came from the section-gang boxcars at the railroad, looking for the women who waited around the bridge—the ones who would go down for a half bottle of wine. The black men came from the railroad tracks too, to stand on the bridge and look down at them. He did not know if they looked at him or if they were only looking at his mother and the women who lined up beside her, to smile and wave and yell "Hey, honey" up to the men. The white people who drove by looked straight ahead. But late one afternoon some white men came and called until the women came out of the lean-tos, and then the men yelled at them and threw empty bottles, trying to hit them. The woman with reddish hair threw the bottles back at them and screamed their own words back to them. The police came. They dragged the people out of their shelters—and they pulled the pieces of tin and cardboard down. The police handcuffed the skinny men with swollen faces; they pushed and kicked them up the crumbling clay sides of the arroyo. They held the women in a circle while they tried to catch the children who had scattered in all directions when they saw the police coming. The men and the women who were too sickdrunk to stand up were dragged away, one cop on each arm. He hid in the tamarics, breathing hard, his heart pounding, smelling the shit on his bare feet. The summer heat descended as the sun went higher in the sky, and he watched them, lying flat on his belly in the dry leaves of tamaric that began to make him itch, and he moved cautiously to scratch his arm and his neck. He watched them tear down the last of the shelters, and they piled the rags and coats they

117

found and sprinkled them with kerosene. Thick black smoke climbed furiously into the cloudless blue sky, hot and windless. He could feel the flies buzzing and crawling around his legs and feet, and he was afraid that the men searching would hear them and find him. But the smell in the remaining grove of tamaric and willow was strong enough to keep them away. The men in dark green coveralls came with steel canisters on their backs, and they sprayed the places where the shelters had been; and in the burned smell of cloth and wood he could smell the long white halls of the place they kept children. At sundown he woke up and caught sight of the headlights of the traffic across the bridge. He stood up slowly and looked restlessly toward the arroyo banks, thinking about food.

It was a warm night and he wandered for a long time in the alleys behind the houses, where the dogs barked when he reached into the tin cans. He ate as he made his way back to the arroyo, chewing the soft bone cartilage of pork ribs he found. He saved the bones and sucked them until he went to sleep, in the tamarics and willows. Late in the night he heard voices, men stumbling and falling down the steep crumbling bank into the arroyo, and he could hear bottles rattle together and the sound of corks being pulled from the bottles. They talked loudly in the language his mother spoke to him, and one man sat with his back against the bank and sang songs until the wine was gone.

He crawled deeper into the tamaric bushes and pulled his knees up to his belly. He looked up at the stars, through the top branches of the willows. He would wait for her, and she would come back to him.

They took more pollen,
more beads, and more prayer sticks,

118

and they went to see old Buzzard.

They arrived at his place in the east.
"Who's out there?
Nobody ever came here before."
"It's us, Hummingbird and Fly."
"Oh. What do you want?"

"We need you to purify our town."
"Well, look here. Your offering isn't
complete. Where's the tobacco?"

(You see, it wasn't easy.)
Fly and Hummingbird
had to fly back to town again.

Robert and Tayo stopped on
the bridge and looked into the riverbed. It had been dry
for a long time, and there were paths in the sand where
the people walked. They were beginning to move. All
along the sandy clay banks there were people, mostly
men, stretched out, sleeping, some of them face down
where they fell, and a few rolled over on their backs or
on their sides, sleeping with their heads on their arms. The
sun was getting hot and the flies were beginning to come
out. They could see them buzzing around the face of a
man under the bridge, smelling the sweetness of the wine
or maybe the vomit down the front of the man's shirt.
Robert shook his head. Tayo felt the choking in his
throat; he blinked his eyes hard and didn't say anything.
A man and woman came walking down the wash below
them and looked up at them on the bridge. "Hey buddy!"
the man yelled up. "You got a dollar you can loan us?"
Robert looked at them and shook his head calmly, but

Tayo started to sweat. He started reaching deep into his pockets for loose coins. The woman's hair was tangled in hairpins which had been pulled loose and hung around her head like ornaments. Her head weaved from side to side as she squinted and tried to focus on Tayo up above her. Her slip was torn and dragging the ground under her skirt; she had a dark bruise on her forehead. He found two quarters and tossed them into the man's outstretched hands, swaying above his head, and both the man and the woman dropped to their knees in the sand to find them. Robert walked away, but Tayo stood there, remembering the little bridge in a park in San Diego where all the soldiers took their dates the night before they shipped out to the South Pacific and stood throwing coins into the shallow pond. He had tossed the coins to them the way he had tossed them from the bridge in San Diego, in a gentle slow arc. Rocky wished out loud that night for a safe return from the war, but Tayo couldn't remember his wish. He watched them stumble and crawl up the loose clay of the steep riverbank. The man pulled the woman up the last few feet. The fly of his pants was unbuttoned and one of his shoes was flopping loose on his foot. They walked toward a bar south of the bridge, to wait for it to open.

They walked like survivors, with dull vacant eyes, their fists clutching the coins he'd thrown to them. They were Navajos, but he had seen Zunis and Lagunas and Hopis there too, walking alone or in twos and threes along the dusty Gallup streets. He didn't know how they got there in the first place, from the reservation to Gallup, but some must have had jobs for a while when they first came, and cheap rooms on the north side of the tracks, where they stayed until they got laid off or fired. Reservation people were the first ones to get laid off because white people in Gallup already knew they wouldn't ask any questions or get angry; they just walked away. They were educated only enough to know they wanted to leave the reservation; when they got to Gallup there weren't many jobs they could get. The men unloaded trucks in the warehouses near the tracks or piled lumber in the lumberyards or pushed wheelbarrows for construction; the women cleaned out motel rooms along Highway 66. The Gallup people knew they didn't have to pay good wages or put up with anything they didn't like, because there were plenty more Indians where these had come from.

It seemed to Tayo that they would go home, sooner or later, when they were hungry and dirty and broke; stand on 666 north of town and wait for someone driving to Keams Canyon or Lukachukai to stop, or borrow two dollars and ride the bus back to Laguna. But Gallup was a dangerous place, and by the time they realized what had happened to them, they must have believed it was too late to go home.

Robert was waiting for him on the hill. "Somebody you used to know?"

"Maybe," Tayo said. The sun was above them now, in a deep blue sky like good turquoise.

He looked back at the bridge, and he made a wish. The same wish Rocky made that night in San Diego: a safe return.

"What kind of medicine man lives in a place like that, in the foothills north of the Ceremonial Grounds?" Auntie wanted to know. Grandma told her, "Never mind. Old man Ku'oosh knows him, and he thinks this man Betonie might help him."

The Gallop Ceremonial had been an annual event for a long time. It was good for the tourist business coming through in the summertime on Highway 66. They liked to see Indians and Indian dances; they wanted a chance to buy Indian jewelry and Navajo rugs. Every year it was organized by the white men there, Turpen, Foutz, Kennedy, and the mayor. Dance groups from the Pueblos were paid to come; they got Plains hoop dancers, and flying-pole dancers from northern Mexico. They organized an all-Indian rodeo and horse races. And the people came, from all the reservations nearby, and some came from farther away; they brought their things to sell to the tourists and they bought things to trade with each other: white deerhides, and feathers, and dried meat or piki bread. The tourists got to see what they wanted; from the grandstand at the Ceremonial grounds they watched the dancers perform, and they watched Indian cowboys ride bucking horses and Brahma bulls. There were wagon races, and the ladies' wood-chopping contest and fry-bread-making race. The Gallup merchants raised prices in motels and restaurants all Ceremonial week, and made a lot of money off the tourists. They sold great amounts of liquor to Indians, and in those years when liquor was illegal for Indians, they made a lot more money because they bootlegged it.

Old Betonie's place looked down on all of it; from the yellow sandrock foothills the whole town spread out below. The old man was tall and his chest was wide; at one time he had been heavier, but old age was consuming everything but the bones. He kept his hair tied back neatly with red yarn in a chongo knot, like the oldtimers wore. He was sitting on an old tin bucket turned upside down by the doorway to his hogan. When he stood up and extended his hand to Robert and Tayo, his motions were strong and unhesitating, as if they belonged to a younger man. He watched Tayo look around at the hogan and then back down at the Ceremonial grounds and city streets in the distance. He nodded his head at Tayo.

"People ask me why I live here," he said, in good English, "I tell them I want to keep track of the people. 'Why over here?' they ask me. 'Because this is where Gallup keeps Indians until Ceremonial time. Then they want to show us off to the tourists.' " He looked down at the riverbed winding through the north side of Gallup. "There," he said, pointing his chin at the bridge, "they sleep over there, in alleys between bars." He turned and pointed to the city dump east of the Ceremonial grounds and rodeo chutes. "They keep us on the north side of the railroad tracks, next to the river and their dump. Where none of them want to live." He laughed. "They don't understand. We know these hills, and we are comfortable here." There was something about the way the old man said the word "comfortable." It had a different meaning—not the comfort of big houses or rich food or even clean streets, but the comfort of belonging with the land, and the peace of being with these hills. But the special meaning the old man had given to the English word was burned away by the glare of the sun on tin cans and broken glass, blinding reflections off the mirrors and chrome of the wrecked cars in the dump below. Tayo felt the old nausea rising up in his stomach, along with a vague feeling that he knew something which he could not remember. The sun was getting hot, and he thought about flies buzzing around their faces as they slept in the weeds along the arroyo. He turned back to Betonie. He didn't know how the medicine man could look down at it every day.

"You know, at one time when my great-grandfather was young, Navajos lived in all these hills." He pointed to the hills and ridges south of the tracks where the white people had built their houses. He nodded at the arroyo cut by the river. "They had little farms along the river. When the railroaders came and the white people began to build their town, the Navajos had to move." The old man laughed suddenly. He slapped his hands on his thighs. His laughter was easy, but Tayo could feel the tiny hairs along his spine spring up. This Betonie didn't talk the way Tayo expected a medicine man to talk. He didn't act like a medicine man at all.

"It strikes me funny," the medicine man said, shaking his head, "people wondering why I live so close to this filthy town. But see, this hogan was here first. Built long before the white people ever came. It is that town down there which is out of place. Not this old medicine man." He laughed again, and Tayo looked at Robert quickly to see what he thought of the old man; but Robert's face was calm, without any mistrust or alarm. When old Betonie had finished talking, Robert stepped over to Tayo and touched his shoulder gently. "I guess I'll go now," he said softly.

Tayo watched him walk down the path from the old man's place, and he could feel cold sweat between his fingers. His heart was pounding, and all he could think about was that if he started running right then, he could still catch up to Robert.

"Go ahead," old Betonie said, "you can go. Most of the Navajos feel the same way about me. You won't be the first one to run away."

Tayo turned to look for Robert, but he was gone. He stared at the dry yellow grass by the old man's feet. The sun's heat was draining his strength away; there was no place to go now except back to the hospital in Los Angeles. They didn't want him at Laguna the way he was.

All along there had been something familiar about the old man. Tayo turned around then to figure out what it was. He looked at his clothes: the old moccasins with splayed-out elkhide soles, the leather stained dark with mud and grease; the gray wool trousers were baggy and worn thin at the knees, and the old man's elbows made brown points through the sleeves of the blue cotton work shirt. He looked at his face. The cheekbones were like the wings of a hawk soaring away from his broad nose; he wore a drooping thick mustache; the hairs were steel gray. Then Tayo looked at his eyes. They were hazel like his own. The medicine man nodded. "My grandmother was a remarkable Mexican with green eyes," he said.

He bent down like the old man did when he passed through the low doorway. Currents of cool air streamed toward the door, and even before his eyes adjusted to the dimness of the room, he could smell its contents; a great variety of herb and root odors were almost hidden by the smell of mountain sage and something as ordinary as curry powder. Behind the smell of dried desert tea he smelled heavier objects: the salty cured smell of old hides sewn into boxes bound in brass; the odor of old newspapers and cardboard, their dust smelling of the years they had taken to decay.

The old man pointed to the back of the circular room. "The west side is built into the hill in the old-style way. Sand and dirt for a roof; just about halfway underground. You can feel it, can't you?"

Tayo nodded. He was standing with his feet in the bright circle of sunlight below the center of the log ceiling open for smoke. The size of the room had not been lost in the clutter of boxes and trunks stacked almost to the ceiling beams.

Old Betonie pointed at a woolly brown goatskin on the floor below the sky hole. Tayo sat down, but he didn't take his eyes off the carboard boxes that filled the big room; the sides of some boxes were broken down, sagging over with old clothing and rags spilling out; others were jammed with the antennas of dry roots and reddish willow twigs tied in neat bundles with old cotton strings. The boxes were stacked crookedly, some stacks leaning into others, with only their opposing angles holding them steady. Inside the boxes without lids, the erect brown string handles of shopping bags poked out; piled to the tops of the WOOLWORTH bags were bouquets of dried sage and the brown leaves of mountain tobacco wrapped in swaths of silvery unspun wool.

He could see bundles of newspapers, their edges curled stiff and brown, barricading piles of telephone books with the years scattered among cities—St. Louis, Seattle, New York, Oakland—and he began to feel another dimension to the old man's room. His heart beat faster, and he felt the blood draining from his legs. He knew the answer before he could shape the question. Light from the door worked paths through the thick bluish green glass of the Coke bottles; his eyes followed the light until he was dizzy and sick. He wanted to dismiss all of it as an old man's rubbish, debris that had fallen out of the years, but the boxes and trunks, the bundles and stacks were plainly part of the pattern: they followed the concentric shadows of the room.

The old man smiled. His teeth were big and white. "Take it easy," he said, "don't try to see everything all at once." He laughed. "We've been gathering these things for a long time—hundreds of years. She was doing it before I was born, and he was working before she came. And on and on back down in time." He stopped, smiling. "Talking like this is just as bad, isn't it? Too big to swallow all at once."

Tayo nodded, but now his eyes were on the ceiling logs where pouches and bags dangled from wooden pegs and square-headed nails. Hard shrunken skin pouches and black leather purses trimmed with hammered silver buttons were things he could understand. They were a medicine man's paraphernalia, laid beside the painted gourd rattles and deer-hoof clackers of the ceremony. But with this old man it did not end there; under the medicine bags and bundles of rawhide on the walls, he saw layers of old calendars, the sequences of years confused and lost as if occasionally the oldest calendars had fallen or been taken out from under the others and then had been replaced on top of the most recent years. A few showed January, as if the months on the underlying pages had no longer been turned or torn away.

Old Betonie waved his hands around the hogan. "And what do I make from all this?" He nodded, moving his head slowly up and down. "Maybe you smelled it when you came in.

"In the old days it was simple. A medicine person could get by without all these things. But nowadays

126

. . ." He let his voice trail off and nodded to let Tayo complete the thought for him.

Tayo studied the pictures and names on the calendars. He recognized names of stores in Phoenix and Albuquerque, but in recent years the old man had favored Santa Fe Railroad calendars that had Indian scenes painted on them—Navajos herding sheep, deer dancers at Cochiti, and little Pueblo children chasing burros. The chills on his neck followed his eyes: he recognized the pictures for the years 1939 and 1940. Josiah used to bring the calendars home every year from the Santa Fe depot; on the reservation these calendars were more common than Coca-Cola calendars. There was no reason to be startled. This old man had only done the same thing. He tried to shake off the feeling by talking.

"I remember those two," he said.

"That gives me some place to start," old Betonie said, lighting up the little brown cigarette he had rolled. "All these things have stories alive in them." He pointed at the Santa Fe calendars. "I'm one of their best customers down there. I rode the train to Chicago in 1903." His eyes were shining then, and he was looking directly into Tayo's eyes. "I know," he said proudly, "people are always surprised when I tell them the places I have traveled." He pointed at the telephone books. "I brought back the books with all the names in them. Keeping track of things." He stroked his mustache as if he were remembering things.

Tayo watched him, trying to decide if the old man was lying. He wasn't sure if they even let Indians ride trains in those days. The old man laughed at the expression on Tayo's face. He wiped his mouth on the sleeve of his shirt.

"She sent me to school. Sherman Institute, Riverside, California. That was the first train I ever rode. I had been watching them from the hills up here all my life. I told her it looked like a snake crawling along the red-rock mesas. I told her I didn't want to go. I was already a big kid then. Bigger than the rest. But she said 'It is carried on in all languages now, so you have to know English too.'" He ran his fingers through his mustache again, still smiling as though he were thinking of other stories to tell. But a single hair came loose from his thick gray mustache, and his attention shifted suddenly to the hair between his fingers. He got up and went to the back of the hogan. Tayo heard the jingle of keys and the tin sound of a footlocker opening; the lock snapped shut and the old man came back and sat down; the hair was gone.

"I don't take any chances," he said as he got settled on the goatskin again. Tayo could hear his own pulse sound in his ears. He wasn't sure what the old man was talking about, but he had an idea. "Didn't anyone ever teach you about these things?"

Tayo shook his head, but he knew the medicine man could see he was lying. He knew what they did with strands of hair they found; he knew what they did with bits of fingernail and toenails they found. He was breathing faster, and he could feel the fear surge over him with each beat of his heart. They didn't want him around. They blamed him. And now they had sent him here, and this would be the end of him. The Gallup police would find his body in the bushes along the big arroyo, and he would be just one of the two or three they'd find dead that week. He thought about running again; he was stronger than the old man and he could fight his way out of this. But the pain of betrayal pushed into his throat like a fist. He blinked back the tears, but he didn't move. He was tired of fighting. If there was no one left to trust, then he had no more reason to live.

The old man laughed and laughed. He laughed, and when his laughter seemed almost to cease, he would shake his head and laugh all over again.

"I was at the World's Fair in St. Lous, Missouri, the year they had Geronimo there on display. The white people were scared to death of him. Some of them even wanted him in leg irons."

Tayo did not look up. Maybe this time he really was crazy. Maybe the medicine man didn't laugh all the time; maybe the dreams and the voices were taking over again.

"If you don't trust me, you better get going before dark. You can't be too careful these days," Betonie said, gesturing toward the footlocker where he kept the hairs. "Anyway, I couldn't help anyone who was afraid of me." He started humming softly to himself, a song that Tayo could hear only faintly, but that reminded him of butterflies darting from flower to flower.

"They sent me to this place after the war. It was white. Everything in that place was white. Except for me. I was invisible. But I wasn't afraid there. I didn't feel things sneaking up behind me. I didn't cry for Rocky or Josiah. There were no voices and no dreams. Maybe I belong back in that place."

Betonie reached into his shirt pocket for the tobacco sack. He rolled a skinny little cigarette in a brown wheat paper and offered the sack to Tayo. He nodded slowly to indicate that he had been listening.

"Thats true," the old man said, "you could go back to that white place." He took a puff from the cigarette and stared down at the red sand floor. Then he looked up suddenly and his eyes were shining; he had a grin on his face. "But if you are going to do that, you might as well go down there, with the rest of them, sleeping in the mud, vomiting cheap wine, rolling over women. Die that way and get it over with." He shook his head and laughed. "In that hospital they don't bury the dead, they keep them in rooms and talk to them."

"There are stories about me," Betonie began in a quiet round voice. "Maybe you have heard some of them. They say I'm crazy. Sometimes they say worse things. But whatever they say, they don't forget me, even when I'm not here." Tayo was wary of his eyes. "That's right," Betonie said, "when I am gone off on the train, a hundred miles from here, those Navajos won't come near this hogan." He smoked for a while and stared at the circle of sunlight on the floor between them. What Tayo could feel was powerful, but there was no way to be sure what it was.

"My uncle Josiah was there that day. Yet I know he couldn't have been there. He was thousands of miles away, at home in Laguna. We were in the Philippine jungles. I understand that. I know he couldn't have been there. But I've got this feeling and it won't go away even though I know he wasn't there. I feel like he was there. I feel like he was there with those Japanese soldiers who died." Tayo's voice was shaking; he could feel the tears pushing into his eyes. Suddenly the feeling was there, as strong as it had been that day in the jungle. "He loved me. He loved me, and I didn't do anything to save him."

"When did he die?"

"While we were gone. He died because there was no one to help him search for the cattle after they were stolen."

"Rocky," Betonie said softly, "tell me about Rocky."

The tears ran along the sides of Tayo's nose and off his chin; as they fell, the hollow inside his chest folded into the black hole, and he waited for the collapse into himself.

"It was the one thing I could have done. For all of them, for all those years they kept me . . . for everything that had happened because of me . . ."

"You've been doing something all along. All this time, and now you are at an important place in this story." He paused. "The Japanese," the medicine man went on, as though he were trying to remember something. "It isn't surprising you saw him with them. You saw who they were. Thirty thousand years ago they were not strangers.

130

You saw what the evil had done: you saw the witchery ranging as wide as this world."

"And these cattle . . .

"The people in Cubero called her the Night Swan. She told him about the cattle. She encouraged him to buy them. Auntie said that—"

The old man waved his arms at Tayo. "Don't tell me about your aunt. I want to know about those cattle and that woman."

"She said something to me once. About our eyes. Hazel-green eyes. I never understood. Was she bad, like Auntie kept saying? Did the cattle kill him—did I let the cattle kill him?"

The old man had jumped up. He was walking around the fire pit, moving behind Tayo as he went around. He was excited, and from time to time he would say something to himself in Navajo.

Betonie dug down into the cardboard boxes until dust flew up around his face. Finally he pulled out a brown spiral notebook with a torn cover; he thumbed through the pages slowly, moving his lips slightly. He sat down again, across from Tayo, with the notebook in his lap.

"I'm beginning to see something," he said with his eyes closed, "yes. Something very important."

The room was cooler than before. The light from the opening in the roof was becoming diffuse and gray. It was sundown. Betonie pointed a finger at him.

"This has been going on for a long long time. They will try to stop you from completing the ceremony."

The hollow inside him was suddenly too small for the anger. "Look," Tayo said through clenched teeth, "I've been sick, and half the time I don't know if I'm still crazy or not. I don't know anything about ceremonies or these things you talk about. I don't know how long anything has been going on. I just need help." The words made his body shake as if they had an intensity of their own which was released as he spoke.

"We all have been waiting for help a long time. But it

131

never has been easy. The people must do it. You must do it." Betonie sounded as if he were explaining something simple but important to a small child. But Tayo's stomach clenched around the words like knives stuck into his guts. There was something large and terrifying in the old man's words. He wanted to yell at the medicine man, to yell the things the white doctors had yelled at him—that he had to think only of himself, and not about the others, that he would never get well as long as he used words like "we" and "us." But he had known the answer all along, even while the white doctors were telling him he could get well and he was trying to believe them: medicine didn't work that way, because the world didn't work that way. His sickness was only part of something larger, and his cure would be found only in something great and inclusive of everything.

"There are some things I have to tell you," Betonie began softly. "The people nowadays have an idea about the ceremonies. They think the ceremonies must be performed exactly as they have always been done, maybe because one slip-up or mistake and the whole ceremony must be stopped and the sand painting destroyed. That much is true. They think that if a singer tampers with any part of the ritual, great harm can be done, great power unleashed." He was quiet for a while, looking up at the sky through the smoke hole. "That much can be true also. But long ago when the people were given these ceremonies, the changing began, if only in the aging of the yellow gourd rattle or the shrinking of the skin around the eagle's claw, if only in the different voices from generation to generation, singing the chants. You see, in many ways, the ceremonies have always been changing."

Tayo nodded; he looked at the medicine pouches hanging from the ceiling and tried to imagine the objects they contained.

"At one time, the ceremonies as they had been performed were enough for the way the world was then. But after the white people came, elements in this world began to shift; and it became necessary to create new ceremonies. I have made changes in the rituals. The people mistrust this greatly, but only this growth keeps the ceremonies strong.

"She taught me this above all else: things which don't shift and grow are dead things. They are things the witchery people want. Witchery works to scare people, to make them fear growth. But it has always been necessary, and more than ever now, it is. Otherwise we won't make it. We won't survive. That's what the witchery is counting on: that we will cling to the ceremonies the way they were, and then their power will triumph, and the people will be no more."

He wanted to believe old Betonie. He wanted to keep the feeling of his words alive inside himself so that he could believe that he might get well. But when the old man left, he was suddenly aware of the old hogan: the red sand floor had been swept unevenly; the boxes were spilling out rags; the trunks were full of the junk and trash an old man saves—notebooks and whisker hairs. The shopping bags were torn, and the weeds and twigs stuck out of rips in the brown paper. The calendars Betonie got for free and the phone books that he picked up in his travels—all of it seemed suddenly so pitiful and small compared to the world he knew the white people had—a world of comfort in the sprawling houses he'd seen in California, a world of plenty in the food he had carried from the officers' mess to dump into garbage cans. The old man's clothes were dirty and old, probably collected like his calendars. The leftover things the whites didn't want. All Betonie owned in the world was in this room. What kind of healing power was in this?

Anger propelled him to his feet; his legs were stiff from sitting for so long. This was where the white people and their promises had left the Indians. All the promises they made to you, Rocky, they weren't any different than the other promises they made.

He walked into the evening air, which was cool and smelled like juniper smoke from the old man's fire. Betonie was sitting by the fire, watching the mutton ribs cook over a grill he had salvaged from the front end of a wrecked car in the dump below. The grill was balanced between two big sandrocks, where the hot coals were banked under the spattering meat. Tayo looked down at the valley, at the lights of the town and the headlights and taillights strung along Highway 66.

"They took almost everything, didn't they?"

The old man looked up from the fire. He shook his head slowly while he turned the meat with a forked stick. "We always come back to that, don't we? It was planned that way. For all the anger and the frustration. And for the guilt too. Indians wake up every morning of their lives to see the land which was stolen, still there, within reach, its theft being flaunted. And the desire is strong to make things right, to take back what was stolen and to stop them from destroying what they have taken. But you see, Tayo, we have done as much fighting as we can with the destroyers and the thieves: as much as we could do and still survive."

Tayo walked over and knelt in front of the ribs roasting over the white coals of the fire.

"Look," Betonie said, pointing east to Mount Taylor towering dark blue with the last twilight. "They only fool themselves when they think it is theirs. The deeds and papers don't mean anything. It is the people who belong to the mountain."

Tayo poked a stick into the coals and watched them lose shape and collapse into white ash. "I wonder sometimes," he said, "because my mother went with white men." He stopped there, unable to say any more. The birth had betrayed his mother and brought shame to the family and to the people.

Old Betonie sat back on his heels and looked off in the distance. "Nothing is that simple," he said, "you don't write off all the white people, just like you don't trust all the Indians." He pointed at the coffeepot in the sand at the edge of the coals, and then at the meat. "You better eat now," he said.

Tayo finished the meat on the mutton ribs and threw the bones to a skinny yellow dog that came out from behind the hogan. Behind the dog a boy about fifteen or sixteen came with an armload of firewood. He knelt by the fire with the kindling; Betonie spoke to him in Navajo and indicated Tayo with a nod of his head.

"This is my helper," he told Tayo. "They call him Shush. That means bear." It was dark, but in the light from the fire Tayo could see there was something strange about the boy, something remote in his eyes, as if he were on a distant mountaintop alone and the fire and hogan and the lights of the town below them did not exist.

He was a small child
learning to get around
by himself.
His family went by wagon
into the mountains near
Fluted Rock.

It was Fall and
they were picking piñons.
I guess he just wandered away
trying to follow his brothers and sisters
into the trees.
His aunt thought he was with his mother,
and she thought he was with her sister.

When they tracked him the next day
his tracks went into the canyon
near the place which belonged

to the bears. They went
as far as they could
to the place
where no human
could go beyond,
and his little footprints
were mixed in with bear tracks.

So they sent word for this medicine man
to come. He knew how
to call the child back again.

There wasn't much time.
The medicine man was running, and his
assistants followed behind him.

They all wore bearweed
tied at their wrists and ankles
and around their necks.

He grunted loudly and scratched on the ground in front
of him
he kept watching the entrance of the bear cave.
He grunted and made a low growling sound.
Pretty soon the little bears came out
because he was making mother bear sounds.
He grunted and growled a little more
and then the child came out.
He was already walking like his sisters
he was already crawling on the ground.

They couldn't just grab the child
They couldn't simply take him back
because he would be in between forever
and probably he would die.

They had to call him
step by step the medicine man

brought the child back.

So, long time ago
they got him back again
but he wasn't quite the same
after that
not like the other children.

Tayo stood up and moved around the fire uneasily; the boy took some ribs and disappeared again behind the hogan. The old man put some wood on the fire. "You don't have to be afraid of him. Some people act like witchery is responsible for everything that happens, when actually witchery only manipulates a small portion." He pointed in the direction the boy had gone. "Accidents happen, and there's little we can do. But don't be so quick to call something good or bad. There are balances and harmonies always shifting, always necessary to maintain. It is very peaceful with the bears; the people say that's the reason human beings seldom return. It is a matter of transitions, you see; the changing, the becoming must be cared for closely. You would do as much for the seedlings as they become plants in the field."

NOTE ON BEAR PEOPLE AND WITCHES

Don't confuse those who go to the bears with the witch people. Human beings who live with the bears do not wear bear skins. They are naked and not conscious of being different from their bear relatives. Witches crawl into skins of dead animals, but they can do nothing but play around with objects and bodies. Living animals are terrified of witches. They smell the death. That's why witches can't get close to them. That's why people keep

137

dogs around their hogans. Dogs howl with fear when witch animals come around.

us have nothing compared to white people;
out their cities and all the machines and food
He says the land is no good, and we must go

The wind came up and fanned the fire. Tayo watched a red flame crawl out from under the white coals; he reached down for a piece of juniper and tossed it in. The fire caught. He rubbed pitch from the wood between his fingers and looked down at Gallup.

"I never told you about Emo," he said, "I never told you what happened to Rocky." He pointed at the lights below. "Something about the lights down there, something about the cars and the neon signs which reminds me of both of them."

"Yes," the old man said, "my grandmother would not leave this hill. She said the whole world could be seen from here."

"Rocky wanted to get away from the reservation; he wanted to make something of himself. In a city somewhere."

"They are down there. Ones like your brother. They are down there."

"He didn't make it though. I was supposed to help him, so he'd make it back. They were counting on him. They were proud of him. I owed them that much. After everything that happened. I owed it to them." He looked at the old man, but he was staring at the lights down below, following the headlights from the west until they were taillights disappearing in the east. He didn't seem to be listening.

"There are no limits to this thing," Betonie said. "When it was set loose, it ranged everywhere, from the mountains and plains to the towns and cities; rivers and

138

oceans never stopped it." The wind was blowing steadily and the old man's voice was almost lost in it.

"Emo plays with these teeth—human teeth—and he says the Indians have nothing compared to white people. He talks about their cities and all the machines and food they have. He says the land is no good, and we must go after what they have, and take it from them." Tayo coughed and tried to clear the tightness from his throat. "Well, I don't know how to say this but it seems that way. All you have to do is look around. And so I wonder," he said, feeling the tightness in his throat squeeze out the tears, "I wonder what good Indian ceremonies can do against the sickness which comes from their wars, their bombs, their lies?"

The old man shook his head. "That is the trickery of the witchcraft," he said. "They want us to believe all evil resides with white people. Then we will look no further to see what is really happening. They want us to separate ourselves from white people, to be ignorant and helpless as we watch our own destruction. But white people are only tools that the witchery manipulates; and I tell you, we can deal with white people, with their machines and their beliefs. We can because we invented white people; it was Indian witchery that made white people in the first place.

Long time ago
in the beginning
there were no white people in this world
there was nothing European.
And this world might have gone on like that
except for one thing:
witchery.
This world was already complete
even without white people.
There was everything
including witchery.

Then it happened.
These witch people got together.
Some came from far far away
across oceans
across mountains.
Some had slanty eyes
others had black skin.
They all got together for a contest
the way people have baseball tournaments nowadays
except this was a contest
in dark things.

So anyway
they all got together
witch people from all directions
witches from all the Pueblos
and all the tribes.
They had Navajo witches there,
some from Hopi, and a few from Zuni.
They were having a witches' conference,
that's what it was
Way up in the lava rock hills
north of Cañoncito
they got together
to fool around in caves
with their animal skins.
Fox, badger, bobcat, and wolf
they circled the fire
and on the fourth time
they jumped into that animal's skin.

But this time it wasn't enough
and one of them
maybe a Sioux or some Eskimos
started showing off.
"That wasn't anything,
watch this."

The contest started like that.
Then some of them lifted the lids
on their big cooking pots,
calling the rest of them over
to take a look:
dead babies simmering in blood
circles of skull cut away
all the brains sucked out.
Witch medicine
to dry and grind into powder
for new victims.

Others untied skin bundles of disgusting objects:
dark flints, cinders from burned hogans where the
dead lay
Whorls of skin
cut from fingertips
sliced from the penis end and clitoris tip.

Finally there was only one
who hadn't shown off charms or powers.
The witch stood in the shadows beyond the fire
and no one ever knew where this witch came from
which tribe
or if it was a woman or a man.
But the important thing was
this witch didn't show off any dark thunder charcoals
or red ant-hill beads.
This one just told them to listen:
"What I have is a story."

At first they all laughed
but this witch said
Okay
go ahead
laugh if you want to
but as I tell the story
it will begin to happen.

141

Set in motion now
set in motion by our witchery
to work for us.

Caves across the ocean
in caves of dark hills
white skin people
like the belly of a fish
covered with hair.

Then they grow away from the earth
then they grow away from the sun
then they grow away from the plants and animals.
They see no life
When they look
they see only objects.
The world is a dead thing for them
the trees and rivers are not alive
the mountains and stones are not alive.
The deer and bear are objects
They see no life.

They fear
They fear the world.
They destroy what they fear.
They fear themselves.

The wind will blow them across the ocean
thousands of them in giant boats
swarming like larva
out of a crushed ant hill.

They will carry objects
which can shoot death
faster than the eye can see.

They will kill the things they fear

all the animals
the people will starve.

They will poison the water
they will spin the water away
and there will be drought
the people will starve.

They will fear what they find
They will fear the people
They kill what they fear.

Entire villages will be wiped out
They will slaughter whole tribes.

Corpses for us
Blood for us
Killing killing killing killing.

And those they do not kill
will die anyway
at the destruction they see
at the loss
at the loss of the children
the loss will destroy the rest.

Stolen rivers and mountains
the stolen land will eat their hearts
and jerk their mouths from the Mother.
The people will starve.

They will bring terrible diseases
the people have never known.
Entire tribes will die out
covered with festered sores
shitting blood
vomiting blood.
Corpses for our work

Set in motion now
set in motion by our witchery
set in motion
to work for us.

They will take this world from ocean to ocean
they will turn on each other
they will destroy each other
Up here
in these hills
they will find the rocks,
rocks with veins of green and yellow and black.
They will lay the final pattern with these rocks
they will lay it across the world
and explode everything.

Set in motion now
set in motion
To destroy
To kill
Objects to work for us
objects to act for us
Performing the witchery
for suffering
for torment
for the still-born
the deformed
the sterile
the dead.

Whirling
whirling
whirling
whirling
set into motion now
set into motion.

So the other witches said
"Okay you win; you take the prize,
but what you said just now—
it isn't so funny
It doesn't sound so good.
We are doing okay without it
we can get along without that kind of thing.
Take it back.
Call that story back."

But the witch just shook its head
at the others in their stinking animal skins, fur
and feathers.
It's already turned loose.
It's already coming.
It can't be called back.

They left on horseback before dawn. The old man rode a skinny pinto mare with hip bones and ribs poking against the hide like springs of an old car seat. But she was strong and moved nimbly up the narrow rocky path north of Betonie's hogan. The old man's helper rode a black pony, hunching low over its neck with his face in the mane. Maybe he rode like that for warmth, because it was cold in those foothills before dawn; the night air of the high mountains was chilled by the light of the stars and the shadows of the moon. The brown gelding stumbled with Tayo; he reined it in and walked it more slowly. Behind them in the valley, the highway was a faint dark vein through the yellow sand and red rock. He smelled piñon and sage in the wind that blew across the stony backbone of the ridge. They left the red sandstone and the valley and rode into the lava-rock foothills and pine of the Chuska Mountains.

"We'll have the second night here," Betonie said, indicating a stone hogan set back from the edge of the rimrock.

Tayo stood near the horses, looking down the path over

the way they had come. The plateaus and canyons spread out below him like clouds falling into each other past the horizon. The world below was distant and small; it was dwarfed by a sky so blue and vast the clouds were lost in it. Far into the south there were smoky blue ridges of the mountain haze at Zuni. He smoothed his hand over the top of his head and felt the sun. The mountain wind was cool; it smelled like springs hidden deep in mossy black stone. He could see no signs of what had been set loose upon the earth: the highways, the towns, even the fences were gone. This was the highest point on the earth: he could feel it. It had nothing to do with measurements or height. It was a special place. He was smiling. He felt strong. He had to touch his own hand to remember what year it was: thick welted scars from the shattered bottle glass.

His mother-in-law suspected something.
She smelled coyote piss one morning.
She told her daughter.
She figured Coyote was doing this.
She knew her son-in-law was missing.

There was no telling what Coyote had done to him.
Four of them went to track the man.
They tracked him to the place he found deer tracks.
They found the place the deer was arrow-wounded
where the man started chasing it.
Then they found the place where Coyote got him.
Sure enough those coyote tracks went right along there
Right around the marks in the sand where the man lay.

The human tracks went off
toward the mountain

where the man must have crawled.
They followed the tracks to a hard oak tree
where he had spent a night.
From there he had crawled some distance farther
and slept under a scrub oak tree.
Then his tracks went to a piñon tree
and then under the juniper where he slept another night.

The tracks went on and on
but finally they caught up with him
sleeping under the wild rose bush.
"What happened? Are you the one
who left four days ago, my grandchild?"
A coyote whine was the only sound he made.
"Four days ago you left,
are you that one, my grandchild?"
The man tried to speak
but only a coyote sound was heard,
and the tail moved back and forth
sweeping ridges in the sand.
He was suffering from thirst and hunger
he was almost too weak to raise his head.
But he nodded his head "yes."

"This is him all right,
but what can we do to save him?"

They ran to the holy places
they asked what might be done.

"At the summit of Dark Mountain
ask the four old Bear People.
They are the only possible hope
they have the power to restore the mind.
Time and again
it has been done."

Big Fly went to tell them.

The old Bear People said they would come
They said
Prepare hard oak
scrub oak
piñon
juniper and wild rose twigs
Make hoops
tie bundles of weeds into hoops.
Make four bundles
tie them with yucca
spruce mixed with charcoal from burned weeds
snakeweed and gramma grass and rock sage.
Make four bundles.

The rainbows were crossed.
They had been his former means of travel.
Their purpose was
to restore this to him.

They made Pollen Boy right in the center of
the white corn painting.
His eyes were blue pollen
his mouth was blue pollen
his neck was too
There were pinches of blue pollen
at his joints.

He sat in the center of the white corn sand painting. The rainbows crossed were in the painting behind him. Betonie's helper scraped the sand away and buried the bottoms of the hoops in little trenches so that they were standing up and spaced apart, with the hard oak closest to him and the wild rose hoop in front of the door. The old man painted a dark mountain range beside the farthest hoop, the next, closer, he painted blue, and moving toward him, he knelt and made the yellow mountains; and in front of him, Betonie painted the white mountain range.

The helper worked in the shadows beyond the dark mountain range; he worked with the black sand, making bear prints side by side. Along the right side of the bear footprints, the old man painted paw prints in blue, and then yellow, and finally white. They finished it together, with a big rainbow arching wide above all the mountain ranges. Betonie gave him a basket with prayer sticks to hold.

en-e-e-ya-a-a-a-a!
en-e-e-ya-a-a-a-a!
en-e-e-ya-a-a-a-a!
en-e-e-ya-a-a-a-a!

In dangerous places you traveled
in danger you traveled
to a dangerous place you traveled
in danger e-hey-ya-ah-na!

To the place
where whirling darkness started its journey
along the edges of the rocks
along the places of the gentle wind
along the edges of blue clouds
along the edges of clear water.

Whirling darkness came up from the North
Whirling darkness moved along to the East
It came along the South
It arrived in the West
Whirling darkness spiraled downward
and it came up in the Middle.

The helper stepped out from the shadows; he was grunting like a bear. He raised his head as if it were heavy for him, and he sniffed the air. He stood up and walked to Tayo; he reached down for the prayer sticks and spoke the words distinctly, pressing the sticks close to his

149

heart. The old man came forward then and cut Tayo across the top of his head; it happened suddenly. He hadn't expected it, but the dark flint was sharp and the cut was short. They both reached for him then; lifting him up by the shoulders, they guided his feet into the bear footprints, and Betonie prayed him through each of the five hoops.

> eh-hey-yah-ah-na!
> eh-hey-yah-ah-na!
> eh-hey-yah-ah-na!
> eh-hey-yah-ah-na!
> eh-hey-yah-ah-na!

Tayo could feel the blood ooze along his scalp; he could feel rivulets in his hair. It moved down his head slowly, onto his face and neck as he stooped through each hoop.

> e-hey-yah-ah-na!
> e-hey-yah-ah-na!
> e-hey-yah-ah-na!
> e-hey-yah-ah-na!

> At the Dark Mountain
> born from the mountain
> walked along the mountain
> I will bring you through my hoop,
> I will bring you back.

> Following my footprints
> walk home
> following my footprints
> Come home, happily
> return belonging to your home
> return to long life and happiness again
> return to long life and happiness.

e-hey-yah-ah-na!
e-hey-yah-ah-na!
e-hey-yah-ah-na!
e-hey-yah-ah-na!

At the Dark Mountain
born from the mountain
moves his hand along the mountain
I have left the zigzag lightning behind
I have left the straight lightning behind

I have the dew,
a sunray falls from me,
I was born from the mountain
I leave a path of wildflowers
A raindrop falls from me
I'm walking home
I'm walking back to belonging
I'm walking home to happiness
I'm walking back to long life.

When he passed through the last hoop
it wasn't finished
They spun him around sunwise
and he recovered
he stood up
The rainbows returned him to his
home, but it wasn't over.
All kinds of evil were still on him.

From the last hoop they led him through the doorway. It was dark and the sky was bright with stars. The chill touched the blood on his head; his arms and legs were shaking. The helper brought him a blanket; they walked him to the edge of the rimrock, and the medicine man told him to sit down. Behind him he heard the sound of wood and brush being broken into kindling. He smelled a fire. They gave him Indian tea to drink and old Betonie told him to sleep.

He dreamed about the speckled cattle. They had seen him and they were scattering between juniper trees, through tall yellow grass, below the mesas near the dripping spring. Some of them had spotted calves who ran behind them, their bony rumps flashing white and disappearing into the trees. He tried to run after them, but it was no use without a horse. They were gone, running southwest again, toward the high, lone-standing mesa the people called Pa'to'ch.

He woke up and he was shivering. He stood up and the blanket covering him slid to the ground. He wanted to leave that night to find the cattle; there would be no peace until he did. He looked around for Betonie and his helper. The horses had been tied by a big piñon tree, but they were gone now. He felt the top of his head where the cut had been made; it wasn't swollen or hot. It didn't hurt. He stood on the edge of the rimrock and looked down below: the canyons and valleys were thick powdery black; their variations of height and depth were marked by a thinner black color. He remembered the black of the sand paintings on the floor of the hogan; the hills and mountains were the mountains and hills they had painted in sand. He took a deep breath of cold mountain air: there were no boundaries; the world below and the sand paintings inside became the same that night. The mountains from all the directions had been gathered there that night.

He heard someone come up from the west side of the ridge. He turned. Betonie looked even taller in the darkness. He motioned for Tayo to sit down. He sat down next to him and reached into his shirt pocket for the tobacco and wheat papers. He rolled a thin cigarette without looking down at his hands, still gazing up at the east sky. He lit it and took little puffs without inhaling the smoke.

"It all started a long time ago. My grandfather, Descheeny, was an old man then. The hunters were returning from the South Peak. They had been hunting deer and

152

drying the meat for two months. The burros were loaded with sacks full of jerky and bundles of stiff dry hides. The Navajos were careful. They didn't want any trouble with the soldiers at the fort in San Mateo. They made their night camp up a narrow deep canyon, northwest of the settlement, and they didn't build any campfires. The night was warm and the sky was bright with stars which flared like fire as they shined. The older men sat wrapped in their blankets, smoking and looking up at the sky to watch for shooting stars. But the young men stood over near the horses, talking in whispers and laughing frequently. They shared a cigarette, and the red light of ash passed back and forth between them in the dark. They didn't want to sit around all night and listen to the old men belch and pluck out chin whiskers until they were snoring. They wanted to ride over toward the settlement just to see if maybe there wasn't some stray horse or lost goats wandering in the hills outside town. There had been no raiding for many years, but they could sense the feeling of riding at night through piñon trees, galloping through the cool wind along the flats.

"The old men were unconcerned. They sat whittling toothpicks from piñon twigs. They knew how it would feel to let the horses run through the cool air; they had been traveling slowly in the dust and sun beside the burros for over a week. They watched the young men untie their horses; someone commented that it was a seductive night, and all the old men laughed and settled back to watch the sky again, and to tell the stories they had for nights like this night.

"The stars gave off a special light, more subtle and luminous than moonlight. The riders could make out the density of the trees and the massive boundaries of the boulders, but were still protected by darkness. When they got close enough that they could smell wood smoke, they pulled the running horses down to a lope and then a trot. The horses were excited and hot; they shook their heads and tried to pull away the reins. The riders could feel their heat and smell the horse sweat. They looked east at the tiny square pattern of the town in the valley that came down from the west slope of the big blue peaks, still solid with snow. They could see a few dim outlines of windows. They rode slowly, listening and watching. They did not expect to find anything, because they knew how careful the Mexicans were with their livestock at night. They were satisfied to ride close enough to smell the wood smoke and hear the village dogs barking in the distance.

"They had turned the horses around, and were riding back to the camp, along a piñon ridge. They had crossed a grassy clearing and were riding into the trees again when their horses stopped suddenly and spun around in panic. It was something about the big piñon tree at the edge of the clearing; the horses shied away from it and blew air through their nostrils when the men tried to ride them near it. They would have left that place, galloping fast, if one of them had not seen a light-colored object fall out of the tree, lightly like a bird. He dismounted and walked over to the tree slowly and picked up the object. It was a blue lace shawl. The others walked over, and they stood together and looked up into the branches of the big tree.

"They boosted a man up to the big branch to bring her down. He moved toward her cautiously, expecting her to fight, but she came down on her own, dropping softly into the dry needles under the tree. She did not cry like captives did, or jabber in her own language with tears running down her face. She held her mouth tight, teeth clenched under her thin lips, and she stared at them with hazel green eyes that had a peculiar night shine of a wolf or bobcat. The wind came out of the trees and blew her loose hair wildly around her wide brown face. Their confidence was caught in the wind: they were chilled as they looked at her. Each man was ready to let her go, to leave that place as fast as possible, but no one wanted to be the one to admit his fear. After all she was only twelve or thirteen, and she would bring a good price.

"They tied her to a small tree in a clearing where they could see her. But she watched them all night, staring at them steadily until they were afraid to look at her. In the morning the old men were silent. They did not joke or laugh as they loaded the burros. They gave her a horse to ride, and doubled up themselves; none of them wanted to get near her. Late in the afternoon they stopped to rest the animals in a canyon surrounded by red-rock mesas. The old men discussed how to get rid of her; nobody said so, but they all knew that they could not simply turn her loose or leave her behind, tied to a tree. They were in trouble now. They would kill her as soon as they found somebody who knew how it should be done. The old men discussed the stupidity of the young men in tones of great contempt. 'It's a good thing for us we are near old Descheeny's place,' one of them said, 'we can get him to help us.'

"Early the next morning they rode into the Chuska Mountains. They stopped at the white clay springs and sent someone up the hill to find Descheeny. They looked at the Mexican captive and then at the burros loaded with meat; they wondered how much Descheeny would charge to get them out of this situation. Descheeny's wives came down the hill first; they watched curiously, and then walked back up the trail.

"'What does she look like?' he asked his wives before they could speak. 'Who?' they said, pretending not to understand him, the way they often did, trying to anger him. But he smiled this time, and got up from his place by the door. 'Don't give me any trouble, ladies,' he said, putting on his old badger fur hat, and reaching for his walking cane, 'or I think I will marry her.'

Descheeny stood on the trail above the spring and watched her. She was kneeling at the edge of the pool, washing herself. Descheeny came down to the hunters who pretended to be adjusting the harnesses and tightening the cinches.

" 'Nice load of meat you have there,' he said, motioning toward the bundles with his chin.

" 'We have something else too, you might have noticed,' the tall man said casually. 'She's quite valuable, but she slows us down. You know how they are. Crying and screaming.' Descheeny smiled at the lies. He shook his head. 'I can see what you have. I will help you out for two or three loads of meat. Otherwise . . .' His voice trailed off and the hunters started whispering among themselves.

"He knew some Spanish. 'I'm too old to bother with you,' he said. 'Tomorrow we'll take you back to your people. We'll assure them that you have not been touched by the men. You can go back to your former life.' Descheeny was pleased with himself; he thought the words sounded suitably generous and sensitive. He watched her face; it was unchanged.

" 'We'll tell your people where you were found. It was up in a tree, wasn't it? In the hills, late at night.' She laughed at him; her nostrils flared and her face was sneering.

" 'You know the answer, old man, don't play games with me. You know what the people there will do with me.'

" 'We don't want that thing around here,' the three sisters told their husband. 'It is a disgrace the way you sleep with her every night. We try to teach our children to avoid touching alien things, but every day they see you do it, you senile old man.' So he moved her to the winter house below the mountains, in the southwest, where the yellow sandrock foothills look over on the river.

"In the middle of the night he heard her moving in the hogan, the soft sounds of basket lids lifted and buckskin bundles unrolling, the rustle of seeds and dry leaves, the clink of eagle claws and wolves' teeth taken on their strings from his bag. Then there was silence.

" 'I hear you, old man. Go back to sleep.'

" 'I get cold without you close to me. Come lay down again.'

" 'I will if you tell me why I hear so many voices in this hogan at night. All these languages I never heard before.'

" 'Come lay down now. I'm shivering.'

"She lay down beside him and pulled the blanket over her mouth, and gradually moved closer to him until she could feel his thin ribs moving up and down. Old Descheeny's heart still pounded when he heard her breathing, and the excitement crawled up his thighs to his belly in anticipation.

" 'I think it is them again.'

" 'Yes.'

" 'They are working for the end of this world, aren't they?'

" 'I think so.'

" 'Sometimes I don't know if the ceremony will be strong enough to stop them. We have to depend on people not even born yet. A hundred years from now.' She could only whisper the words because he was holding her close to him now.

" 'You Mexicans have no patience,' he said, stroking her belly, 'it never has been easy. It will take a long long time and many more stories like this one before they are laid low.' She rolled over on top of him quickly.

" 'There is something else which takes a long time happening,' she said in a low voice. 'Why do I bother to lay down with you, old man?'

"Old age made him fearless. He flexed the old chants and the beliefs like a mountain-oak bow. He had been watching the sky before she came, the planets and con-stellations wheeling and shifting the patterns of the old stories. He saw the transition, and he was ready. Some of the old singers could see new shadows across the moon; they could make out new darkness between the stars. They sent Descheeny the patients they couldn't cure, the victims of this new evil set loose upon the world.

"He reasoned that because it was set loose by witch-ery of all the world, and brought to them by the whites, the ceremony against it must be the same. When she came, she didn't fool him for long. She had come for his ceremonies, for the chants and the stories they grew from.

" 'This is the only way,' she told him. 'It cannot be done alone. We must have power from everywhere. Even the power we can get from the whites.'

"Although the people detected changes in the ceremonies Descheeny performed, they tolerated them because of his acknowledged power to aid victims tainted by Chris-tianity or liquor. But after the Mexican captive came, they were terrified, and few of them stayed to see the conclusion of his ceremonies. But by then, Descheeny was getting ready to die anyway, and he could not be bothered with isolated cures.

"He gazed into his smoky quartz crystal and she stared into the fire, and they plotted the course of the ceremony by the direction of dark night winds and by the colors of the clay in drought-ridden valleys.

"The day I was born they saw the color of my eyes, and they took me from the village. The Spaniards in the town looked at me, and the Catholic priest said, 'Let her die.' They blamed the Root Woman for this birth and they told her to leave the village before dark. She waited until they had gone, and she went to the old trash pile in the arroyo where they left me. She took me north to El Paso, and years later she laughed about how long she had waited for me in that village full of dirty stupid people. Sometimes she was bitter because of what they had done to her in the end, after all the years she had helped them. 'Sometimes I have to shake my head,' she'd say, 'because human beings deserve exactly what they get.' "

The people asked,
"Did you find him?"
"Yes, but we forgot something.
Tobacco."
But there was no tobacco
so Fly and Hummingbird had to fly
all the way back down
to the fourth world below
to ask our mother where
they could get some tobacco.

"We came back again,"
they told our mother.
"Maybe you need something?"
"Tobacco."
"Go ask caterpillar."

"There was a child. The Mexican woman gave her to Descheeny's daughters to raise. The half sisters taught her to fear her mother. Many years later she had a child. When I was weaned, my grandmother came and took me. My mother and my old aunts did not resist because it all had been settled before Descheeny died."

Betonie paused and blew smoke rings up at the sky. Tayo stretched out his legs in front of him. He was thinking about the ceremony the medicine man had performed over him, testing it against the old feeling, the sick hollow in his belly formed by the memories of Rocky and Josiah, and all the years of Auntie's eyes and her teeth set hard on edge. He could feel the ceremony like the rawhide thongs of the medicine pouch, straining to hold back the voices, the dreams, faces in the jungle in the L.A. depot, the smoky silence of solid white walls.

"One night or nine nights won't do it any more," the medicine man said; "the ceremony isn't finished yet." He was drawing in the dirt with his finger. "Remember these stars," he said. "I've seen them and I've seen the spotted cattle; I've seen a mountain and I've seen a woman."

The wind came up and caught the sleeves of Tayo's shirt. He smelled wood smoke and sage in the old man's clothes. He reached for the billfold in his hip pocket. "I want to pay you for the ceremony you did tonight."

Old Betonie shook his head. "This has been going on for a long long time now. It's up to you. Don't let them stop you. Don't let them finish off this world."

The dry skin
was still stuck
to his body.
But the effects
of the witchery
of the evil thing
began to leave
his body.
The effects of the witchery
of the evil thing
in his surroundings
began to turn away.

160

It had gone a great distance
It had gone below the North.

                                    The truck driver stopped at
San Fidel to dump a load of diesel fuel. Tayo went inside
the station to buy candy; he had not eaten since he had
left Betonie and his helper up in the mountains. The room
smelled like rubber from the loops of fan belts hanging
from the ceiling. Cases of motor oil were stacked in front
of the counter; the cans had a dull oil film on them. The
desk behind the counter was covered with yellow and
pink slips of paper, invoices and bills with a half cup of
cold coffee sitting on top of them. Above the desk, on a
calendar, a smiling blond girl, in a baton twirler's shiny
blue suit with white boots to her knees, had her arms
flung around the neck of a palomino horse. She was holding a bottle of Coca-Cola in one hand. He stared at the
calendar for a long time; the horse's mane was bleached
white, and there was no trace of dust on its coat. The
hooves were waxed with dark polish, shining like metal.
The woman's eyes and the display of her teeth made him
remember the glassy eyes of the stuffed bobcat above the
bar in Bibo. The teeth were the same. He turned away
from the calendar; he felt sick, like a walking shadow,
faint and wispy, his sense of balance still swaying from
the ride in the cab of the tank truck. All the windows of
the candy machine had red sold-out flags in them.
    The station man came inside. He looked at Tayo suspi-
ciously, as if he thought Tayo might be drunk, or in
there to steal something. In his anger Tayo imagined
movie images of himself turning the pockets of his jeans
inside out, unbuttoning his shirt to prove he had stolen
nothing. A confrontation would have been too easy, and
he was not going to let them stop him; he asked the man
where he could buy some candy.

"Down the road," he said, not looking up from the cash register. His milky white face was shaded with the stubble of a red beard. There were white hairs scattered among the red, and the skin across his forehead and at the corner of each eye was wrinkled as if he had been frowning for a long time. The backs of his hands were covered with curly reddish hair; the fingers were black and oily. He had never seen a white person so clearly before. He had to turn away. All those things old Betonie had told him were swirling inside his head, doing strange things; he wanted to laugh. He wanted to laugh at the station man who did not even know that his existence and the existence of all white people had been conceived by witchery.

He told the truck driver he didn't need to ride any farther. The sun was behind him and a warm dry wind from the southwest was blowing enough to cool the sweat on his forehead, and to dry out the wet cloth under the arms of his shirt. He walked down the ditch beside the highway, below the shoulder of the highway. He didn't want any more rides. He wanted to walk until he recognized himself again. Grasshoppers buzzed out of the weeds ahead of him; they were fading to a dry yellow color, from their bright green color of spring. Their wings flashed reflections of sun when they jumped. He looked down at the weeds and grass. He stepped carefully, pushing the toe of his boot into the weeds first to make sure the grasshoppers were gone before he set his foot down into the crackling leathery stalks of dead sunflowers. Across the highway, behind the bar at Cerritos there was a big corn field, but the plants were short and thin, and their leaves were faded yellow like the grasshoppers. There would be only a few cobs on each plant, and the kernels would be small and deformed. He wondered what the Mexicans at Cubero thought. Their cattle were thin too. What did they do? Drop down on their knees in the chapel, sweaty straw hats in their hands, to smell the candle wax and watch the flickering red and blue votive lights? Pray up to the plaster Jesus in rose-colored robes, his arms reaching out? "Help us, forgive us."

He heard a truck slowing down on the highway behind him. He turned around and saw Harley hanging out the window, waving at him. He swung the door open before the old green truck had come to a stop and stumbled out of the seat grinning, holding a bottle of Garden Deluxe Tokay in each hand Harley patted him on the back and pushed him toward the truck. Tayo could see Leroy was driving, but there was someone else in the truck, someone sitting in the middle, between them.

"Hey buddy—meet Helen Jean," Harley said, and winked crookedly, as if he had been drinking for a while. She was wearing tight blue western pants and a frilly pink western blouse. She didn't say anything, but she smiled and moved closer to Leroy. Leroy grinned at Tayo. She rubbed her leg against Leroy, but she was staring out the window while she did it, as if her mind were somewhere else. Leroy and Harley were happy; they had wine and two six-packs, and they didn't watch her the way Tayo did. Her perfume was close and heavy; breathing it was like swallowing big red roses; it choked him. He turned his face to the fresh air rushing in the window.

"Good thing you're skinny, buddy. Otherwise we couldn't shut the door!" Leroy shifted through the gears. The woman grinned at him because she was straddling the gear stick and he kept brushing against her thigh whenever he shifted gears. Harley nudged her in the ribs with an elbow and offered her the bottle.

"Look at her! She drinks like a pro," Harley said, delighted. "We found her in Gallup last night, didn't we?"

Leroy nodded. His eyes were bloodshot.

Harley passed him the bottle. Tayo shook his head. "You want a beer?"

Tayo shook his head and pointed to his stomach.

"Sick? Hey Leroy, this guy says he's sick! We know

163

how to cure him, don't we, Helen Jean?" She nodded. Tayo could see the lines at the corners of her eyes and a slight curve of flesh under her chin. Her hair was short and curled tight, and her eyelashes were stiff with mascara; she kept reaching into her tooled leather purse between her feet for her lipstick, rubbing it back and forth until her lips were thick and red. She wasn't much older than they were.

Tayo leaned out the window to make more room in the cab, but Harley, Helen Jean, and Leroy enjoyed squeezing close. He wanted to be still walking, but he knew them too well. It was no use to refuse a ride from them when they were drunk, because they'd follow him along the shoulder of the highway for ten miles in low gear until he got in with them. He wanted to catch a grasshopper and hold it close to his face, to look at its big flat eyes and shiny thin legs with stripes of black and brown like beadwork, making tiny intricate designs. The last time he held one, Rocky was with him, and they had stained their finger tips brown with the tobacco juice the grasshoppers spit.

"Hey!" Harley said. "What you watching?"

"Grasshoppers."

She giggled.

Harley shook his head and made him hold the wine bottle. "Here. You better have some. You're in bad shape, isn't he, Leroy? Watching grasshoppers when we've got Helen Jean here to watch, eh?" He laughed again.

The bottle was sticky. It was almost empty. He watched the weeds in the ditch speeding by. In another month the grasshoppers would be dead; autumn wind and old age would chill them bone white, leaving their hollow shells to swirl with the dry leaves in the ditch.

"Hey! You like my truck?"

Tayo nodded.

"Where'd you get it?"

"No money down! Pay at the first of the month!"

"If they catch him!" Harley laughed.

"Yeah! They have to catch me first!"

Harley bounced up and down on the seat laughing. "They owed it to us—we traded it for some of the land they stole from us!"

Helen Jean didn't smile, but she said, "Gypped you again! This thing isn't even worth a half acre!"

Tayo laughed then, too, because it was true. He could smell fumes from a loud busted muffler, and he was going to make a joke about how the white people sold junk pickups to Indians so they could drive around until they asphyxiated themselves; but it wasn't that funny. Not really.

They were getting close to Laguna, crossing the overpass by New Laguna; Leroy shifted into second gear for the hill.

"Thanks for the ride," Tayo said. "You can let me out any place along here." He gave the wine bottle to Helen Jean. She steadied it between her thighs, and pulled the cork out again.

"Easy, easy!" she said to Leroy. "You guys already spilled one bottle over me." She was either an Apache or a Ute. Her face was angular, and something about her nose and eyes reminded him of a hawk.

Leroy slowed down and pulled off the right shoulder of the highway.

"Hey! Wait! He's going with us. Aren't you, Tayo? Huh, buddy!" Harley had Tayo by the arm and was leaning close to him, breathing wine fumes in his face. Harley was sweating and his face was shiny. They had been his friends for a long time; they were the only ones left now. He hesitated and Harley saw it. He started whooping and slapping Tayo on the back; Leroy revved up the engine and threw it into low gear. The rear wheels spun sand and pebbles against the fenders, and the truck skidded and swerved back on the pavement. He did a speed shift into second gear and gunned it across the bridge, up the hill past Willie Creager's garage. Helen

Jean squealed and laughed because Leroy's driving threw them hard against each other; Harley had his arms around her neck, bellowing out war whoops and laughs. The old truck was vibrating hard; the steering was loose and the front end wandered across the white line into the other lane, and each time a car was coming at them head-on before Leroy wrestled the wheel around and steered the truck over again. White people selling Indians junk cars and trucks reminded Tayo of the Army captain in the 1860s who made a gift of wool blankets to the Apaches: the entire stack of blankets was infected with smallpox. But he was laughing anyway, the bumps shaking laughter out of him, like feathers out of an old pillow, until he was limp and there were tears in his eyes.

"We'll give you a cure! We know how, don't we?" Harley was bouncing on the seat, and he made the whole truck sway on its weak springs. Helen Jean squealed, and the bottle of wine she was holding splashed all over them. Tayo grabbed it and swallowed what was left in the bottle.

"Drink it! Drink it! It's good for you! You'll get better! Get this man to the cold Coors hospital! Hurry up!"

Leroy pressed the gas pedal to the floorboard, and the speedometer dial spun around and around before it fluttered at 65. The engine whined with the strain, and the heat-guage needle was pointing at 212. Tayo could smell hot oil and rubber, but Leroy kept it wide open past Mesita.

Up ahead, he could see where the highway dipped across an arroyo. But Leroy didn't slow down, and the old truck bounced, and landed hard on the other side of the dip. Their heads hit the roof of the cab, and Harley said this was better than a carnival ride at the Laguna fiesta. Tayo sank down into sensations—the truck vibrating and bouncing down the road, the bodies squeezed around him tight, the smell of perfume and sweat and wine, and the rushing fresh air cooling the sweat. Everything made them laugh, until they were laughing at their own noises and laughter. He didn't have to remember anything, he didn't have to feel anything but this; and he wished the truck would never stop moving, that they could ride like that forever.

Leroy parked the truck under the elm trees at the Y bar. Wine bottles and beer cans were scattered everywhere, broken and flattened by tires. Leroy turned off the key, but he left it in gear, so when he took his foot off the clutch, the truck lurched forward suddenly. Harley was helping Helen Jean get out, and the sudden lurch threw her against him. They both collapsed on the ground, laughing. The contents of her tooled leather purse with the rose designs had spilled all around her. She picked up her billfold, but they all got down on their hands and knees, crawling around to pick up little brass tubes of lipstick and her mirror and powder puff. Harley grabbed the mirror out of her hand and pranced around one of the elm trees, pretending to be "chickish muggy," someone who swished around, exercising his back muscles as he walked.

"Hey, Harley!" Tayo yelled. "You can't fool us any more! We know you are one of those guys! Where's your lipstick and nail polish?"

Harley took mincing steps and dropped the mirror into Helen's purse. "I'll race you to a cold beer!" he said as he took off, running to the door of the bar.

Harley and Leroy raced for the screen door, leaving Tayo behind with Helen Jean. She was giggling to herself, taking big steps and setting her feet down stiffly, as though she weren't sure the ground would hold her. They stepped over a Navajo sleeping on the shady side of the wooden steps. The juke box was playing a Mexican polka and Harley was dancing around by himself. There were some Mexicans from the section gang drinking beer at a table in the corner and three Navajos slouching on stools at the bar. The Mexicans could see she was drunk, and they were already getting ideas about her.

The way the men looked at her tensed Tayo's hands into fists. He didn't feel the fun or the laughter any more. His back was rigid; he sat down stiffly in the chair Leroy pulled out for him. Harley kept Helen Jean between himself and Tayo, and away from Leroy. He should have been worrying about the Mexicans in the corner, not Leroy. But Harley was up again, ordering a round of Coors, feeding quarters into the juke box as he punched the buttons for all the Hank Williams songs.

Helen Jean was smiling coyly at one of the Mexicans. Tayo tried to focus his eyes in the dim light to see which one, but there was a buzzing inside his head that made his eyes lose focus. He swallowed more beer, trying to clear away the dull ache; and he decided then he was too tired to care what she did.

"It wouldn't have worked anyway," Harley was saying in a loud voice; "between this beer belly of mine and her big belly, there would have been too much distance!" He laughed and looked at Helen Jean to see if she liked his story. She moved her eyes away quickly from the tall Mexican with long sideburns. She stared down at the table, smiling to herself.

The Mexicans stood up; the tall one put his cap on slowly and pulled it to one side of his head seductively. He watched her steadily; he didn't care if the Indians noticed. He nodded, and she smiled. Harley had the bottle tilted all the way, nursing the last drops of beer. He was too drunk and too happy to see what was happening. Leroy's shirttail was coming loose from his jeans, and when he answered Harley he had trouble making the words come out.

Helen Jean reached down by her feet for her purse.

She hesitated and looked at Tayo. She giggled and said, "I have to go pee"; he nodded and finished off the beer. Harley and Leroy never even saw her go.

She had been thinking about it that morning when they left Gallup. Something had reminded her; maybe it was the people in the bar talking about the Gallup Ceremonial coming in two weeks. She had left Towac about then, August, one year ago. Left the reservation for good to find a job. She hadn't thought about it until then. Maybe it was because she was with these reservation Indians, out drinking with them and dancing in Gallup with all the other reservation Indians. Maybe someone had even talked about Towac.

She took the money she had saved—money the missionary lady paid her for cooking—and she stopped by Emma's to tell them good-bye. But the padlock was hooked through the hasp on the door, and it was locked, which meant Emma would be gone all day. Maybe to Cortez. So she left without seeing her little sisters, because she planned to come back on the bus, every weekend, to visit, and to bring money to help them out.

These Laguna guys were about the worst she'd run into, especially that guy they picked up walking along the highway; he acted funny. Too quiet, and not very friendly. She wanted to get away from them. They weren't mean like the two Oklahoma guys who beat her up one afternoon in a parked car behind the El Fidel. Pawnees, they said. Normandy. Omaha Beach. They beat her up—took turns holding and hitting her. They yelled at her because they both wanted her; they had been buddies all through the war together, and she was trying to split them up, they said. These Lagunas wouldn't beat her up, except she didn't know for sure about the quiet one. But Harley and Leroy, they were okay. She just didn't want to be driving around, way out in the sticks, with these reservation guys, even if they were war vets.

It was just a feeling she'd had since that morning. Thinking about Ceremonial time coming again. She hadn't sent any letters to Emma or the girls. She meant to do it; she had even written letters, in the evenings, on Stephanie's pink stationery at the little table in the kitchen they all shared. But she saved the letters in unsealed envelopes, waiting for a couple of dollar bills to send along.

It didn't work out. Her roommates were nice, but they had to have rent money, and she had to buy her share of the food. All day one Saturday the girls gave each other curly permanent waves and plucked out their eyebrows, penciling a thin arc over each eye. Monday she borrowed Elaine's blue dress, and she went down to the Kimo theater to apply for the job they advertised in the theater window. The man told her to wait in the lobby. It smelled like cold popcorn and burned-out cigarettes. She was too shy to ask him what the job was, or to tell him she knew how to type. She looked at the doors marked PRIVATE and OFFICE and tried to imagine what the desks looked like and what kind of typewriter they had. He didn't smile or look at her directly. "You can start today," he said, "but you might want to change your clothes." She stood in front of him, afraid to ask what was wrong with her clothes. He turned and motioned for her to follow. At the end of the corridor he pulled open a door, and she saw a push broom, and a scrub bucket. "Oh," she said. She always smiled when she was embarrassed. "How much do you pay?" "Seventy-five cents an hour," he said, walking away.

These Laguna guys were fun all right. And they sure spent their money. She didn't even know if there would be any money left when she asked them to help her out a little. Her roommates got tired of helping her out. They thought she was a secretary; they kept asking her what she did with all her money. She lied; she said she had to send it back home to Emma and the girls. She got dressed every day and left for work when they did. She changed her clothes in the ladies' lounge. But it wasn't working out. The man at the theater waited for her now; he watched her go down to the ladies' lounge. She wasn't surprised the day she heard the door open and close and she saw his brown shoes under the door of the toilet stall.

These Indians who fought in the war were full of stories about all the places they'd seen. San Diego, Oakland, Germany, the Philippines. The first few times she heard them talk, she believed everything. That was right after she got to town, and the girls took her out one weekend. She had walked around, staring up at the tall buildings, and all the big neon signs on Central Avenue. Every time she rode an elevator then, she thought of the old people at home, who shook their heads at the mention of elevators and tall buildings or juke boxes that could play a hundred different records. The old Utes said it was a lie; there were no such things. But she saw it every day, and for a long time when she saw these things, she felt embarrassed for the old people at home, who did not believe in these things. So she was careful not to make the same kind of mistake herself; and she believed all the stories the guys told. They had ribbons and medals they carried in their wallets; and if the U.S. Government decorated them, they must be okay.

She knew where to find them—which downtown bars they liked. She knew the veterans' disability checks came out around the first of the month. She learned these things after she quit her job at the Kimo. She walked by the El Fidel, that day she quit, and she could hear them laughing and whooping it up inside, so she knew they were Indians. That day she went in only to ask for a loan, because the girls were getting behind with the rent. The guys told her to sit down. She asked for a Coke, and they told the bartender to put rum in it.

"How do you like that!" they said, laughing and patting each other on the back. "Nothing like this at Towac, huh?"

She sat with them all afternoon. It was dim in there, and cool because they had a table near the fan. In July the streets and sidewalks were too hot to touch. She looked for work, but every day when it started to get hot, she walked past the El Fidel to see who was there. They were happy to see her; they introduced her to their other buddies. Late in the afternoon, when she got up to leave, she would ask someone to help her out a little. By then they would be feeling pretty good. Someone always helped her out with five or maybe ten dollars. "We used to do this every night during the war," one of them told her. "In San Diego one time, we bought the whole bar—all the soldiers and their girls—a round of drinks. The bartender shook his head; he told us, 'I know it's you Indians, without even looking. No one ever did that until the Indian soldiers came around.'"

They told her other stories too. Later on, when they started looking at her and sitting closer to her. The sergeant from Isleta still wore his khaki shirt with the stripes on the arm. As he reached over to pour her more beer, he rubbed his shaky arm against her side to feel the swell of her breast. She wasn't surprised then either. She knew if they helped her out, they would get friendly with her too. He had already told her a story about blowing up a bunker full of Japs. The story ended with him pulling out his wallet to show her a little bronze star on a blue ribbon. "Another thing was the women. The white women in California. Boy! You never saw anything like it! They couldn't get enough of us, huh?" "No!" all the others at the table would shout. "See," the sergeant said, looking a little crookedly at her, "I'll tell you about this one who was in love with me." He nodded deliberately. "Yeah, she was. I told her I was already married back home, but she didn't care. Boy, you shoulda seen her blond hair! She had it all curled. And she was built like this up front." He held his brown hands out in front of his chest and grinned at the others. He turned back to her and breathed heavily into her ear. "Hey, let's go someplace where I can tell you about it."

But she didn't want to go with him. "Tell me here," she said, "I want to finish my drink."

"Her name was Doreen. She only needed the money because her mother was a cripple. She wasn't like the others. She went with me because she loved me. I could still have her if I went back to California."

One of the guys at the table, an Apache, yelled at the Isleta sergeant. "She told that to all the guys. Doreen. That's what she called herself. Sure she liked Indians! Because they were dumb guys like you!"

The Apache had been watching Helen Jean; he had been watching the Isleta rub up against her. The Isleta grabbed her arm. "Let's go," he said. She didn't move. The Apache jumped up, ready to fight.

"She doesn't want to go with you," the Apache said.

The Isleta turned to her; his eyes were pinched with rage. "You bitch! You think you're better than a white woman?" He slapped her across the face. Her teeth cut her tongue and the inside of her mouth. Tears ran down her face. The Apache grabbed him, and they started pushing at each other, in a staggering circle on the dance floor. The other guys were cheering for a fight. They forgot about her.

She knew all the stories, about white women in San Diego and Oakland and L.A. Always blond or redhead, nice girls with sick or crippled parents at home. It didn't make any difference to her. They drank until they couldn't walk without holding on to her. She asked them for money then, money to send back to Emma at Towac: for the little girls. Then they stumbled up the steps to the Hudson Hotel. If she took long enough in the toilet, they usually passed out on the bed.

Even in the wintertime, when the rooms at the Hudson were cold and the window by the bed had frost on it, they sweated beer; and they lay on her so heavily that it was difficult to breathe. Their mouths were wet and soured with beer, and when they pushed themselves down on her, they felt small and soft between her thighs. She stared at the stains on the ceiling, and waited until they gave up or fell asleep, and then she rolled out from under them.

She looked at these Laguna guys. They had been treated first class once, with their uniforms. As long as there had been a war and the white people were afraid of the Japs and Hitler. But these Indians got fooled when they thought it would last. She was tired of pretending with them, tired of making believe it had lasted. It was almost a year since she had left Towac. There was something about Gallup that made her think about it. She didn't like the looks of the Indian women she saw in Gallup, dancing at Eddie's club with the drunks that stumbled around the floor with them. Their hair was dirty and straight. They'd shaved off their eyebrows, but the hairs were growing back and they didn't bother to pencil them any more. Their blouses had buttons missing and were fastened with safety pins. Their western pants were splitting out at the seams; there were stains around the crotch.

She reached into her purse for the little pink compact and looked in the mirror. Her hair was cut short and was tightly curled. It needed to be washed, but at least it wasn't long or straight. She touched up her left eyebrow and put on lipstick. She didn't like the looks of the country around here either. Rocks and sand, arroyos and no trees. After spending all her life at Towac, she didn't need to be wasting her time there, in the middle of nowhere, some place worse than the reservation she had left. If she hung around any longer with these guys, that's how she'd end up. Like the rest of the Indians. She smiled at the Mexican; he winked at her. He had the cash from his railroad pay check on the table in front of him. He'd help her out, give her some to send back to Towac. And this time she was really going to send some money to Emma, and she wasn't going to waste any more time fooling around with Indian war heroes.

He sat back in the chair and rested his head against the cool plaster wall. Through the sound of the juke box he could hear the Navajo, sitting now with his back against the screen door, singing songs. There was something familiar in the songs, and he remembered old Betonie's singing; something in his belly stirred faintly; but it was too far away now. He crawled deeper into the black gauzy web where he could rest in the silence, where his coming and going through this world was no more than a star falling across the night sky. He left behind the pain and buzzing in his head; they were shut out by the wide dark distance.

Someone was yelling. Someone was shaking him out of the tall tree he was in. He thought it might be old Betonie telling him to get on his way, telling him that he'd slept too long and there were the cattle to find, and the stars, the mountain, and the woman.

He started to answer old Betonie, to tell him he hadn't forgotten.

"I'm going," he said.

"You're damn right you're going!" the white man said. "Your pal got the shit kicked out of him, and I don't want no more trouble here."

The last bright rays of sunlight split his head in half, like a big ax splitting logs for winter kindling. He put his hand over his eyes to shade them. He moved down the steps carefully, remembering the Navajo who had been sitting there, singing. But he was gone and the Mexicans were gone too; and the sky was deep orange and scarlet, all the way across to Mount Taylor. Leroy was kneeling over Harley, balancing himself unsteadily with one hand. His shirttail was loose, making a little skirt around his slim hips. He was saying, "Harley, buddy, did they hurt you?" Leroy's lips were bloody and swollen where they'd hit him. Harley was breathing peacefully, passed out or knocked out, Tayo couldn't tell. There was a big cut above his left eyebrow, but the blood had already crusted over it.

They carried Harley to the truck; his legs dragged behind him, wobbling and leaving long toe marks in the dirt. They propped him up between them, with Tayo behind the wheel. Leroy was slumped against the door, passed out. He searched the dashboard for the knob to turn on the headlights. When he pulled it, the knob came loose in his hands; he was too tired and sick to laugh at this truck, but he would have if Helen Jean had been there. Because she said it: gypped again.

At twilight the earth was darker than the sky, and it was difficult to see if any of Romero's sheep or goats were grazing along the edge of the pavement. The tourist traffic on Highway 66 was gone now, and Tayo imagined white people eating mashed potatoes and gravy in some steamy Grants café.

During that last summer they had ridden across these flats to round up the speckled cattle and brand the calves. He took the pickup across the dip slowly, almost tenderly, as if the old truck were the blind white mule too old to be treated roughly any more. He was thinking about Harley and Leroy; about Helen Jean and himself. How much longer would they last? How long before one of them got stabbed in a bar fight, not just knocked out? How long before this old truck swerved off the road or head-on into a bus? But it didn't make much difference anyway. The drinking and hell raising were just things they did, as he had done sitting at the ranch all afternoon, watching the yellow cat bite the air for flies; passing the time away, waiting for it to end.

Someone groaned; he looked over to see who it was. He smelled vomit. Harley had thrown up all over himself. Tayo rolled down the window and drove with his head outside, the way train engineers did, the air rushing at his face as he watched the white lines of the highway fall past the truck.

He pulled off the highway at Mesita, and reached over and shook Leroy by the arm. He mumbled and pushed Tayo's hand away. He shut off the engine and looked at the village. The lights of the houses were as scattered and dim as far-away stars. He left the keys in the ignition and rolled up the window in case the wind blew that night. One of them had pissed, and the rubber mat at Leroy's feet was wet, and with the windows rolled up the urine smell steamed around him. He gagged as he pushed the door open, and something gave way in his belly. He vomited out everything he had drunk with them, and when that was gone, he was still kneeling on the road beside the truck, holding his heaving belly, trying to vomit out everything—all the past, all his life.

The Scalp Ceremony lay to rest the Japanese souls in the green humid jungles, and it satisfied the female giant who fed on the dreams of warriors. But there was something else now, as Betonie said: it was everything they had seen—the cities, the tall buildings, the noise and the lights, the power of their weapons and machines. They were never the same after that: they had seen what the white people had made from the stolen land. It was the story of the white shell beads all over again, the white shell beads, stolen from a grave and found by a man as he walked along a trail one day. He carried the beautiful white shell beads on the end of a stick because he suspected where they came from; he left them hanging in the branches of a piñon tree. And although he had never touched them, they haunted him; all he could think of, all he dreamed of, were these white shell beads hanging in that tree. He could not eat, and he could not work. He lost touch with the life he had lived before the day he found those beads; and the man he had been before that day was lost somewhere on that trail where he first saw the beads. Every day they had to look at the land, from horizon to horizon, and every day the loss was with them; it was the dead unburied, and the mourning of the lost going on forever. So they tried to sink the loss in booze, and silence their grief with war stories about their courage, defending the land they had already lost.

He followed the wagon road to Laguna, going by memory and the edges of old ruts. The air was cool, and he could smell the dampness that came out with the stars. Old Betonie might explain it this way—Tayo didn't know for sure: there were transitions that had to be made in order to become whole again, in order to be the people our Mother would remember; transitions, like the boy walking in bear country being called back softly.

Up North
around Reedleaf Town
there was this Ck'o'yo magician
they called Kaup'a'ta or the Gambler.

He was tall
and he had a handsome face
but he always wore spruce greens around his head,
over his eyes.
He dressed in the finest white buckskins
his moccasins were perfectly sewn.
He had strings of sky blue turquoise
strings of red coral in his ears.
In all ways
the Gambler was very good to look at.

His house was high
in the peaks of the Zuni mountains
and he waited for people to wander
up to his place.
He kept the gambling sticks all stacked up
ready for them.

He walked and turned around for them
to show off his fancy clothes and expensive beads.
Then he told them he would gamble with them—
their clothes, their beads for his.
Most people wore their old clothes
when they went hunting in the mountains;
so they figured they didn't have much to lose.
Anyway, they might win all his fine things.
Not many could pass up his offer.

But the people didn't know.
They ate the blue cornmeal
he offered them.
They didn't know
he mixed human blood with it.
Visitors who ate it
didn't have a chance.
He got power over them that way,
and when they started gambling with him

they did not stop until they lost
everything they owned.
And when they were naked
and he had everything
he'd say

"I tell you what
since I'm so good and generous
I'll give you one last chance.
See that rawhide bag hanging
on the north wall over there?
If you can guess what is in that bag
I'll give you back all your clothes and beads
and everything I have here too—
these feather blankets
all these strings of coral beads
these fine white bucksin moccasins.
But if you don't guess right
you lose your life."

They were in his power.
They had lost everything.
It was their last chance.
So they usually said "okay"
but they never guessed
what was in the bag.

He hung them upside down in his storeroom,
side by side with the other victims.
He cut out their hearts
and let their blood run down
into the bins of blue cornmeal.

That is what the ck'o'yo Kaup'a'ta, Gambler did,
up there
in the Zuni mountains.
And one time
he even captured the stormclouds.

He won everything from them
but since they can't be killed,
all he could do
was lock them up
in four rooms of his house—
the clouds of the east in the east room
the clouds of the south in the south room
the clouds of the west in the west room
the clouds of the north in the north room.

The Sun is their father.
Every morning he wakes them up.
But one morning he went
first to the north top of the west mountain
then to the west top of the south mounain
and then to the south top of the east mountain;
and finally, it was on the east top of the north mountain
he realized they were gone.

For three years the stormclouds disappeared
while the Gambler held them prisoners.
The land was drying up
the people and animals were starving.

They are his children
so he went looking for them.
He took blue pollen and yellow pollen
he took tobacco and coral beads;
and he walked into the open country
below the mesas.
There, in a sandy place by a blue flower vine,
Spiderwoman was waiting for him.

"Grandson," she said.
"I hear your voice," he answered
"but where are you?"
"Down here, by your feet."
He looked down at the ground and saw a little hole.

"I brought you something, Grandma."
"Why thank you, Grandson,
I can always use these things," she said.

"The stormclouds are missing."
"That Ck'o'yo Kaup'a'ta the Gambler has them locked up,"
she told him.
"How will I get them back?"

"It won't be easy, Grandson,
but here,
take this medicine.
Blow it on the Gambler's black ducks
who guard his place.
Take him by surprise.
The next thing is:
don't eat anything he offers you.
Go ahead
gamble with him.
Let him think he has you too.
Then he will make you his offer—
your life for a chance to win everything:
even his life.
He will say
"What do I have hanging in that leather bag
on my east wall?"
You say "Maybe some shiny pebbles,"
then you pause a while and say "Let me think."
Then guess again,
say "Maybe some mosquitoes."
He'll begin to rub his flint blade and say
"This is your last chance."
But this time you will guess
"The Pleiades!"
He'll jump up and say "Heheya'! You are the first to
guess."
Next he will point to a woven cotton bag

182

                    hanging on the south wall.
He will say
          "What is it I have in there?"
You'll say
          "Could it be some bumblebees?"
          He'll laugh and say "No!"
"Maybe some butterflies, the small yellow kind."
"Maybe some tiny black ants," you'll say.
     "No!" Kaup'a'ta will be smiling then.
          "This is it," he'll say.

     But this is the last time, Grandson,
you say "Maybe you have Orion in there."
          And then
          everything—
     his clothing, his beads, his heart
          and the rainclouds
               will be yours."

          "Okay, Grandma, I'll go."
He took the medicine into the Zuni mountains.
He left the trail and walked high on one of the peaks.

     The black ducks rushed at him
     but he blew the medicine on them
          before they could squawk.

     He came up behind the Gambler
          practicing with the sticks
          on the floor of his house.

     "I'm fasting," he told Kaup'a'ta,
when he offered him the blue cornmeal
          "but thanks anyway."
     Sun Man pulled out his things:
          four sets of new clothes
          two pairs of new moccasins
          two strings of white shell beads

Kaup'a'ta smiled when he saw these things
    "We'll gamble all night," he said.

        It happened
    just the way Spiderwoman said:
    When he had lost everything
    Kaup'a'ta gave him a last chance.
    The Gambler bet everything he had
that Sun Man couldn't guess what he had
    in the bag on the east wall.
    Kaup'a'ta was betting his life
        that he couldn't guess
what was in the sack hanging from the south wall.

    "Heheya'! You guessed right!
Take this black flint knife, Sun Man,
go ahead, cut out my heart, kill me."
    Kaup'a'ta lay down on the floor
    with his head toward the east.
But Sun Man knew Kaup'a'ta was magical
    and he couldn't be killed anyway.
    Kaup'a'ta was going to lie there
    and pretend to be dead.

So Sun Man knew what to do:
    He took the flint blade
and he cut out the Gambler's eyes
    He threw them into the south sky
and they became the horizon stars of autumn.

Then he opened the doors of the four rooms
    and he called to the stormclouds:
        "My children," he said
I have found you!
Come on out. Come home again.
Your mother, the earth is crying for you.
Come home, children, come home."

"What are you doing here?"

The voice came from the yard. She was standing under an apricot tree, partially hidden by a bushy canopy of gnarled limbs sweeping so close to the earth the slender leaves touched the ground in the wind. The shadows made her skin and hair look dark.

"I couldn't drive past the washed-out bridge. So I left the truck there and rode the horse." The sun had gone down, behind the mesa below the rimrock. The sky and clouds on the horizon were bright red.

"Who sent you?"

"I'm looking for some cattle. They belong to my uncle."

"Somebody sent you," she said, and he noticed she was holding a small willow staff, slightly curved at one end. A cool wind blew down from the northwest rim of the mountain plateau above them and rattled the apricot leaves. He got off the mare and loosened the cinch; the horse tried to shake off sweat and fatigue. The leather and steel fittings on the saddle and bridle clashed together violently. She stepped out from under the tree then. She was wearing a man's shirt tucked into a yellow skirt that hung below her knees. Pale buckskin moccasins reached the edge of her skirt. The silver buttons up the side of each moccasin had rainbirds carved on them. She wasn't much older than he was, but she wore her hair long, like the old women did, pinned back in a knot.

"Can I get some water for the horse?"

She gestered with her chin in the direction of the corral. Her eyes slanted up with her cheekbones like the face of an antelope dancer's mask.

"Help yourself," she said.

Her skin was light brown; she had ocher eyes. She

stood in the yard and watched him lead the mare away.

The wind was blowing harder, and the mare's long tail streamed around them like tall dune grass; the corral gate bumped back and forth in the wind. The mare was thirsty; she sank her nostrils under water and came up only to breathe. He rubbed her behind the ears where the bridle made sweaty creases in the hair. He smelled leather wet with horse sweat, and damp clay from the edge of the pool where the mare stood knee-deep; he smelled winter coming in the wind.

He tied the horse in the corral and pulled off the saddle. He untied his bedroll from the back of the saddle and looked for a sandy sheltered place to unroll his bed. The wind and sand were blowing so hard he didn't hear her walk up from behind. He turned and she was there.

"Come inside," she said loud enough to be heard over the wind. She pulled the handwoven blanket up around her shoulders and head, and walked into the stinging sand with her head bowed. He followed her with his head down and his eyes squeezed shut against the sand; but he did not miss the designs woven across the blanket in four colors: patterns of storm clouds in white and gray; black lightning scattered through brown wind.

He followed her down the long screen porch to a narrow pine door. When she opened it, he smelled dried apricots and juniper wood burning. The inner walls were massive and all the doorways were low. The smell of clay and mountain sage stirred old memories. He touched a whitewashed wall as he went through a doorway, and rubbed the powdery clay between his fingers. His heart was beating fast, and his hands were damp with sweat.

The fireplace was in the corner of the room; the flames blazed up, snapping the kindling and sucking at the wind that came down the chimney. He stood in front of the fire and held out his hands to get warm.

"Sit down. Eat."

He took off his jacket and laid it on the bench beside him. He watched her move lids and pots on the small cookstove. She put a bowl and spoon in front of him. The chili was thick, red like fresh blood, and full of dried corn and fresh venison. She stood by the window and looked outside.

"The sky is clear. You can see the stars tonight." She spoke without turning around. He felt a chill bristle across his neck, and it was difficult to swallow the mouthful of stew.

He had watched the sky every night, looking for the pattern of stars the old man drew on the ground that night. Late in September he saw them in the north.

He had left Laguna before dawn and drove all day until he came to the big arroyo where years of summer rain had gradually eroded the clay bank away from the narrow plank bridge, cutting a deep new channel between the road and the bridge.

He got up from the table and walked back through the rooms. He pushed the porch screen door wide open and looked up at the sky: Old Betonie's stars were there.

So they flew
all the way up again.
They went to a place in the West

(See, these things were complicated. . . .)
They called outside his house
"You downstairs, how are things?"
"Okay," he said, "come down."
They went down inside.
"Maybe you want something?"
"Yes. We need tobacco."
Caterpillar spread out

187

dry corn husks on the floor.
He rubbed his hands together
and tobacco fell into the corn husks.
Then he folded up the husks
and gave the tobacco to them.

He watched her face, and her
eyes never shifted; they were with him while she moved
out of her clothes and while she slipped his jeans down
his legs, stroking his thighs. She unbuttoned his shirt, and
all he was aware of was the heat of his own breathing and
the warmth radiating from his belly, pulsing between his
legs. He was afraid of being lost, so he repeated trail
marks to himself: this is my mouth tasting the salt of her
brown breasts; this is my voice calling out to her. He
eased himself deeper within her and felt the warmth close
around him like river sand, softly giving way under foot,
then closing firmly around the ankle in cloudy warm
water. But he did not get lost, and he smiled at her as she
held his hips and pulled him closer. He let the motion
carry him, and he could feel the momentum within, at
first almost imperceptible, gathering in his belly. When it
came, it was the edge of a steep riverbank crumbling
under the downpour until suddenly it all broke loose and
collapsed into itself.

He rearranged the goat hides under the blankets and
rolled over on his back. Under his leg he could feel the
damp wide leaf pattern that had soaked into the blanket
where she lay.

He dreamed about the cattle that night. It was a continuous dream that was not interrupted even when she
reached out for him again and pulled him on top of her.
He went on dreaming while he moved inside her, and

when he heard her whisper, he saw them scatter over the crest of a round bare hill, running away from him, scattering out around him like ripples in still water.

She got up before dawn. When she left, he got dressed and followed her. The air felt damp and cold like the ground after the snow has melted into it, making it dense and rich. He stood on the steps and looked at the morning stars in the west. He breathed deeply, and each breath had a distinct smell of snow from the north, of ponderosa pine on the rimrock above; finally he smelled horses from the direction of the corral, and he smiled. Being alive was all right then: he had not breathed like that for a long time.

He walked to the corral and untied the mare. He led her to the tall grass around the pool and held the reins while she grazed, watching how she took great mouthfuls, working the bit with her tongue so that it didn't interfere with chewing the grass. He squatted down by the pool and watched the dawn spreading across the sky like yellow wings. The mare jingled the steel shanks of the bit with her grazing, and he remembered the sound of the bells in late November, when the air carried the jingling like snowflakes in the wind. Before dawn, southeast of the village, the bells would announce their approach, the sound shimmering across the sand hills, followed by the clacking of turtleshell rattles—all these sounds gathering with the dawn. Coming closer to the river, faintly at first, faint as the pale yellow light emerging across the southeast horizon, the sounds gathered intensity from the swelling colors of dawn. And at the moment the sun came over the edge of the horizon, they suddenly appeared on the riverbank, the Ka't'sina approaching the river crossing.

He stood up. He knew the people had a song for the sunrise.

Sunrise!
We come at sunrise
to greet you.

We call you
at sunrise.
Father of the clouds
you are beautiful
at sunrise.
Sunrise!

He repeated the words as he remembered them, not sure if they were the right ones, but feeling they were right, feeling the instant of the dawn was an event which in a single moment gathered all things together—the last stars, the mountaintops, the clouds, and the winds—celebrating this coming. The power of each day spilled over the hills in great silence. Sunrise. He ended the prayer with "sunrise" because he knew the Dawn people began and ended all their words with "sunrise."

The horse had stopped grazing and was standing still; whether she had eaten all the grass she could reach and was waiting for him to move her, or whether she had paused the way the mule deer stop grazing at dawn, he did not know. Maybe the dawn woke the instinct in the dim memory of the blood when horses had been as wild as the deer and at sunrise went into the trees and thickets to hide.

He tied her in the corral again and walked back to the house. The massive walls had been plastered with red clay mud, but the weather had exposed the straw in the plaster; under a broken tin rain gutter, plaster was peeling away, exposing brown adobe bricks. He tried to determine when it had been built, but except for the sagging screen all around the long porch, the house was like the mesas around it: years had little relation to it. Along the south wall, tall orange sunflowers were still blooming among dry corn stalks; the wind of the night before had twisted the sunflowers around the brittle corn stalks, so that in the early morning light the dried-up corn plants were bearing big orange sunflowers that dusted the hard-packed earth beneath them with orange pollen. Somebody had planted blue morning-glories below each of the four wide windows, and the vines of the blue flowers were climbing cotton strings that had been nailed to the window frames. The morning-glories were open wide, themselves the color of the sky, with thin white clouds spreading from the center of the blossoms into the bright blue.

She fed him cold roast venison and coffee. She sat at the other end of the table examining buckskin bundles and rawhide pouches. Occasionally she laid a round shiny pebble on the table, and once he saw animal teeth and claws in one bundle she unwrapped. He wanted to ask her what she was doing, but something about the way she ignored his eyes kept him quiet. She worked intently with the rocks. A few were light colored and appeared to be sandstone, an ocher yellow sandstone with a pow-dery fine texture he had never seen before. She un-wrapped a pinkish gray stone from a muslin cloth and laid it on the table beside a powdery blue stone; she rolled the strings that had been wrapped around the mus-lin bundle into a tight ball, and looked at him abruptly. She still said nothing, but worked more slowly now, conscious that he was watching. She reached into a flour sack by her feet and brought out bundles of freshly gathered plants. She sniffed them and blew on them before she matched the plants with the stones, put-ting a spring of blue-gray mountain sage with the blue stone. The dark yellow plant from the rocky mesa top smelled like wet tobacco; she laid it beside the ocher sandstone. And then she pulled out a long vine covered with tiny white flowers with six sharp petals like fallen stars. She shook the vine gently, and small black ants that had been clinging to the leathery green vine fell to the floor, making a circle around her feet until the crumbs around the stove lured them away. Sunshine from the window made a big square on the floor, and something in the silence of the room was warm and comfortable like this sunlight.

He finished the coffee in the tin cup and stood up. "Thank you," he said. She looked up from the vine and nodded.

The trail was parallel to the top of the orange sandrock mesa. It was almost too narrow for a horse, and the mare sent a stream of pebbles and small rocks rolling down the steep slopes. He leaned forward over her shoulders to make the climb easier. The sun was moving higher into the sky, and the cliffs of the mesa radiated the sun's warmth. He stopped her near the top and tied his jacket behind the saddle, over the bedroll and sack of food. He looked at the sky: it had a bright blue intensity that only autumn and the movement of the sun from its summer place in the sky could give it. He studied the sky all the rest of the way up; the mare had only one direction to go because the trail had become too narrow even for her to turn around. At the top, the wind was cold. He stopped to put on his jacket and rest the mare. Below, the house was hidden by the foothills, but the country beyond it spread out before him in all directions. To the east was the Rio Puerco Valley, where the river had cut a deep narrow arroyo that now carried the water too low to benefit the valley land. Years of wind and no rain had finally stripped the valley down to dark gray clay, where only the bluish salt bush could grow. Beyond the Rio Puerco, to the southeast, he could see the blue mountains east of the Rio Grande, where the rich valley was full of their cities. But from this place there was no sign the white people had ever come to this land; they had no existence then, except as he remembered them. So for a while he forgot, and sought out the southern peaks that were thin blue and skeletal in the great distance.

The mountain had been named for the swirling veils of clouds, the membranes of foggy mist clinging to the peaks, then leaving them covered with snow. This morning the mountain was dusted with snow, and the bluegray clouds were unwinding from the peaks. He pulled

192

the mare away from her grazing and remounted. He trotted her west, across the grassy flat toward the *cerros*, gently rounded hills of dark lava rock which were covered with a thin crust of topsoil and grass, edged with thickets of scrub oak. The pine trees grew in groves along the ridges above the dry lake-bed flats; but as he rode closer to the mountain, the land ascended into a solid pine forest, and the scrub oak and grass grew only in small clearings.

The white ranchers called this place North Top, but he remembered it by the story Josiah had told him about a hunter who walked into a grassy meadow up here and found a mountain-lion cub chasing butterflies; as long as the hunter sang a song to the cub, it continued to play. But when the hunter thought of the cub's mother and was afraid, the mountain-lion cub was startled, and ran away. The Laguna people had always hunted up there. They went up the slopes of the cone-shaped peaks in the summer, when the deer were reddish brown, the hair short and shining while they browsed in meadows above the treeline to avoid the heat. In late fall, as the deer moved down with each snowstorm, the people hunted the foothills and *cerros* and the grassy dry lake flats of the big plateau. And finally, in the winter, when the deer had heavy dark coats and the bitter snow winds drove them down twisting narrow trails, the Laguna hunters found them, fat from acorns and piñons growing in the narrow steep canyons below the rim.

All but a small part of the mountain had been taken. The reservation boundary included only a canyon above Encinal and a few miles of timber on the plateau. The rest of the land was taken by the National Forest and by the state which later sold it to white ranchers who came from Texas in the early 1900s. In the twenties and thirties the loggers had come, and they stripped the canyons below the rim and cut great clearings on the plateau slopes. The logging companies hired full-time hunters who fed entire logging camps, taking ten or fifteen deer each week and fifty wild turkeys in one month. The loggers shot the bears and mountain lions for sport. And it was then the Laguna people understood that the land had been taken, because they couldn't stop these white people from coming to destroy the animals and the land. It was then too that the holy men at Laguna and Acoma warned the people that the balance of the world had been disturbed and the people could expect droughts and harder days to come.

White ranchers pastured cattle there, especially during the dry years when no grass grew below the mountain. They fattened them on the plateau during the summer, and brought them down to the buyers in late fall. Tayo rode past white-faced Herefords standing around a windmill; they stared at him and at the horse stupidly. He did not expect to find Josiah's cattle near Herefords, because the spotted cattle were so rangy and wild; but without Betonie he wouldn't have hoped to find the cattle at all. Until the previous night, old Betonie's vision of stars, cattle, a woman, and a mountain had seemed remote; he had been wary, especially after he found the stars, and they were in the north. It seemed more likely to find the spotted cattle in the south, far far in the south—the direction they had always gone. The last time Josiah had seen them, the cattle had been wandering southwest along the boundary between the reservation and state land. When Tayo told Robert he was going north, up into the mountains to look for the cattle, Robert shrugged his shoulders and shook his head. "Maybe," he said, "maybe. I guess once somebody got them, they could have taken them just about anywhere." So he had gone, not expecting to find anything more than the winter constellation in the north sky overhead; but suddenly Betonie's vision was a story he could feel happening—from the stars and the woman, the mountain and the cattle would come.

Tayo stopped the mare by a pine tree on a ridge near a scrub-oak thicket. He tied the lariat rope around her neck and slipped off the bridle to let her graze. He untied the food sack from behind the saddle and walked over to the tree. Layers of reddish brown pine needles sank softly under his feet, and he brushed aside the pine cones before he sat down. From where he sat, the world looked as if it were more than half blue sky closing around like a dome. The sun was leaning into the southwest sky. He chewed the jerky as carefully as the mare chewed the grass, pushing against cords of gristle with his tongue, feeling the slippery fibers give way between his teeth. He swallowed the last piece of jerky and felt it roll with the urgency and excitement in his belly.

The Texans who bought the land fenced it and posted signs in English and Spanish warning trespassers to keep out. But the people from the land grants and the people from Laguna and Acoma ignored the signs and hunted deer; occasionally, the Mexicans took a cow. So later on, the ranchers hired men to patrol on horseback, carrying .30-30s in saddle scabbards. But the armed riders made little difference because there were miles and miles of fence and two or three hunters could easily slip between them. Still, he would have to be careful. When he located the cattle, he would drive them back. He had the bill of sale from Ulibarri buttoned in his shirt pocket just in case.

He got up feeling happy and excited. He would take the cattle home again, and they would follow the plans Josiah had made and raise a new breed of cattle that could live in spite of drought and hard weather. He tied the lunch sack under the bedroll and pulled the bridle back over the mare's ears. He rode west along the south rim of the plateaus, watching for sudden movements that were speckled white. The barbed wire fence paralleled the rim, and he could see bits of belly hair the deer left on the barbed wire where their trails crossed the fence. Fences had never stopped the speckled cattle either, but there was no sign they had been there. So he rode north, looking for another fence that might be holding them.

He rode miles across dry lake flats and over rocky *cerros* until he came to a high fence of heavy-gauge steel mesh with three strands of barbed wire across the top. It was a fence that could hold the spotted cattle. The white man, Floyd Lee, called it a wolf-proof fence; but he had poisoned and shot all the wolves in the hills, and the people knew what the fence was for: a thousand dollars a mile to keep Indians and Mexicans out; a thousand dollars a mile to lock the mountain in steel wire, to make the land his.

He was examining the fence and the way the wire was buried underground so animals could not crawl or dig under it, when from the corner of his eye he saw something move. They were too far away for him to see the brands, and the light brown spots were difficult to make out on their light hides, but they moved like deer, on long thin legs. It was them.

They were strung out on the south slope of a round lava rock hill, moving west along the fence line. He watched them disappear over a ridge, and in a few minutes he saw the lead cow reappear on the far slope, still following the fence line. They had worn a path into the ground along the south boundary fence, walking relentlessly back and forth from east to west, as if waiting for some chance to escape, for some big pine to blow down in the wind and tear open a gate to the south. South: the direction was lodged deep in their bones.

He moved quickly; his hands were shaking. The mare snorted and shied away from the sudden motions. He held the reins tight and moved closer to her, slowly, speaking softly. He patted her neck until she was calm again. He looked at the hill where the cattle had disappeared, and fumbled untying the saddle strings; he pulled the bedroll loose and reached into the folds of the blankets. Next to a rope the most important tool a rider carried was a pair of fencing pliers. Hundreds of miles of barbed-wire fence marked boundaries and kept the cattle and horses from wandering. Josiah taught him to watch for loose strands of wire and breaks in the fence; he taught Tayo how to mend them before any livestock strayed off reservation land. He helped Tayo stitch a leather holster for the pliers one evening after supper, and he reminded him that you never knew when you might be traveling some place and a fence might get in your way. Josiah had nodded toward Mount Taylor when he said it.

He pulled on his work gloves, and he cut through four strands of heavy steel wire before he realized he was standing where anyone might see him. He looked around quickly for a fence rider on horseback or a patrol in a pickup truck. His heart was pounding, and he remembered the hide-and-go-seek games of a long time ago, when he had lain flat on the ground, trying hard not to pee in his pants. He threw down the pliers and pulled off the gloves. He could think more clearly after he pissed. There was no reason to hurry. The cattle would be easy to find because they stayed close to the south boundary fence. In a few hours it would be dark, and he could go after them. It would be simple. There was no reason to hurry or make foolish mistakes.

He tied the mare in a clearing surrounded by a thicket of scrub oak. He sat under a scrub oak and picked up acorns from the ground around him. The oak leaves were already fading from dark green to light yellow, and within the week they would turn gold and bright red. The acorns were losing their green color too, and the hulls were beginning to dry out. By the time the leaves fell and the acorns dropped, he would be home with the cattle.

The sun was hanging low in the branches of the pines at the top of the ridge; the thicket and clearing were in deep shadow. The wind rustled the oak leaves, and the mare's shit sent steam into the cold air. He crouched down with his hands in his pockets and the collar of his jacket pulled up to his ears. Up here, winter was already close. He ate another piece of jerky and a handful of parched corn, waiting for the dark. He swallowed water from the canteen and watched the sky for the autumn evening stars to appear.

He fed the mare a handful of parched corn and lifted her unshod hooves to check for damage from the sharp lava rock. He didn't know how well she could run at at night over this rocky, unfamiliar country. The dry lake flats and scrub-oak ridges could be confusing. The rolling hills scattered with lava rock and the pine ridges between clearings were almost indistinguishable from one another. He had been fooled by them before when he had gone hunting with Rocky and Robert and Josiah. They had left the truck parked in plain view, at the edge of a pine ridge. But at the end of the day, when he and Rocky had started walking back, they expected to see the old green truck parked on every ridge that came into sight. They weren't lost, because they knew where they were, but the green truck was lost. They kept hiking across dry lake flats and over oak- and pine-covered ridges, saying to each other, "This time, this will be the place," until finally Josiah and Robert came bouncing over the rocky flats in the green truck and picked them up.

Tayo rode the mare slowly along the fence, looking for a place that could be easily located, even at night. He would have only one chance to drive the cattle through the hole in the fence, and while he searched desperately for the opening, they could scatter in every direction. He stopped by a dead pine. Lightning had split it down the middle, and around the charred core, where the bark had peeled away, the tree had weathered silver. Behind it there was an outcrop of lava that made a knob on top of the ridge. He dismounted and went to work on the wire.

The strands of wire were four inches apart and a quarter of an inch thick. He had to stop to shake the muscle cramps from his hands. The moon was rising early. He worked on his knees, cutting away the wire at ground level, where it continued under the surface six inches deep to discourage coyotes and wolves from digging under it. He tried to clear a place to kneel, but the ground was almost solid with pebbles and rocks. After the first ten feet of cutting and bending back wire, his knees went numb; he felt cold air on his skin and knew that his Levis were worn through at both knees. He was thinking about the cattle and how they had ended up on Floyd Lee's land. If he had seen the cattle on land-grant land or in some Acoma's corral, he wouldn't have hesitated to say "stolen." But something inside him made him hesitate to say it now that the cattle were on a white man's ranch. He had a crazy desire to believe that there had been some mistake, that Floyd Lee had gotten them innocently, maybe buying them from the real thieves. Why did he hesitate to accuse a white man of stealing but not a Mexican or an Indian? He took off his gloves and stuck his hands inside his jacket to wipe the broken blisters on his shirt. Sweat made the raw skin sting all the way up both arms, leaving his shoulders with a dull ache. He knew then he had learned the lie by heart—the lie which they had wanted him to learn: only brown-skinned people were thieves; white people didn't steal, because they always had the money to buy whatever they wanted.

The lie. He cut into the wire as if cutting away at the lie inside himself. The liars had fooled everyone, white people and Indians alike; as long as people believed the lies, they would never be able to see what had been done to them or what they were doing to each other. He wiped the sweat off his face onto the sleeve of his jacket. He stood back and looked at the gaping cut in the wire. If the white people never looked beyond the lie, to see that theirs was a nation built on stolen land, then they would never be able to understand how they had been used by the witchery; they would never know that they were still being manipulated by those who knew how to stir the ingredients together: white thievery and injustice boiling up the anger and hatred that would finally destroy the world: the starving against the fat, the colored against the white. The destroyers had only to set it into motion, and sit back to count the casualties. But it was more than a body count: the lies devoured white hearts, and for more than two hundred years white people had worked to fill their emptiness; they tried to glut the hollowness with patriotic wars and with great technology and the wealth it brought. And always they had been fooling themselves, and they knew it.

The cut in the fence was a good twenty feet wide, large enough for the cattle to find. He walked back to the horse and put away the pliers. He poured water over the raw skin on his hands and drank what was left in the canteen; he pissed one more time.

The moon was bright, and the rolling hills and dry lake flats reflected a silvery light illusion that everything was as visible as if seen in broad daylight. But the mare stumbled and threw him hard against the saddle horn, and he realized how deceptive the moonlight was; exposed root tips and dark rocks waited in deep shadows cast by the moon. Their lies would destroy this world.

The trail was splashed with cow manure, and he reined the mare in frequently to lean down from the saddle to see how fresh it was. The farther west the trail went, the higher it was; the pines were tall and thick, and brushy piñon and cedar filled the spaces between the big trees, blocking out nearly all the light. He walked the mare, letting her find a way along the trail where trees and brush had closed in on both sides. He kept his head low, and his eyes closed for protection against the pine needles and sharp branches.

He stopped on the edge of the clearing. The air was much colder. He had been so intent on finding the cattle that he had forgotten all the events of the past days and past years. Hunting the cattle was good for that. Old Betonie was right. It was a cure for that, and maybe for other things too. The spotted cattle wouldn't be lost any more, scattered through his dreams, driven by his hesitation to admit they had been stolen, that the land—all of it—had been stolen from them. The anticipation of what he might find was strung tight in his belly; suddenly the tension snapped and hurled him into the empty room where the ticking of the clock behind the curtains had ceased. He stopped the mare. The silence was inside, in his belly; there was no longer any hurry. The ride into the mountain had branched into all directions of time. He knew then why the oldtimers could only speak of yesterday and tomorrow in terms of the present moment: the only certainty; and this present sense of being was qualified with bare hints of yesterday or tomorrow, by saying, "I go up to the mountain tomorrow." The ck'o'yo Kaup'a'ta somewhere is stacking his gambling sticks and waiting for a visitor; Rocky and I are walking across the ridge in the moonlight; Josiah and Robert are waiting for us. This night is a single night; and there has never been any other.

In the clearing he expected to see them: some standing, others lying down, the color of their hides reflecting the moon like snow on the mountain peaks. But he found nothing, and at the seventh or eighth clearing he stopped to listen for them; there was only the rattle of the bit as the mare chewed the grass she had sneaked when they stopped. He jerked her head up from the grass to rid her of any ideas she might have about grazing.

His anger excluded everything but the horse. If he did not break her of the habit right now, she would try to get away with it all the time. He remembered the old black gelding: as long as Josiah had been there watching, the old black horse loped slowly around the big corral; it stood patiently while Rocky slid down its shoulder and then boosted Tayo up. But after Josiah went inside the shed to repair bridles, the old horse began to test them. It no longer loped; it trotted. Tayo's teeth rattled together and he had to grip the wiry mane with both hands; his bottom hurt from bouncing against the sharp backbone; and when it felt the loose reins, the black gelding stopped trotting and walked over to the tender green tumbleweed shoots that grew along the fence. Rocky ran over and handed the reins back up to him, and he yelled at the old horse and kicked both heels into its ribs. It raised its head and seemed surprised for a moment, but Tayo wasn't strong enough to pull the big head around or keep it away from the weeds; and the gelding went back to nibbling weeds again, acting as if the two little boys were not there. They didn't want Josiah to know that the old horse had won, because Josiah always said that if they couldn't make the horse behave, then they had no business riding it. So they pretended they were tired of riding, and let the old horse loose. As it lumbered out of the corral toward the river, they pelted it with rocks and sticks, and Rocky yelled at it. Josiah came out of the shed to see what all the noise was about; he scolded them for throwing rocks at the old horse, but he had a hard time to keep from smiling.

"So that old horse won, huh?" he said, almost laughing. "Even got you throwing rocks and yelling at him."

He reined the mare in tight and kept his heels hard against her sides to let her know he meant business. Josiah had always shown them how ridiculous violence and anger were; beating the mare would not make the spotted cattle appear.

He stopped at a wide shallow stream and dismounted while the mare drank. She had traveled for hours without water; now she swelled out her sides drinking. She let out a deep sigh when she was finished and shook herself; she was tired. As he led her away from the stream, he felt the muscles in his thighs get shivery, and his knees were tight and sore from hours in the saddle and from kneeling on the rocks to cut the wire. His hands hurt, and his fingers were still swollen with blisters from the pliers. He knew what was happening. In the sky above the clearing, Orion had fallen over the south edge; he was running out of night. His stomach tensed up again. Whatever night this was, he still had a big hole cut in their fence, and he had to find the cattle and get them out before the fence riders found the break. They would be after him then, tracking him, hunting him down as they had hunted the last few bears on the mountain. His chest was aching with anger. What ever made him think he could do this? The woman under the apricot tree meant nothing at all; it was all in his own head. When they caught him, they'd send him back to the crazy house for sure. He was trapped now, tricked into trying something that could never work.

He still had time to get back. He could pull the sections of wire together and twist the strands into place, and then ride like hell off the mountains. They'd never know who did it; they'd blame Mexicans from Marquez. It would be the smartest thing he could do. All the rest—old Betonie and his stargazing, the woman in her storm-pattern blanket—all that was crazy, the kind of old-time superstition the teachers at Indian school used to warn him and Rocky about. Like the first time in science class, when the teacher brought in a tubful of dead frogs, bloated with formaldehyde, and the Navajos all left the room; the teacher said those old beliefs were stupid. The Jemez girl raised her hand and said the people always told the kids not to kill frogs, because the frogs would get angry and send so much rain there would be floods. The science teacher laughed loudly, for a long time; he even had to wipe tears from his eyes. "Look at these frogs," he said, pointing at the discolored rubbery bodies and clouded eyes. "Do you think they could do any-thing? Where are all the floods? We dissect them in this class every year." As the Army doctors had told him: it was all superstition, seeing Josiah when they shot those goddamn Japs; it was all superstition, believing that the rain had stopped coming because he had cursed it.

A strange paralysis accompanied his thoughts; a sudden overwhelming fatigue took hold, and his heart pounded furiously, and he panted trying to walk only a few feet from the place he had tied the mare. His knees buckled, and he fell into the old pine needles and cones under a tree. This was the end. He wouldn't even be able to try to escape; they would find him collapsed under the tree.

His face was in the pine needles where he could smell all the tree, from roots deep in the damp earth to the moonlight blue branches, the highest tips swaying in the wind. The odors wrapped around him in a clear layer that sucked away the substance of his muscle and bone; his body became insubstantial, so that even if the fence riders came looking for him with their .30–30s loaded and cocked, they would see him only as a shadow under the tree.

The mountain lion came out from a grove of oak trees in the middle of the clearing. He did not walk or leap or run; his motions were like the shimmering of tall grass in the wind. He came across the meadow, moving into the wind. Tayo watched it with his head against the ground, conscious of pine needles tangled in his hair. He waited for the mare to shy away from the yellow form that moved toward them; but the horse was upwind and did not stir. The eyes caught twin reflections of the moon; the glittering yellow light penetrated his chest and he inhaled suddenly. Relentless motion was the lion's greatest beauty, moving like mountain clouds with the wind, changing substance and color in rhythm with the contours of the mountain peaks: dark as lava rock, and suddenly as bright as a field of snow. When the mountain lion stopped in front of him, it was not hesitation, but a chance for the moonlight to catch up with him. Tayo got to his knees slowly and held out his hand.

"Mountain lion," he whispered, "mountain lion, becoming what you are with each breath, your substance changing with the earth and the sky." The mountain lion blinked his eyes; there was no fear. He gazed at him for another instant and then sniffed the southeast wind before he crossed the stream and disappeared into the trees, his outline lingering like yellow smoke, then suddenly gone.

The horse was stamping her front feet and blowing her nostrils open wide to catch the mountain-lion smell that was on the wind now. Tayo stroked her neck and made sure the rope was tied securely to the tree. He went into the clearing where the mountain lion had stood; he knelt and touched the footprints, tracing his finger around the delicate edges of dust the paw prints had made, deep round imprints, each toe a distinctive swirl. He kept his back to the wind and poured yellow pollen from Josiah's tobacco sack into the cup of his hand. He leaned close to the earth and sprinkled pinches of yellow pollen into the four footprints. Mountain lion, the hunter. Mountain lion, the hunter's helper.

He rode the mare west again, in the direction the mountain lion had come from. The sound of the wind in the pine branches and the smell of snow from the mountain made him alert.

At dawn he stopped on a grassy ridge to watch the sun rise; he let the mare graze, part of the cycle of restoration. Inside him the muddy water turmoil was settling to the bottom, and streaks of clarity were slowly emerging. Gathering the spotted cattle was only one color of sand falling from the fingertips; the design was still growing, but already long ago it had encircled him.

When he turned away from the sun to mount the mare, he saw the spotted cattle, grazing in a dry lake flat below the ridge. They were facing southeast, grazing in a herd. They had smelled the horse and rider and were looking up at the ridge; his motion sent them running, with grass still hanging from wet lips. They ran as Robert said they did, wilder than antelope, smarter than elk about human beings. Their memory of people endured long after all other traces of domestication were gone; and he was counting on another instinct: the dim memory of direction which lured them always south, to the Mexican desert where they were born.

They ran southeast, in the direction he wanted them to go, with tails straight out behind their manure-stained haunches, running more like deer than cattle, moving from thicket to thicket for cover, avoiding the clearings. They favored trails too low and brushy for horses and riders. He let the mare run far behind them, confident of their direction. The cold air whipped tears in his eyes, but he felt good; they were gathered before him, headed for home. They took the trail they had worn along the fence and followed it east; he watched to be sure none of them circled back, but the old direction was persistent even in the half-grown calves. He slowed the mare to a lope and let the cattle go. The horse was tiring; she had frothy sweat on her shoulders and neck. If he followed the cattle too closely or pushed them too fast, they might break and scatter; they might miss the opening in the fence. He watched them appear briefly, crossing a ridge about a half mile ahead; they had already slowed from a dead run to a trot.

The sky was washed pale blue by the glare of the sun; there were no clouds, but he could feel a strong wind from the west at his back, and he knew there would be storm clouds before noon. In the distance up ahead he occasionally caught glimpses of the cattle, trotting steadily; they appeared in clearings and disappeared into oak thickets again, still following the south boundary fence to the east.

The tension in the muscles of his neck and shoulders unwound with each breath he took. He smiled and patted the mare on the neck; the hair was still damp and stiff with sweat. He slowed her to a walk, confident that the cattle would veer through the break in the fence and continue south down the trail off the mountain plateau. He kicked his boots loose from the stirrups and stretched his legs; the tendons and muscles unlocked from the flexed position of the saddle. He had proved something to himself; it wasn't as strong as it had once been. It was changing, unraveling like the yarn of a dark heavy blanket wrapped around a corpse, the dusy rotted strands of darkness unwinding, giving way to the air; its smothering pressure was lifting from the bones of his skull.

From the corner of his eye he saw them, at first mistaking them for a strand of his own hair caught by the wind. But when he turned there were two riders approaching from the north. He whipped the mare into a dead run, crouching low over her neck, trying to guide her over the rocky, uneven terrain, down the steep slope of a ridge. They were about a mile away when he first saw them, so he would try to find a deep grove of pine where he could stay until they passed. He strained to see if the cattle were still in sight, wondering if the riders had seen them. The bill of sale in his shirt pocket would mean very little to armed patrolmen chasing a trespasser. He pressed his heels into the mare's sides to make her run faster, but the lava rock was already scattering from under her feet, and she was fighting to keep her balance. He looked over to see if they were on the hilltop behind him yet; they weren't, so he reined the mare in, to save some of her strength. He wiped the tears that the wind whipped in his eyes onto the sleeve of his jacket and tried to focus on the ridges and flats ahead, searching for the lava-rock knob and the lightning-struck pine that marked the hole in the fence.

He opened his eyes to a bright blue sky and clouds that were full, but very high: and for an instant he was waking up years before, on a nameless island in the Pacific. He thought he had been hit, and he began to call for Rocky to help. Then he saw the color of his sleeve of his shirt, and felt the dry lava pebbles pressing into his raw hands.

He could remember seeing the sunny bright day and the faint autumn colors emerging in the scrub oak; he remembered thinking how funny it was to be in such trouble in the middle of the day, when it was nighttime and darkness that were suspected occasions of danger. He remembered seeing the skeleton pine tree in the distance, above a bowl-shaped dry lake bed, and the last cow bolting through the opening in the wire, kicking her heels at the wire as she plunged through, disappearing over the horizon. He remembered all this clearly, even the way the mare fell, her front legs sliding in the rocks, and the slow shivering roll of her body as she fell.

The smell of mountain sage surrounded him, and he realized he had skidded through a sage bush; twigs of sage and oak leaves were caught in his hair and crumbled down the back of his neck. When he tried to move, the inside of his head pounded; so he lay flat and spat out the gritty mountain clay. His ribs hurt when he breathed, but he could move his fingers and lift both legs. He closed his eyes, telling himself that he could afford to rest a while longer, lying to himself the way he had on cold winter mornings when the room was still dark and there was no fire in the stove.

"Where are you going so goddamn fast?" the voice was hostile, and it had a drawling Texan sound. He raised himself up on one hand and looked at them. They were both tall and lanky, with light brown hair; and except for their faces they were the same: boots scuffed and dusty, jeans faded to the same shade of blue; even their shirt-sleeves were rolled to the elbow in the same manner. But the one with the narrow face was agitated and angry. He kept demanding to know what Tayo was doing there.

"Poaching deer?" he said, stepping so close to Tayo's hand that he could feel weeds, crushed by the boot, pressing against his fingers; and for an instant he thought he might step on his hand to make him talk.

"Maybe you were rustling yourself a little beef, huh?" He would let them believe anything they wanted. The other man had a small round face and no chin, but his eyes were calm.

"Are you hurt?" he said. "Can you stand up?" He put his hand on Tayo's left arm and squatted down beside him to get a better grip. Tayo kept thinking about the cattle and the gaping hole in the fence; but they didn't act as if they had noticed anything except him. Behind the drumming pain inside his head, he had one thought: to keep them occupied with him, to keep them away from the next ridge.

"You better go back for the truck," the cowboy with the round face said. "I think he might be hurt."

"Shit! There's nothing wrong with the son of a bitch! Let him ride behind the saddle with me."

As they pulled him to his feet, his vision spun away, pulling his head into a shower of bright lights. He stumbled against the big palomino; it snorted and shied away.

"Whoa! You jackass! Whoa!" They boosted him up, behind the creamy-colored tooled leather saddle. His ears buzzed and he had to grip the saddle strings tightly to stay erect. The horse sidestepped nervously, feeling the awkward load shifting from side to side on its back. Just as the Texan swung his long thin leg over the saddle, Tayo leaned over and vomited all over the sagebrush.

The pain swelled out of his head, pounding through his ears until it hit his belly, and waves of nausea surged up. The sun was going down, and the round-faced man was hunched over on a boulder, with his back to the cold wind. He had his hands in his pockets and was chewing tobacco, working his jaws furiously and spitting savagely, sending the brown juice all over the ground around his feet. He saw that Tayo was awake, but he didn't speak. The skin on the cowboy's face was wrinkled; it had been rubbed dry and red by the wind and sun. Under the blue bandanna he wore around his throat, the skin was still milky and tender. He wasn't much older than Tayo; maybe they both had been in the war together. He acted as if he wanted to forget the whole thing and let the Indian go. But the Texan had gone back for the truck; he wanted to take the Indian back. Maybe because their boss expected them to do something once in a while: shoot a coyote or catch a Mexican. But it was getting late, and the wind was bitter with the snowstorm that had masked the peaks. It would be dark by the time they got him back to the ranch headquarters, and then they would have to drive him all the way to the jail in Grants. It was a lot of trouble just for an Indian; maybe it would be too much trouble, and they would let him go.

Black pebbles and the ancient gray cinders the mountain had thrown poked into his backbone. He closed his eyes but did not sleep. He felt cold gusts of wind scattering dry oak leaves in the grass. He listened to the cowboy collect tobacco juice in his mouth and the squirting liquid sound when he spat. He was aware of the center beneath him; it soaked into his body from the ground through the torn skin on his hands, covered with powdery black dirt. The magnetism of the center spread over him smoothly like rainwater down his neck and shoulders; the vacant cool sensation glided over the pain like feather-down wings. It was pulling him back, close to the earth, where the core was cool and silent as mountain stone, and even with the noise and pain in his head he knew how it would be: a returning rather than a separation. He was relieved because he feared leaving people he loved. But lying above the center that pulled him down closer felt more familiar to him than any embrace he could remember; and he was sinking into the elemental arms of mountain silence. Only his skull resisted; and the resistance increased the pain to a shrill whine. He visualized each piece of his own skull, fingering each curve, each hollow, testing its thickness for a final thin membrane worn thin by time and the witchery of dead ash and mushroomed bullets. He searched thin walls, weak sutures of spindle bones above the ear for thresholds. He knew if he left his skull unguarded, if he let himself sleep, it would happen: the resistance would leak out and take with it all barriers, all boundaries; he would seep into the earth and rest with the center, where the voice of the silence was familiar and the density of the dark earth loved him. He could secure the thresholds with molten pain and remain; or he could let go and flow back. It was up to him.

He heard the truck motor stop and door slam. The voices were muffled by the distance, but the Texan had not come back alone.

"Hey! I found something! Remember those lion tracks we found last spring? Well there's fresh ones all over the place! Around the number twelve windmill. A big son of a bitch! Tracks the size of my palm!" The new voice was high pitched with excitement.

The cowboy got up from the boulder stiffly and spat out the last of the tobacco wad.

"Well, what about this guy?" he said. "I thought you wanted to take him in."

The Texan cleared his throat. "Shit," he said, "greasers and Indians—we can run them down anytime. But it's been a couple of years since anybody up here got a mountain lion."

"Okay, okay. You were the one that wanted to mess with him, not me."

"Shit, by the time we got him back, the lion would be long gone."

"Just leave him where he is and let's go get the lion hounds before it gets dark."

"Yeah, we taught him a lesson," the Texan said, his voice fading in and out with the wind. "These goddamn Indians got to learn whose property this is!"

When he woke up again they were gone, and the wind

had calmed down; but the air was heavy and damp. The sky was full of storm clouds. The pain and the pounding inside his head were gone, but when he sat up he had to move slowly to avoid jarring the soreness inside his skull. His feet and hands were numb from the cold, and his legs were stiff from lying still so long. He sat rubbing his legs and feet, with a cold breeze at his back. If he went a few yards over the top of the ridge, he would be in the scrub oaks, out of the storm.

The oaks grew thick and close to the ground. He knelt at the edge of the thicket, looking until he found a narrow winding trail through the fringes of oak. The deer made trails through every thicket, and some of the big thickets had two or three trails running parallel to the top of the ridge; they moved into the thickets after sunrise and spent their days in the thickets, sleeping and feeding on acorns, crossing a clearing only to reach another stand of scrub oak. The leaves accumulated in deep layers of years, and his feet sank under the new copper leaves that had already fallen this year. The deer made beds in shallow niches deep within the thickets where the oaks grew tall and made canopies of limbs and branches.

He lay in a shallow depression and heaped piles of dry leaves over himself until he felt warm again. He looked up through the branches and the leaves, which were yellow and soft, ready to fall; the sky was heavy and dark, and purple veins striated the gray swollen clouds dragging their bellies full of snow over the mountaintop. The smell of snow had a cold damp edge, and a clarity that summer rain never had. The scent touched him deep behind his belly, and he could feel the old anticipation stirring as it had when he was a child waiting for the first snowflakes to fall.

He lay there and hated them. Not for what they wanted to do with him, but for what they did to the earth with their machines, and to the animals with their packs of dogs and their guns. It happened again and again, and the people had to watch, unable to save or to protect any of the things that were so important to them. He ground his teeth together; there must be something he could do to still the vague, constant fear unraveling inside him: the earth and the animals might not know; they might not understand that he was not one of them; he was not one of the destroyers. He wanted to kick the soft white bodies into the Atlantic Ocean; he wanted to scream to all of them that they were trespassers and thieves. He wanted to follow them as they hunted the mountain lion, to shoot them and their howling dogs with their own guns. The destroyers had sent them to ruin this world, and day by day they were doing it. He wanted to scream at Indians like Harley and Helen Jean and Emo that the white things they admired and desired so much—the bright city lights and loud music, the soft sweet food and the cars—all these things had been stolen, torn out of Indian land: raw living materials for their ck'o'yo manipulation. The people had been taught to despise themselves because they were left with barren land and dry rivers. But they were wrong. It was the white people who had nothing; it was the white people who were suffering as thieves do, never able to forget that their pride was wrapped in something stolen, something that had never been, and could never be, theirs. The destroyers had tricked the white people as completely as they had fooled the Indians, and now only a few people understood how the filthy deception worked; only a few people knew that the lie was destroying the white people faster than it was destroying Indian people. But the effects were hidden, evident only in the sterility of their art, which continued to feed off the vitality of other cultures, and in the dissolution of their consciousness into dead objects: the plastic and neon, the concrete and steel. Hollow and lifeless as a witchery clay figure. And what little still remained to white people was shriveled like a seed hoarded too long, shrunken past its time, and split open now, to expose a fragile, pale leaf stem, perfectly formed and dead.

It was still dark when he woke up, and he could feel flakes of snow blowing in the wind. He couldn't see if the sky in the east was getting light yet, because the storm clouds were still dense and low. He shook the snow off his hair; the oak leaves had held a shell of snow around him. He stood up and brushed the leaf dust away and pissed a yellow steaming slash through the snow.

He walked southeast. He went slowly because his whole body was sore and because the snow was rapidly covering the ground, even the big rocks, making it difficult to follow the trail even as the darkness dissolved into gray light. The sky was dense and gray; it was difficult to estimate distances. He turned and looked back in the direction of the mountain, but it was hidden in a swirling mass of wet clouds. He ate a handful of snow, blinking the flakes off his eyelashes as he tried to face the direction the storm was coming from, because the cowboys had gone that way. A gust of wind brought the center of the storm down, and big flakes fluttered around his head like summer moths crowding the sky, rising high over the edges of wet black lava and the tips of yellow grass.

The snow was covering everything, burying the mountain lion's tracks and obliterating his scent. The white men and their lion hounds could never track the lion now. He walked with the wind at his back. It would cover all signs of the cattle too; the wet flakes would cling to the fence wire and freeze into a white crust; and the wire he had cut away and the gaping hole in the fence would be lost in the whiteout, hidden in snow on snow. Under his feet the dark mountain clay was saturated, making it slippery and soft; the ranch roads would be impassable with sticky mud, and it would be days before the cowboys could patrol the fences again. He smiled. Inside, his belly was smooth and soft, following the contours of the hills and holding the silence of the snow. He looked back at the way he had come: the snow-flakes were swirling in tall chimneys of wind, filling his tracks like pollen sprinkled in the mountain lion's foot-prints. He shook his head the way the deer shook snow away and yelled out "ahooouuuh!" Then he ran across the last wide flat to the plateau rim.

The snow packed under his feet with a hollow sound. The big snowflakes still crowded behind him like the gauzy curtains in the woman's house. He stood on the rimrock and looked over the edge, down on the dark evergreens and piñon trees growing thick on the steep canyon slopes. He had to walk about a hundred yards north to find the place where the trail went down be-tween two big piñon trees. He pulled a piñon cone from the snowy branches and shook the fat brown piñons into his hand. He ate them as he walked, cracking the shells one by one, working the nut meat loose with his tongue. He spit the shells into the snow below the trail and tried to see into the distance below the mesa, over the edge of the steep trail where her house was. Then behind him he heard someone singing. A man singing a chant. He stopped and listened. His stomach froze tight, and sweat ran down his ribs. His heart was pounding, but he was more startled than afraid.

> Hey-ya-ah-na-ah! Hey-ya-ah-na-ah!
> Ku-ru-tsu-eh-ah-eh-na! Ku-ru-tsu-eh-ah-eh-na!
> to the east below
> to the south below
> the winter people come.

> Hey-ya-ah-na-ah! Hey-ya-ah-na-ah!
> Ku-ru-tsu-eh-ah-na! Ku-ru-tsu-eh-ah-eh-na!
> from the west above
> from the north above
> the winter people come.

eh-ah-na-ah!
eh-ah-na-ah!

antlers of wind
hooves of snow
eyes glitter ice
eyes glitter ice
eh-ah-na-ah!
eh-ah-na-ah!
antlers of wind
antlers of wind
eh-ah-na-ah! eh-ah-na-ah!

The voice faded in and out, sometimes muffled or lost in the wind. He recognized phrases of the song; he had heard the hunters sing it, late in October, while they waited for the deer to be driven down from the high slopes by the cold winds and the snow. He waited until the hunter saw him before he spoke. He was carrying a small fork-horned buck across his shoulders, steadying the load by gripping the antlers in one hand and the hind legs in the other. He smiled when he saw Tayo.

He wore his hair long, tied back with white cotton string in the old style the men used to wear. He had long strings of sky-blue turquoise in his ears, and silver rings on four fingers of each hand. His face was wide and brown, and the skin was smooth and soft like an old woman's. Instead of a jacket, he was wearing a long fur vest sewn with gray rabbit pelts. The fur was old, and there were small bald patches where the bare skin showed through. The elbows of the brown flannel shirt were worn thin, as if his elbow bone might poke through anytime. But the cap he wore over his ears was made from tawny thick fur which shone when the wind ruffled through it; it looked like mountain-lion skin.

"You been hunting?" he asked, sliding the carcass down from his shoulders into the snow. Tayo noticed that he had already tied delicate blue feathers to the tips of the antlers.

"I was looking for some cattle."

"They are probably down below by now," he said, gesturing at the snow around them and the flakes still falling from the sky. Tayo nodded; he was looking at the old rifle slung across the hunter's back.

"That's an old one," he said, helping the hunter lift the deer up on his shoulders again.

"But it works good," he answered, starting down the trail ahead of Tayo, "it works real good. That's the main thing." He started singing again, this time it wasn't a Laguna song; it sounded like a Jemez song or maybe one from Zuni. He didn't want to interrupt the hunter to ask, but he was wondering where he was from, and where he had learned the Laguna song.

All he could see as he walked down the trail was snow, blurring the boundaries between the earth and the sky. At the bottom of the trail he stopped and kicked away the snow until wet sand was exposed. He was looking for some trace of the cattle, manure or some sign they had been there. The hunter shook his head.

"You better come inside first and have something to eat. You can look for them later." Tayo followed him to the yard. The leaves of the apricot tree were solid with snow. He looked toward the corral for the mare and the cattle, but it was snowing too hard to see anything. He smelled piñon smoke. The hunter motioned for him to step inside.

They stood side by side in front of the corner fireplace. The flames crackled and hissed when they shook the snow from their clothes. The wet leather of Tayo's boots and the hunter's elkskin leggings made steam rise around them like mountain fog after a storm. Tayo looked into the flames for a long time, feeling stronger and more calm as he got dry. When he finally turned around, they were together, the hunter kneeling beside the woman, placing pinches of cornmeal on the deer's nose, whispering to it.

They sat across from him at the table. When they had finished eating, the hunter stood up and pointed out the window.

"The tree," he said to her, "you better fold up the blanket before the snow breaks the branches."

"I'm going out. I'll shake the snow off the branches," Tayo said, remembering how one spring when a late snow fell he had helped Josiah and Rocky shake the budded apple trees. She nodded, and walked into the bedroom. The black storm-pattern blanket was spread open across the gray flagstone. He watched her fold it.

He walked to the tree. It was a dome of snow with only the edges and tips of the leaves scattered green across the white. The early storm had caught the tree vulnerable with leaves that caught the snow and held it in drifts until the branches dragged the ground. He slipped his gloves out of his jacket pocket and took hold of the boughs gently, remembering that it was an old tree and the limbs were brittle. He shook the snow off carefully, moving around the tree from the east to the south, and from the west to the north, his breath steaming out in front of him. By the time he had shaken a circle of snow in a pile around the tree, the storm had passed. The mesas to the east were obscured by veils of falling snow, and the sky above them was dark blue. But overhead the snowflakes became sparse and floated down slowly on their own weight, now that the wind was gone. To the west the sky was opening into a high gray overcast, and where the clouds were rubbed thin, the streaks of sky were almost blue.

The mare whinnied, and he smiled at the way horses remember those who feed them. She was leaning against the corral gate with her ears pointed at him, alert. She pawed the snow impatiently and pushed her warm nose into his hands. There was a brown crust of blood on the raw skin of her forelegs where she had fallen. Tayo walked her to see how she moved, if she was lame. She followed him eagerly.

"Do you expect me to feed you after the way you dumped me up there?" He scratched her neck, feeling the thick winter hair; a few days before, it had been a summer coat and now suddenly the winter preparations had been made. He pushed her back from the gate and closed it.

She was combing her hair by the window, watching the sky. He watched her take sections of long hair in her hand and comb it with a crude wooden comb. There was something about the way she moved her arms around her head, and the soft shift of her breasts with each stroke of the comb, even her breathing, which was intimate. His face felt hot, and he looked away quickly before the hunter walked in.

"Aren't you going to ask me?"

"About what?" He tried to keep his voice calm and soft, but he was afraid she was referring to the night they slept together.

"You didn't even ask me what I thought when your horse came back to the corral without you."

"Oh."

"You haven't asked me about your spotted cattle either." She was smiling at him now, as if she had guessed the source of his embarrassment.

"I was going to ask you, but I didn't know if—ah, I mean, I wasn't sure if your husband—" She dropped the comb in her lap and clapped her hands together, laughing. The hunter came in from the back room.

"She's giving you a bad time, huh?" he said. He smiled too, but Tayo felt sweat between each of his fingers.

"She's got your cattle, you know." Tayo nodded and glanced at her; she was grinning at him and watching his face while the hunter spoke.

"Which way did they come down?"

He wanted to sound casual, but all he could think

about was how the hunter seemed to know that he and the woman had met before.

"Yesterday afternoon," she said, "early. They came running down the big arroyo which comes down from the high canyon."

"But how did you catch them?"

"They went just like the run-off goes after a rainstorm, running right down the middle of the arroyo into the trap. That's why it's there. Livestock come down off the mountain that way. All I had to do was go down and close the gate behind them." She twisted her hair around her fingers and pinned it into a knot again. "We catch our horses the same way." She stood up.

"Come on. I'll show you."

He followed her down the steep trail into the big arroyo. He traced it back into the canyon with his eyes; the gray banks cut a winding track, its curves and twists the print of a snake's belly across the sand. It was only a continuation of the deep canyon orifice that revealed the interior layers of the mountain plateau. The gray clay was slippery, and it stuck to the soles of his boots. The trap for livestock was simple. The people had made such traps for a long time because they were easy to build and because they enable one or two people alone to corral many horses or cattle. The trap took advantage of the way horses and cattle, once they had been driven into a dry arroyo bed, would usually continue following the course of the arroyo because the sides of the banks were steep and difficult to escape; they could be driven deep into an arroyo that way until the banks were fifteen or twenty feet high, making it impossible for horses or cattle to escape. Arroyos might be dry for years, but when heavy rains did come, the run-off carried boulders and logs down the arroyo, where they snagged weeds and sticks and other debris. With a little work the debris could be shifted, small logs and dry limbs placed between boulders to form a barrier that only flood water could pour through.

He couldn't see the barrier to this trap, because it had been carefully built around a curve in the bank where the animals could not see it until after they had gone through the opening. Almost anything could be used for a gate, but, here, unskinned juniper poles had been strung together with baling wire, making them almost indistinguishable from the other driftwood and dry brush collected around the boulders and logs on either side of the gate. Once the animals were inside the trap, it was easy to drag the gate across the opening.

The storm left the sky thin and dappled gray, like a molted snakeskin. "An early snow," he said, "maybe it will be a wet winter. A good year next year."

She didn't say anything; she was stepping carefully over the snow, which had drifted in some places deeper than the tops of her moccasins. The clay and snow were churned into a muddy trench along the gate where the cattle had milled around, pushing their bony heads against the juniper poles, working for another escape.

He followed her inside and pulled the gate closed behind them. She walked close to the arroyo bank to avoid the manure and mud. The cattle backed into the far left corner of the barrier; their eyes were wide and frightened, and some were pawing the mud. Their breathing formed a single cloud of steam that drifted up, floating away over the banks of the arroyo. As they walked closer, the cows crowded closer together, and some of them lowered their heads and snorted as if they were fending off coyotes. He didn't like being on foot in the corral with them, because he suspected that human beings mattered very little to them, and it was only the size of the horse, not the rider, which they respected. But the woman was not afraid. She stepped closer to the cattle, bending down to inspect their bellies and legs, walking a half circle in the muddy snow, looking at all of them. They watched her tensely.

The snow had melted into their hides, washing out the dirt and manure, leaving them silky white; the spots were golden brown. The butterfly brand and Auntie's rafter 4 were barely visible through the heavy new growth of winter hair. Josiah had wanted something more than the stupid drooling Herefords the white ranchers had, something more than animals that had to be driven to water like sheep, and whose bellies shrank around their ribs before they would eat cactus or climb the ridges for brush and bark.

"My uncle was looking for cattle that could survive drought and hard years."

She stepped back from them and nodded her head. Her moccasins were muddy.

"It's a wonder you got this many back again," she said. "Look." She pointed at the necks of the cows closest to her. Rope burns left dark scabby welts in half circles. Strips of hide were missing around their fetlocks.

"Texas roping," she said. "They wanted these Mexican cattle because they are fast and tough. And no loss to them when they happen to break the legs or the neck."

He had never heard it called Texas roping before; he knew it as steer roping, because they used old stringy Mexican steers rather than more expensive cows or calves. It had come from Texas with the cowboys, and it was almost too simple: they rode massive powerful roping horses that were capable of jerking down a steer running full speed, knocking the animal unconscious and frequently injuring or killing it. It was the sport of aging cowboys, too slow and heavy to dismount to wrestle down and tie the animal as they did in calf roping and team tying. He had seen it only once. At the rodeo grounds in Grants. The steer had to stay down for ten seconds before the roper's time could be recorded. The jackpot had been three hundred dollars that day, and the red-faced white man who took it turned in a record time: six seconds; but when the men loosened the rope on the steer's neck, it did not move. They dragged it away behind two horses, one of the forelegs dangling in the hide, shattered. The anger made him lightheaded, but he did not talk about this other dimension of their perversion which, like the hunting of the mountain lion, was their idea of "sport" and fun.

They walked back to the corral. She watched him shake the snow off the saddle blanket and lead the mare to drink at the spring. He looked up at the sky; the sun was in the center of the south sky, covered with high gray clouds.

"I wonder if they'll come looking for the cattle?"

She shrugged her shoulders, unconcerned.

"They won't come down here," she said.

"Why not?"

She gave him a look that chilled him. She must have seen his fear because she smiled and said, "Because of all the snow up there. What else?" She was teasing again. He shook his head.

"I'll get back here and get them as soon as I can," he told her. He took a long time tightening the cinch and checking the leather lacing in the stirrups. He wanted to say something to let her know how good it felt to have her standing close to him. But the hunter was still in the house, so he said nothing. As he stepped over to tie the bedroll behind the saddle, he brushed against her side gently, and she smiled. She knew. She walked close to him as he led the mare out of the corral gate. She pointed at the dusky clouds in the northeast sky.

"It will be cold tonight. The mud and snow will freeze."

"I hope so," he said, "otherwise, the truck will get stuck so deep we won't be able to get it out until next spring." She laughed and nodded.

"Good-bye," he said.

"I'll be seeing you," she said.

When he turned to wave at her, she was gone.

Robert stayed in the big stake-bed truck they had borrowed from their cousin Romero. Tayo went to the door. The apricot tree had dropped yellow leaves all around its dark arched branches, and the wind now scattered them around Tayo's feet. His knocking echoed far inside. He couldn't smell any wood smoke and he heard no sounds inside. He pushed the door open and went in. He could see his own breath as he walked through the empty rooms to the kitchen. He smelled clay and old pine from the vigas in the ceiling. The kerosene lamps were gone, and the coffeepot was pushed to the back of the stove. He stepped through the low doorway into the back room where they had slept together. The curly goat hides and the blankets were gone. The bare plaster floor was swept clean. But on the north wall of the room there was an old war shield hanging from a wooden peg set into the white clay wall. He did not remember seeing it before. It was made from a hide, elk or maybe buffalo, heavy and stiff enough to stop stones and arrows; long dry years had shrunk and split the edges, and it had lost the round shape. At first he thought the hide had turned black from age, but he touched it and realized it had been painted black. There were small white spots of paint all over the shield. He stepped back: it was a star map of the overhead sky in late September. It was the Big Star constellation old Betonie had drawn in the sand.

"Nobody home," he told Robert. The cattle had been driven from the trap in the arroyo to the corral, where they could water in the pond.

"Somebody fed them good," Robert said, pointing at the pile of dry cornstalks on the ground in the corral. He backed the big truck up to the loading chute. Tayo swung the tailgate open. He stood in the corral behind

224

the cattle and waved his arms at them until one by one they hesitantly stepped into the back of the cattle truck.

"They look real good, Tayo," Robert said. "Somebody's been looking after them for you."

"So old Betonie did some good after all," old Grandma kept saying. She was sitting by her kerosene stove, cracking piñons with her front teeth. She had been sick in early December, and her corner by the stove still smelled like Vicks and Ben-Gay. She wore the old black cardigan all the time now, even on warm days, and she insisted on keeping her legs wrapped up in strips of an old wool blanket.

"You're all right now, aren't you, sonny?"

"Yeah, Grandma, I'm okay now." He was cleaning the .22, getting ready to go out after rabbits. Auntie looked at him, but when he looked up at her, she turned away to the stove to the simmering stew and boiling coffee. She had been watching him; she was waiting. She didn't trust the peace they had in the house now. She was waiting.

He dreamed with her, dreams that lasted all night, dreams full of warm deep caressing and lingering desire which left him sleeping peacefully until dawn, when he would wake up at the first dim light with her presence and the feeling that she had been with him all night. He got up then, moving quietly in the dark house, hearing the snores of Robert and old Grandma. Auntie slept too quietly, and on these mornings when he buttoned up his jacket and went out the door, he imagined she was watching him.

He stood on the edge of the sandrock shelf that underlay Laguna and looked east across the river before dawn. "Sunrise, sunrise." His words made vapor in the cold morning, and he felt he was living with her this way. He walked back to the house, with the sun climbing behind him, warming his back, and he chopped wood and waited until he smelled smoke from the stovepipe. Then he carried an armload of kindling inside. Sometimes Auntie looked at him in a way that could only mean she was recalling the winters before, when he had lain in the bed vomiting and crying.

He had been working with Robert every day, hauling loads of juniper and piñon for the woodpile, bringing coal from Cañoncito to shovel into the shed. They checked on the speckled cattle once a week to see if they had left the canyons around the springs; but the cattle seemed content to stay there, at least for the winter. They took soda pop and comic books to Pinkie at sheep camp.

Pinkie leaned against the juniper logs of the sheep pen. He kept his thin arms pulled close to his sides and his hands jammed tight in the front pockets of his jeans. He wasn't paying any attention to Robert or Tayo, who were examining the old ewes. He stared off in the distance toward Gallup. The shirttails of his short-sleeve pearl-button western shirt flapped around him in the wind. He never tucked in shirttails, not even in the Army, he said, where he spent a month in the brig for it. His face was sullen when he talked about it.

They wrestled with a pregnant ewe that bleated and tried to jerk her manure-stained hind legs from their hands. They didn't want to throw her down, and Tayo looked up from the struggling animal to see if Pinkie was coming to help out by grabbing hold of her head. But he was looking the other way, oblivious to the scuffling and noise, opening the blades on his pocketknife, one by one, and stabbing them into the juniper post.

When they were ready to leave that day, Pinkie came out of the little stone sheep-camp house. He was wearing his sunglasses with the dark blue lenses and a new black cowboy hat. He carried the rest of his things in a shopping bag. Tayo moved over on the truck seat to make room for him. Nobody said anything because Pinkie had already stayed at sheep camp a week longer than he ever had before.

"Drop me off at the highway," he said.

The March winds were warm, and they melted the snow. The road was rutted in sticky red mud, and Robert had to put the truck in low gear and gun it to cross the flats by Prairie Dog hill. They bounced and skidded, and Pinkie braced his hand against the dashboard. The wheels slipped but then pulled again, and Tayo could feel by the momentum of the truck that they'd make it. They stopped at the highway to wipe the mud off the windshield. Pinkie got out. He pulled his hat down low over his eyes and picked up his shopping bag. He walked down the highway with his thumb high in the air, and he didn't look back. He was going "up the line," to walk, hitchhike, and maybe ride in Leroy's truck, up Highway 66 to Dixie Tavern, San Fidel, Cerritos, all the way to Gallup and back again, with stops in between— Bibo, the Y—until the money ran out.

He was dreaming of her arms around him strong, when the rain on the tin roof woke him up. But the feeling he had, the love he felt from her, remained. The wet earth smell came in the window that Robert had propped open with an old shoe the night before. He was overwhelmed by the love he felt for her; tears filled his eyes and the ache in his throat ran deep into his chest. He ran down the hill to the river, through the light rain until the pain faded like fog mist. He stood and watched the rainy dawn, and he knew he would find her again.

A few days before the end of May he told them he was going to the ranch to stay. Robert nodded; he was busy with the fields at New Laguna, and, this way, Tayo could look after the cattle and new calves. Auntie looked up from a black book of Church devotions, one she'd been reading since Easter. She looked satisfied, as if she had been waiting all winter for him to say something like that.

"I don't want any of those others around. They can do their drinking some place else. Not at our place." Her face was stiff, and her lips barely moved as she spoke. She had expected that sooner or later he would want to go off with the others, Pinkie and Harley and the rest of them, to go drinking and hell raising—to give her more to worry over—the same things his mother had done, to bring disgrace to the family.

"Gather up some Indian tea for me," old Grandma called to him from the back room. "You hear me? I said pick me some tea." She came through the door shuffling more slowly than last year, using her cane all the time now. She still wore her black sweater and the blanket leggings, although the weather had been warm for some time now. When she sat down next to her stove, her movements were stiff and slow.

"One more thing," old Grandma said, "one more thing, Tayo. Old man Ku'oosh came around the other day. He said maybe pretty soon you would have something to

228

tell them. He said maybe you would go talk to them sometime."

After Robert had driven away, he walked around. The yellow striped cat and the black goat followed him. The cat pounced on grasshoppers in the green tumbleweeds and ate them from the curve of her claws. The goat lagged behind to nibble sprouts of new grass before tossing her head and bounding after him to catch up again. The red clay flats had dried into brittle curls where the standing water had been baked out by the sun. But shining under the sun as far as he could see down the valley, many more puddles remained, full of red muddy water. The valley was green, from the yellow sandstone mesas in the northwest to the black lava hills to the south. But it was not the green color of the jungles, suffocating and strangling the earth. The new growth covered the earth lightly, each blade of grass, each leaf and stem with space between as if planted by a thin summer wind. There were no dusty red winds spinning across the flats this year.

The gray mule was gone, his bones unfolding somewhere on the red dirt, bleaching white and thin in the sun. The changes pulled against themselves inside him; the mule had been blind and old. But his room was the same, the creaking bedsprings and frame pushed into the southeast corner below the small window. The terror of the dreaming he had done on the bed was gone, uprooted from his belly; and the woman had filled the hollow spaces with new dreams.

The buzzing of grasshopper wings came from the weeds in the yard, and the sound made his backbone loose. He lay back in the red dust on the old mattress and closed his eyes. The dreams had been terror at loss, at something lost forever; but nothing was lost; all was retained between the sky and the earth, and within himself. He had lost nothing. The snow-covered mountain remained, without regard to titles of ownership or the white ranchers who thought they possessed it. They logged the trees, they killed the deer, bear, and mountain lions, they built their fences high; but the mountain was far greater than any or all of these things. The mountain outdistanced their destruction, just as love had outdistanced death. The mountain could not be lost to them, because it was in their bones; Josiah and Rocky were not far away. They were close; they had always been close. And he loved them then as he had always loved them, the feeling pulsing over him as strong as it had ever been. They loved him that way; he could still feel the love they had for him. The damage that had been done had never reached this feeling. This feeling was their life, vitality locked deep in blood memory, and the people were strong, and the fifth world endured, and nothing was ever lost as long as the love remained.

He got up and went outside. The sun was behind the clouds, and the air was cool. There were blue-bellied clouds hanging low over the mountain peaks, and he could hear thunder faintly in the distance. He walked north along the road. A year before he had ridden the blind mule, and Harley rode the burro. Pa'to'ch was standing high and clear; months and years had no relation to the colors of gray slate and yellow sandstone circling it. Only the sky had changed, washed clear of the dust and haze which had swirled off the red clay flats the summer before. He could smell wild flowers growing in the weeds and grass beside the road, and he heard the big bumblebees and the smaller bees sucking the blossoms. The flowers were all colors of yellow that day—silky yellow petals like wild canary feathers, and blossoms as dark as the center of the sun.

He found flowers that had no bees, and gathered yellow pollen gently with a small blue feather from Josiah's pouch; he imitated the gentleness of the bees as they brushed their sticky-haired feet and bellies softly against the flowers.

He continued north, looking to the yellows and the

orange of the sandrock cliffs ahead, and to the narrow sandrock canyons that cut deep into the mesa, exposing the springs. He was wondering about the speckled cattle, whether they had pushed their way through the fence and were halfway to Mexico by now. They had been so difficult to control in the beginning; they had taken so much from Josiah.

He left the road and took a trail that cut directly to the cliffs, winding up the chalky gray hill where the mesa plateau ended in crumbling shale above the red clay flats. The sun felt good; he could smell the juniper and piñon still damp from the rain. The wind carried a wild honey smell from meadows of beeweed. The trail dipped into a shallow wash. The sand was washed pale and smooth by rainwater and wind. He knelt and touched it. He pulled off his boots and socks and dug his toes deep into the damp sand; then he started walking again. Up ahead, a snake stopped and raised its head alertly; the tongue slid in and out and then stopped when it located him. It was a light yellow snake, covered with bright copper spots, like the wild flowers pulled loose and traveling. It crossed the wash and wound its way up the slope, disappearing into the grass. He knelt over the arching tracks the snake left in the sand and filled the delicate imprints with yellow pollen. As far as he could see, in all directions, the world was alive. He could feel the motion pushing out of the damp earth into the sunshine—the yellow spotted snake the first to emerge, carrying this message on his back to the people.

She was walking through the sunflowers, holding the blue silk shawl around her shoulders in one hand, carrying the long curved willow stick in the other. She turned to him as soon as he saw her, as if she had been waiting. The nights of soft dreaming of her were suddenly locked tight in his chest, and his heart beat fast.

"I'm camped up by the spring," she said, pointing at

231

the canyon ahead of them. "Here, this way. I'll show you."

She sat in the shade of the willows that grew beside the pool, below the overhang of the cliff. She sat with her legs straight out in front of her, holding the red calico skirt in both hands, pulled tight around her legs like trousers. She wiggled her bare toes and looked up at the sandstone cliffs where the swallows were inside their round mud nests, making high-pitched noises. The shadows of the willow leaves made her skin look mottled and dark, the way the iron deposits streaked the yellow sandstone cliffs dark orange.

He squatted in the sand at the edge of the pool and looked into the shallow clear water. The sand at the bottom caught the color of the sun, and tiny green leaves grew out of this color, suspended in the still water. Shiny black water beetles pushed across the bottom of the pool, leaving trails of tiny air bubbles twisting to the surface. Except for the rustle of the swallows, and a mourning dove calling from the mouth of the canyon, it was quiet. The sunlight moved up and down his back like hands, and he felt the muscles of his neck and belly relax; he lay down beside the pool, across from her, and closed his eyes.

He dreamed he made love with her there. He felt the warm sand on his toes and knees; he felt her body, and it was as warm as the sand, and he couldn't feel where her body ended and the sand began. He woke up and she was gone; his fists were full of sand and he was sweating. The sun had moved across the sky, and he knew he had slept for hours. He washed his face in the water; the surface water was still warm, so he plunged his hands deep into the cool layer above the yellow sand. As he walked from the pool to the place she had been sitting, the moisture on his hands and face evaporated. He looked for an imprint of her feet or the outline that the cloth of her skirt made in the sand. As he moved through the grass around the pool, a small green frog wiggled out of the weeds ahead of him, and splashed into the pool. He felt shaky inside: what if there were no traces of her, no lines of sand pressed by her body, no delicate track of her blue shawl trailing into the weeds?

The imprints were there; he traced his fingers lightly along them. He had not dreamed her; she was there as certainly as the sparrows had been there, leaving spindly scratches in the mud.

"I'm over here," she said. Her voice came from the east side of the narrow canyon. He scrambled over the big rocks; a chipmunk skittered ahead of him; he was afraid she would disappear like the echo her voice made. His bare feet and the ends of his toes were raw from the sandrock. He stood on the boulder above her, breathing hard. She was sitting on the edge of a sandy bank beside a big moonflower plant. The blue silk shawl was spread open by her feet, and she had filled it with freshly dug roots and leaves from many different plants. She gathered up the shawl without looking at him and climbed up the rock to join him.

They climbed a steep trail where niches for toes and fingers had been worn into the yellow sandrock after centuries of use. She pulled herself to the top with a branch of bearberry shrub, and offered him her hand. Coming over the edge, the canyon and the rock of the cliff seemed suddenly gone as if he had stepped from the earth into the sky; where they were, the sky was more than half the world; it enclosed the mesa top where they stood.

"You never told me your name," he said.

"I'm a Montaño," she said. "You can call me Ts'eh. That's my nickname because my Indian name is so long. All of us kids did that."

He nodded. "We did that too, at home. Nicknames." He thought about Rocky then; his baptismal name had been Augustine, and "Rocky" had been as close as he had wanted to come to the Indian name old Grandma's

233

sister had given him. "You have brothers and sisters," he said, wanting to find out about her.

"Yes," she said, looking off into the distance, toward the Black Mountains in the south. "We are all very close, a very close family."

He started to ask where they were then, where they lived, because he had only met the hunter; but her eyes were shining, and they told him things that her words never said.

"I have a sister who lives way down that way. She's married to a Navajo from Red Lake." She pointed south, in the direction she was looking. "Another lives near Flagstaff. My brother's in Jemez." She stopped suddenly and laughed. "You know what they say about the Montaños." The tone of her voice said that of course he knew what the people said about her family, but Tayo couldn't remember hearing of that family.

"Up here, we don't have to worry about those things." She was right. They would leave the questions of lineage, clan, and family name to the people in the village, to someone like Auntie who had to know everything about anyone.

They walked back together. In the distance he could see the spotted cattle scattered across the valley between the mesas; the yellow bull their cousin Romero lent them was grazing a distance from the cows, as if he still feared their horns. Their hides reflected the color of the sunset like clouds on the west horizon.

"How did you know I'd be here?" he said, still watching the cattle.

She laughed and shook her head. "The way you talk!" she said. "I was here almost a week before you came. How did you know that I'd be here? Tell me that first."

He went with her to learn about the roots and plants she had gathered. When she found a place she got comfortable, spreading her blue shawl on the ground after she had cleared the area of pebbles and little sticks and made sure no ants were disturbed. She sat flat on the ground and bent over close to the plants, examining them for a long time, from the petals, sprinkled with pollen, down the stem to each leaf, and finally to the base, where she carefully dug the sand away from the roots.

"This one contains the color of the sky after a summer rainstorm. I'll take it from here and plant it in another place, a canyon where it hasn't rained for a while."

While she gathered plants, he watched the cattle grazing in the tall yellow rice grass that grew above the arroyo just to the edge of the juniper trees. They had stopped moving south. They had worked the direction out of their systems and had settled into the place. Josiah would have said that it was because they were so smart, and they could tell a good place when they found it: springs and good grazing. And what about Romero's yellow bull, he could hear Josiah say, winking when he said that; but the speckled cows had not seen the yellow bull that way, at least not in the beginning.

Romero's bull was short-legged and broad, and his color was yellow sandrock broken loose from a cliff. He had small yellow eyes and a hump in his neck. Romero found him standing on three legs at the Prewitt rodeo grounds the day after a rodeo. The left front leg was hanging at a broken angle, and none of the white people at Prewitt wanted to bother with the bull because the meat would be tough. Romero told them he would haul the bull away for free.

Romero said he didn't know how dangerous the bull might be after being a rodeo bull. But the horns were sawed off blunt, and he had only three good legs, so Romero took him home and doctored him. He said he worked on the animal in the loading chute, but the bull stood still and never fought while Romero worked on him. Romero busted up an orange crate and used the wooden slats for a splint that he tied up with strips of old bed sheet. It was a perfect job, Romero said, only the damn bull had rubbed the leg against the corral posts and loosened the splint too soon. That's why the leg healed a little crooked. If he'd just left it alone, it would have been almost as good as new, Romero said.

The speckled cows had watched the bull step out of the horse trailer, and when he sniffed them out and started to approach them, they crowded together, shaking their heads and the curved horns, threatening with wild eyes. They had moved suddenly, like a whirlwind, dust and sand flying up from their hooves as they chased him back toward the truck and horse trailer. But there he spun around suddenly to face them, and they scattered. He watched them disappear into the junipers of the wide canyon to the west, and then he switched his stubby tail around his haunches a few times, and trotted after them.

The yellow bull grazed in open view, but the speckled cows stayed in the juniper, listening like deer to Tayo's approach, their spotted hides blending into the sandy talus of the big mesa. Gradually they appeared, cautiously joining the yellow bull. Tayo sat motionless with his back against the small cottonwood tree growing in the wash. The cows kept their bodies between him and the new calves, but occasionally a calf bolted away, bucking and leaping in a wide arc, returning finally to its mother when it tired of playing. Tayo's heart beat fast; he could see Josiah's vision emerging, he could see the story taking form in bone and muscle.

236

"There's only one more I need," she said, pointing her chin in the direction of the gunny sacks full of roots and plants. "It won't be ready for a while, but I'll show you which one it is, and maybe you can gather it for me, in case I have to go before it's ready."

Tayo had been drowsing in the sun with his back against the cliff rock; he sat up stiffly and looked at her.

"In case of what?" His heartbeat was fast and unsteady. Her eyes had distance in them; when he looked at her he saw miles spreading into canyons and hills. She knelt down beside him, and he saw tears.

"Out there," she whispered, "things are always moving, always shifting. I hear them sometimes at night."

They walked west across the long mesa where the old ones had piled stones in circles, high above the flat sandstone mesa top far above the canyons and springs.

"This one," she said, pointing at a tall dark green plant with round pointed leaves, deep veined like fossil shells. The flat seed pods were still thick and green, but later, in the fall, the skin would dry thin, and cold winds would strip away the hull to the last translucent membrane, holding the dark eyes of the seed inside it.

"What color of sky is inside this one?"

She shook her head. "This isn't for color," she said. "It's for light. The light of the stars, and the moon penetrating the night." It was too dense and green to be taken then; if the stem were broken then, before the final season, its wet flowing vitality would be lost in a single breath.

"I'll remember it," he said. "I'll gather it for you if you're not here."

Their days together had a gravity emanating from the mesas and arroyos, and it replaced the rhythm that had been interrupted so long ago; now the old memories were less than the constriction of a single throat muscle. She was with him again, a heartbeat unbroken where time subsided into dawn, and the sunset gave way to the stars, wheeling across the night. The breaking and crushing were gone, and the love pushed inside his chest, and when he cried now, it was because she loved him so much.

Robert came at the end of the summer. He had come only once before, when he took the goat and the cat back to Laguna and he stopped to see if Tayo needed anything. Robert had not asked any questions then, about why Tayo was sleeping out there when he could have stayed over at the ranch. This time Tayo could see something different, although they walked up the valley together as they had when Robert came before, looking at the spotted cattle, examining the calves. When they got back to the place Robert parked the truck, Robert looked uneasy.

"What should I tell them at Laguna?" Robert was looking up at the thunderclouds rolling in from the Black Mountains in the south. The roads out that way had been muddy all summer, and he didn't want to get struck that day. Tayo shook his head. A hawk circled high above them, gliding on air currents from the approaching storm. Thunder echoed against the cliffs, but Robert did not go. He took his hat off and wiped his forehead on his shirt sleeve.

"They want you to come home. They are worried about you. They think you might need the doctors again."

"Oh." His stomach fell into a crevice. His hands felt cold.

"Old man Ku'oosh and some of the others are wondering too why you haven't come. They thought maybe there might be something you should tell them." The words caught in his throat, and he coughed. "And Emo has been saying things about you. He's been talking about how you went crazy and are alone out here. He talks bullshit about caves and animals."

Tayo had never heard Robert talk that way before; he had never seen him angry before. Tayo felt light-headed and weak. Robert sounded sad.

"You know how people are about things like that. White people are that way too. The Army might send someone to take you back." Lightning flashed across the dark blue clouds, but for Tayo, the bolt zigzagged slowly up the dark mountain peaks of cloud, taking longer than Robert's words had taken to reach him.

"Maybe if you came back for a while. You know, so they could see that you are all right. So you could talk to them, and then they could see what a liar Emo is."

He nodded at Robert, but he was involved with other things: memories and shifting sounds heard in the night, diamond patterns, black on white; the energy of the designs spiraled deep, then protruded suddenly into three-dimensional summits, their depth and height dizzy and shifting with the eye.

Raindrops rattled on the hood of the pickup. Robert kicked at the left front tire; the recap was beginning to peel loose.

"Thanks," Tayo said, "thanks for telling me."

He watched Robert drive away. The rain ran down his hair into his shirt; it had grown below his ears and touched his neck. He thought of Emo then, always with a GI haircut.

"Death isn't much," she said. She was sitting on the sand, with her feet out straight in front, arranging short willow twigs into bundles, tying them with fluffy cotton string that she had twisted by hand. They had found a calf in the arroyo that morning; small black ants were already making trails across the head, from the nose to the eyes. The belly was bloating out as the sun climbed higher in the sky.

"Sometimes they don't make it. That's all. It isn't very far away." She looked up at him intently, and then continued.

"There are much worse things, you know. The destroyers: they work to see how much can be lost, how much can be forgotten. They destroy the feeling people have for each other."

He took a deep breath; it hurt his chest. He thought of Josiah then, and Rocky.

"Their highest ambition is to gut human beings while they are still breathing, to hold the heart still beating so the victim will never feel anything again. When they finish, you watch yourself from a distance and you can't even cry—not even for yourself."

He recognized it then: the thick white skin that had enclosed him, silencing the sensations of living, the love as well as the grief; and he had been left with only the hum of the tissues that enclosed him. He never knew how long he had been lost there, in that hospital in Los Angeles.

"They are all around now. Only destruction is capable of arousing a sensation, the remains of something alive in them; and each time they do it, the scar thickens, and they feel less and less, yet still hungering for more." She gathered up the bundles of twigs and started walking southwest.

"Old Betonie said there was some way to stop—"

"It all depends," she said. "How far you are willing to go?"

They walked together over the sandy ridge above the wash, across stones that had tumbled down from the clay mortar of walls washed away by time, the geometric patterns of rooms and kivas flowing into the white arroyo sand, where even the shards of pottery were rolled to pebbles, all their colors and designs soaked back into the earth.

The position of the sun in the sky was delicate, transitional; and the season was unmistakable. The sky was the early morning color of autumn: Jemez turquoise, edged with thin quartz clouds. He breathed deeply, trying to inhale the immensity of it, trying to take it all inside himself, the way the arroyo sand swallowed time.

She was looking at Pa'to'ch, and the hair was blowing around her face. He could feel where she had come from, and he understood where she would always be.

The she-elk was bigger than life, painted in pale lavender clay on the south face of sandstone, along the base of the cliff. Her great belly was swollen with new life as she leaped across the yellow sandrock, startled forever across the curve of cliff rock, ears flung back to catch a sound behind her. The priests who painted her each year always cried when they stood back from the cliff and saw her. "A'moo'ooh! A'moo'ooh! you are so beautiful! You carry all that life! A'moo'ooh! With you, the cliff comes alive."

They restacked the stones that had fallen. She laid the willow sticks she had tied inside the small square enclosure, and he laid a flat sandstone over the opening at the top. The rain and wind were overtaking her, rubbing away the details of her legs; the sun was bleaching her hooves into faint outlines, merging into the cliff.

"It's almost gone," he said.

"The clay is washing away," she said. "Nobody has come to paint it since the war. But as long as you remember what you have seen, then nothing is gone. As long as you remember, it is part of this story we have together."

They stayed until the sun had gone to the end of the valley and the she-elk was a dark blue shadow on the cliff.

She laid a dry piñon branch on the coals; smoke curled out of the gray scaly bark like woolly hair until yellow flames burst around it. He saw her face in the light that came suddenly and bright; she was crying. He wanted to kneel down and put his arms around her and tell her not to cry, but his connection with the ground was solid; his arms clasped his knees to his chest like arms of another person, pulling numb legs to a strange chest. Only his brain moved, wet and heavy against the contours of his skull, favoring curvatures of bone and concave niches. When he spoke, it was from a mouth independent of himself, and he had to listen to the sound of the words to know what he was saying.

"What is it? Why are you crying?" The anger in his voice surprised him. She looked at him. The skin on her face was darker where she had smeared the tears with the back of her hand.

242

"The end of the story. They want to change it. They want it to end here, the way all their stories end, encircling slowly to choke the life away. The violence of the struggle excites them, and the killing soothes them. They have their stories about us—Indian people who are only marking time and waiting for the end. And they would end this story right here, with you fighting to your death alone in these hills. Doctors from the hospital and the BIA police come. Some of the old men from Laguna come too. They drive over there in their patrol cars." She pointed across the big arroyo to the place where the sandy wagon road was washed out. "They walk this way. The doctors have medicine to quiet you. The others bring guns. Emo has told them you are crazy, that you live in the cave here and you think you are a Jap soldier. They are all afraid of you." Her eyes filled with tears again. "They'll call to you. Friendly voices. If you come quietly, they will take you and lock you in the white walls of the hospital. But if you don't go with them, they'll hunt you down, and take you any way they can. Because this is the only ending they understand."

"How do you know?"

His stomach churned up a hot taste in his throat. She stared up at the sky for a long time; a shooting star arched from west to east, scattering light behind it like dust on a trail. When she did not answer, he knew; like old Betonie, she could see reflections in sandrock pools of rainwater, images shifting in the flames of juniper fire; she heard voices, low and distant in the night.

"One thing," she said finally, looking down at the red coals in the ring of white ash, "there are only a few others with Emo. The rest have been fooled; they're being used. Tools. The Army people don't know. They don't know about stories or the struggle for the ending to the story. White people are always busy. They will ask themselves: what is one Indian veteran living in a cave in the middle of some reservation? They won't have much time for you. The only reason they come is because Emo called them."

"And the old men from home?"

"They come very reluctantly, because the Government people ask them to come along. They don't like white people coming around anyway. The only thing is: they haven't been able to agree."

"Agree on what?"

"They are trying to decide who you are."

She poked the coals with a stick. "If they didn't find you right away, the white people would get impatient." He nodded and smiled; the squeezing around his chest faded. He knew the rest of the story.

"They won't want to climb around these hills. They're afraid of snakes. Their Government cars will get stuck in sand and muddy places. The old men will get tired of sitting in the hot sun, watching the white men act like fools. They'll all go home," Tayo said.

"That leaves Emo and the others," she said, unrolling their blankets on the sand, "and that part won't be easy."

He held her fiercely all night, as if together their sweat and the heat of their breathing could lock out the moaning voices of the dark whirling winds. Together they made a place, remote and calm as the stars that lay across the sky. He woke up in the night and found that place as he moved close to her again. Before dawn he felt her breathing close to his face, and when he opened his eyes, she was smiling at him.

The cattle stood motionless in the thick yellow light from the edge of the sun, visible above the horizon. There was a density to the light which seemed to hold them, as if the sudden warmth had stopped them, and they did not move when she and Tayo walked past. Their eyes shone yellow, and the hairs of their hides caught needles of light. She stopped to examine the cattle. He stood feeling the sun on his face the way the cattle did, until she turned and faced him.

"It's almost completed," she said. "We are coming to the end soon."

The canyon was full of long early shadows where night lingered, a damp smell in the breeze. The fire left a flat circle of white ash on the yellow sand, and Tayo remembered Betonie's sand painting and the warning that the new ceremonies were not like the old ones; but he had never said they were not complete, only different.

She spread her blue silk shawl open and laid her things in the middle. She had done her washing the day before and had spread the wet clothes over willows to dry. When he went to get them for her, the blouses and skirts were like bright wings of butterflies settled on the branches. He was careful not to snag them as he took them off the willows, and he folded them awkwardly before he took them back. She laughed when she saw the blouses and skirts, and refolded them. She tucked the pouches of seeds and the small smooth stones between the folded clothes, and she rolled bundles of cattail reeds and willow twigs in a skirt. She tied the shawl into a bundle and balanced it on top of her head the way Tayo had seen the old women at Laguna do. She grinned at him.

"See," she said, parading in front of him, "this is the way I will go. Just like this."

She looked around to see if she had forgotten anything. The imminence of her leaving made him press his feet hard against the ground.

"I'll walk you to the road," he said.

They walked close together, arms around each other's waist, pulling each other close. A mourning dove called from the tall grass along the wash, and below the cliffs the speckled cattle were grazing. Every step formed another word, thick like yellow pitch oozing from a broken piñon limb, words pressing inside his chest until it hurt: don't leave me. But he sucked air through clenched teeth and breathed hard, trapping those words inside. She stopped by a juniper tree at the edge of the road and set her bundle on the ground. The road curved through red clay and junipers uphill to the northeast. Behind them the road dropped down the gray shale hill to the clay flats of the valley. A year ago he and Harley had ridden down the road on the burro and mule, but this time the grass along the road was green and thick, and to the east, south, and west, as far as he could see, the land was green again.

"Remember," she said, "remember everything." He hugged her close and closed his eyes tight over the tears. She picked up the bundle and balanced it on her head with one hand.

"I'll see you," she said, starting down the road. At the top of the hill she turned and waved to him.

He woke up choking on humid jungle air, but when he pushed back the blanket he was in the cave, and it was his own sweat and heavy breathing that made the air seem damp. The dream had been dark wet sand, shifting above water, quicksand with no bottom or top, no edges; it had quivered and heaved in spasms until he choked.

He knew better than to walk the road. He climbed up the big boulders, feeling his way slowly, remembering ledges and cracks in the cliff wide enough for a person to climb to the top of the mesa. He moved each foot carefully because the sound of rocks rolling down and dry branches breaking would echo in the canyon, and if they were close enough, they would know he was getting away. His heart was pounding. They were coming to end it their way.

He lay flat on his belly and looked down a hundred feet into the canyon. His lungs were burning, and his sides ached. He listened for them, but for a long time he heard nothing in the bottom of the narrow canyon but gusts of wind that strayed over the rim of sandrock and blew his hair in his eyes. The moon lacked only a night of being full, and the flat bare sandrock on the mesa top reflected its light like snow, and he could see his way clearly.

He ran north until he hit the wood-hauling road, and he followed it east to the Acoma boundary fence. He trotted along the fence.

He stopped to rest, and swallowed back his own heavy breathing until he thought his chest would burst; but he had to listen for sounds behind him. The wind was blowing from the west, and it was difficult to be certain but he thought he heard the low hum of an engine.

The wind shifted, and it was from the south then, at his back, and it pushed him along. He was running easily and thinking about what he had to do.

On the ridge south of Engine Rock, he stopped to look down at the Acoma valley and the road. Enchanted Mesa was a dark silvered shadow rising up from the valley into the sky. There weren't any headlights on the road. He listened, but there was only the wind stirring in the juniper branches, rustling the grass around him. It was a restless, dry wind that felt as if it blew out of dusty thin years of the past; it smelled of emptiness and loss.

He had to bring it back on them. There was no other way. He worked his way down the side of the ridge, winding back and forth across the slope, the way horses did to keep their footing.

He eased his feet in, holding the fluted steel edge of the culvert with both hands. He slid his legs and hips inside and ducked his head under. The curved ridges of the culvert pressed against his spine, and he could feel tiny pebbles and fine sand that had been washed inside. He pushed the dry tumbleweeds farther into the pipe with his feet and tried to get comfortable; he would stay there until morning. Then he would wait for someone from Acoma to drive by, someone who didn't know about him. The Government didn't go to work until eight o'clock, and by then he would be far away.

He woke up when the sky was dark gray, the transition from night already started. Blackbirds swarmed above the junipers; their noise increased with the dawn light and they fluttered and circled their roosting places restlessly. The moon had gone down, and only a few stars still blinked in the west. He slid out of the culvert slowly; his legs were stiff from being drawn up near his belly for warmth. He pulled the collar of his Levi jacket up around his chin and shoved his hands into his pockets. It was still dark along the ground and among the trees, but the sky was getting lighter, the blue gray streaked with red light, like a belly opening under a knife. A frail luminous glow pushed out between the edges of horizon and clouds.

He watched the shadows carefully, checking up and down the wood-hauling road that came down the broken shale ridge and intersected the Acoma road. There had been no vehicles all night, but he had to make sure they weren't waiting somewhere for daylight. The tall yellow rice grass and the broken gray shale ridge were undisturbed by outlines of darker objects that did not belong with the junipers and yuccas. Nothing moved up there. To the west the yellow sandstone cliffs were beginning to catch the light. In the distance he saw the windmill where he and Josiah had chased the spotted cattle after they had wandered through the Acoma fence. Somewhere around there the first gray mule had eaten a poison weed and died; the bones would be scattered in the tall grass around the windmill. It was too early to think of bones, even old gray mule bones, but he realized that all along the valley the cliffs were full of shallow caves and overhangs with springs. But there were other caves too, deeper and darker. He turned away. The cloudy yellow sandstone of Enchanted Mesa was still smoky blue before dawn, and only a faint hint of yellow light touched the highest point of the mesa. All things seemed to converge there: roads and wagon trails, canyons with springs, cliff paintings and shrines, the memory of Josiah with his cattle; but the other was distinct and strong like the violet-flowered weed that killed the mule, and the black markings on the cliffs, deep caves along the valley the Spaniards followed to their attack on Acoma. Yet at that moment in the sunrise, it was all so beautiful, everything, from all directions, evenly, perfectly, balancing day with night, summer months with winter. The valley was enclosing this totality, like the mind holding all thoughts together in a single moment.

The strength came from here, from this feeling. It had always been there. He stood there with the sun on his face, and he thought maybe he might make it after all.

He walked north on the Acoma road until the culvert and windmill were out of sight. The sun was climbing, and he could hear warbling meadow birds and mourning doves calling from the tall grass beside the road. The sun was nearing its autumn place in the sky, each day dropping lower, leaving more and more of the sky undilute blue. Before he could hear it, he felt the presence of something else; maybe he felt it through the soles of his boots on the road: vibrations of a vehicle approaching from behind. He stopped and listened until he could hear it, still in the distance; and he started looking for places on the side of the road where he could hide. He argued with himself that he was safe again; he felt strong, and the dread of the night before was gone. But he remembered the Army doctors in their dark green Government cars, and he moved suddenly from the road into the juniper trees. He knelt and looked between the sparse bottom branches of the tree; it seemed like a long time, and his hands were full of cold sweat when the pickup truck finally appeared. It was moving very slowly, the engine whining in low gear. Leroy's truck. Leroy and Harley. His stomach smoothed out and he felt loose. He was smiling and suddenly close to tears because they had come when he needed friends most. He stepped out from behind the juniper tree and waved both arms above his head.

Harley leaned out the window on one elbow. He was wearing a short-sleeve Hawaiian shirt with red and white flowers all over it, and he had a pair of dark glasses in his shirt pocket. Leroy was wearing an old Army shirt with the sleeves cut off at the shoulders. Tayo knew why Harley was driving; Leroy was so drunk that when he opened the door for Tayo, the door handle pulled him off the seat and halfway to the ground. Leroy swayed on the running board, holding the door handle tight, until Tayo steadied him and helped him back inside.

"Thanks, buddy," Leroy said, staring straight ahead, slouching down on the seat.

Harley reached into the big shopping bag and pulled out a can of beer. He handed Tayo the opener. "You're just in time for our party," he said.

"Oh."

"Celebrating the day we enlisted. When was it you and Rocky signed up?"

Tayo shook his head; suddenly he felt thin and dizzy. He was exhausted; even shoving Leroy back into the truck had made him sweat and breathe hard.

"I don't remember," he said, forcing out the words. He was still holding the beer in one hand and the opener in the other. Harley's breath smelled like wine; his eyes were bloodshot and now he was driving the truck fast, talking all the time.

"Hey man, open it! Start drinking! We're gonna have a party!"

Harley poked Leroy in the ribs with an elbow. "Open it for him!"

Leroy reached for the opener and beer can unsteadily. He jerked the opener out of Tayo's hand and it fell on the floorboards.

"Ah shit!" Leroy slurred the words.

"I'll get it." The blood rushed to Tayo's head and he felt around the floorboards blindly for the opener. He

250

gave it to Leroy and sat back on the seat with his eyes closed, breathing hard.

"Hey! Are you sick or something?"

Tayo shook his head. Harley must have heard the rumors Emo had started.

"Just tired, that's all."

Harley didn't slow down for the ruts or bumps, and the truck bounced hard. Leroy leaned hard against Tayo. "Goddamn it, Harley!" Leroy yelled. "I can't open it when you drive that way!"

"Shit! You're too drunk to open it! Here! Let me!" Harley let go of the steering wheel and grabbed the opener and beer can; he leaned over the steering wheel, steadying it with his chest while he punched open the can. Beer spurted out in a foamy spray. Harley shoved it into Tayo's lap. He held his hand over it tight. His shirt and pants were soaked with beer. Leroy was laughing; there was beer dripping off his face. Harley had the accelerator all the way to the floor. The truck was swaying from one side of the road to the other, spinning up rocks and gravel that struck the underside of the truck.

"Hey! You gonna drink it or spill it?"

Leroy laughed while Tayo tried to get the can to his mouth without spilling it or being thrown against the dashboard. The foam was warm; it stung his tongue.

"You guys got a head start on me, don't you?"

"We been at it all night," Leroy said, blinking his eyes, trying to focus on Tayo's face. "Driving around all night, huh, Harley, didn't we?"

"Never listen to a drunk," Harley said to Tayo. "This guy doesn't remember nothing. We were in Gallup last night."

Tayo tried to look at Harley's face when he said that, but Harley was looking away, over his elbow out the window. He swallowed some more warm beer and tried to think calmly. The pickup had come from the south, down the Acoma road, so how could they have been in

Gallup the night before unless they had taken the wagon road and come over the mesa the back way from Mc-Cartys? But they usually stayed on 66, where there was a bar every ten or fifteen miles, or "every six-pack," as Harley liked to say. Harley and Leroy were his buddies. His friends. But he was feeling something terrible inside, and his heart was beating hard now, from what Leroy had said about "driving around all night"; they had come from the direction he had come, behind him, following him. He gripped the can tight, trying to squeeze away the shaking in his hands.

He finished the beer and threw the can out the window. He looked back and watched it bounce into the tall grass and tumbleweeds beside the road. He breathed deeply and closed his eyes. He had to relax and get hold of these thoughts before they scattered in all directions like a herd of sheep. These guys were his friends.

Leroy fumbled with another beer. "Too damn drunk to open them any more! Have to sober up some before I can open any more."

Tayo opened it for him. He opened one for himself and leaned back on the seat. Beer made the feeling recede and slowed down the beating of his heart. The truck's motion and the beer were soothing; the steel and glass closed out everything. The sky, the land were distant then; trees and hills moved past the windshield glass like movie film. It would be easy to get lost in this place of theirs, where the past, even a few hours before, suddenly lost its impact and seemed like a vague dream compared to these sensations: the motion, vibrations of wheels against the road, the warmth of beer in the belly, and the steel cab snug around them. He would rest there, and not think about the night before. He needed to rest for a while, and not think about the story or the ceremony. Otherwise, it would make him crazy and even suspicious of his friends; and without friends he didn't have a chance of completing the ceremony.

She had been right once already when she told him to

leave the springs. So he would hang around with Harley and Leroy; everyone would understand that: riding around, drinking with his buddies. They wouldn't be suspicious then; they wouldn't think he was crazy. He'd just be another drunk Indian, that's all.

He woke up sweating. The sun was shining through the windshield, and the windows were rolled up. The truck was parked at the foot of a rocky little hill covered with cholla. Harley and Leroy were gone. The heat in the cab made him weak and sluggish. He rolled down the window and hung his head out. The beer vomit ran down the truck door into dry weeds. His head was pounding, and he was thirsty. He got out of the truck and could hardly stand up; the muscles of his legs were stiff. He looked around to see where Harley and Leroy were. The country was dry, and the hills were covered with dark lava rock. The earth was eroded to gray clay, and deep arroyos cut through the length of the valley between the mesas. These were the hills northwest of Cañoncito. He sat down on a big gray rock by a cholla. Grayish green salt bushes had taken over the areas between the crisscross of big arroyos. South, in the distance, he could see one big cottonwood tree, the only bright green in that valley. It was growing on the edge of the deepest arroyo, its web of roots exposed, held upright only by a single connecting root. The bank of the arroyo was undercut so deeply that a strong gust of wind would topple the big tree.

A dry hot wind glided up and down the canyon restlessly, shaking the salt bushes and sweeping dust over the tire tracks. His head hurt every time he took a step; shock waves of a foot against the ground registered on skull drums. He was looking for footprints. He listened, and there was nothing but the sound of the wind, like a hawk sweeping close to the ground, whirring wings of wind that called back years long past and the people lost in them, all returning briefly in a gust of wind. The feeling lasted only as long as the sound, but he wanted to go with them, to be swept away. It was difficult then to call up the feeling the stories had, the feeling of Ts'eh and old Betonie. It was easier to feel and to believe the rumors. Crazy. Crazy Indian. Seeing things. Imagining things.

The sun was hot and the sweat was crawling down his head like little black ants. Then he saw their footprints going up the hill; he could see the pebbles and rocks they had knocked loose and the dry grass crushed under boot heel prints.

Tayo was halfway to the top of the hill before he stopped; suddenly it hit him, in the belly, and spread to his chest in a single surge: he knew then that they were not his friends but had turned against him, and the knowledge left him hollow and dry inside, like the locust's shell. He was not sure why he was crying, for the betrayal or because they were lost. Then he heard voices, low and steady tones from the top of the hill. He didn't like the way his heart pounded, because it kept him from hearing, but his head was clear and his legs were solid. Fear made him remember important things. He moved down the hill, careful not to knock loose any rocks or step in the dry tumbleweeds. He knew why he had felt weak and sick; he knew why he had lost the feeling Ts'eh had given him, and why he had doubted the ceremony: this was their place, and he was vulnerable.

He lifted the hood of the truck and started pulling at the ignition wires, trying to remember how the guys overseas hot-wired Army jeeps. He reached under the truck seat and found a rusty screwdriver. The wires were a tangled bundle and his hands were shaking. His mouth was dry and his tongue stuck to his lips when he tried to moisten them. He looked up at the top of the hill, and then around at the sky and the canyon. The sun was moving down in the sky, but the heat still danced above the salt bushes in the canyon. He slipped the screw driver into his lip pocket and started running.

When years before they had first come to the people living on the Cebolleta land grant, they had not said what kind of mineral it was. They were driving U.S. Government cars, and they paid the land-grant association five thousand dollars not to ask questions about the test holes they were drilling. The cloudy orange sandstone mesas and the canyons between them were dry that year; ever since the New Mexico territorial government took the northeast half of the grant, there had not been enough land to feed the cattle anyway. It was over-grazed; rain eroded big arroyos in the gray clay, and the salt bush took hold. There was nothing there the people could use anyway, no silver or gold. The drought had killed off most of the cattle by then, so it really didn't matter if a square mile of land around the mine area was off limits, with high barbed-wire fences around it, and signs in both Spanish and English warning them to keep out.

Early in the spring of 1943, the mine began to flood with water from subterranean springs. They hauled in big pumps and compressors on flat-bed trucks from Albuquerque. The big trucks sank past their axles in the blow sand, and they hired men from Bibo and Moquino to dig around the tandem wheels and to attach tow chains from the trucks to the big tow truck that came. But later in the summer the mine flooded again, and this time no pumps or compressors were sent. They had enough of what they needed, and the mine was closed, but the barbed-wire fences and the guards remained until August 1945. By then they had other sources of uranium, and it was not top secret any more. Big gray vans came and hauled the machinery away. They left behind only the barbed-wire fences, the watchman's shack, and the hole in the earth. Cebolleta people salvaged lumber and tin from the shack, but they had no use for the barbed wire any more; the last bony cattle wandering the dry canyons had died in choking summer duststorms.

Waves of heat caught him, and his legs and lungs were vapor without sensation; only his memory of running and breathing kept him moving and alive. He stumbled and ran behind the sun, not following but dragged with it across arroyos, over mesas and hills. At sundown he was lying on the sand at the bottom of the long mesa, feeling the heat recede from the air and from his body into the earth. The wind came up and he shivered.

He crawled through the strands of barbed wire. Twilight was giving way to darkness. He scooped water off the top of thick green moss that clogged the steel water trough under the windmill. The water was still warm from the sun and it tasted bitter. He sat on the edge of the trough and looked across the wide canyon at the dark mine shaft. Maybe the uranium made the water taste that way. The sandstone and dirt they had taken from inside the mesa was piled in mounds, in long rows, like fresh graves.

Old Grandma told him while he was still sick and weak, lying in the darkened room. She shuffled in and sat down on the edge of his bed. "I have been thinking of something," she said. "It happened while you were gone. I had to get up, the way I do, to use the chamber pot. It was still dark; everyone else was still sleeping. But as I walked back from the kitchen to my bed there was a flash of light through the window. So big, so bright even my old clouded-up eyes could see it. It must have filled the whole southeast sky. I thought I was seeing the sun rise again, but it faded away, and by that time all the dogs around here were barking, like the time that bear was prowling around the trash pile. You remember that, sonny, how they barked. 'My, my,' I said to myself, 'I never thought I would see anything so bright again.'" She was patting his arm as she talked, tapping out the story with her hand. "Your auntie laughed at me when I told her what I saw. But later on that day, Romero came around. He said he saw it too. So bright that it blinded him for a moment; then later on he could still see it flashing when he closed his eyes." She paused, as if she were trying to think of the right words. "You know, I have never understood that thing I saw. Later on there was something about it in the newspaper. Strongest thing on this earth. Biggest explosion that ever happened— that's what the newspaper said." She was shaking her head slowly from side to side. "Now I only wonder why, grandson. Why did they make a thing like that?"

"I don't know, Grandma," he had answered then. But now he knew.

He had been so close to it, caught up in it for so long that its simplicity struck him deep inside his chest: Trinity Site, where they exploded the first atomic bomb, was only three hundred miles to the southeast, at White Sands. And the top-secret laboratories where the bomb had been created were deep in the Jemez Mountains, on land the Government took from Cochiti Pueblo: Los Alamos, only a hundred miles northeast of him now, still surrounded by high electric fences and the ponderosa pine and tawny sandrock of the Jemez mountain canyon where the shrine of the twin mountain lions had always been. There was no end to it; it knew no boundaries; and he had arrived at the point of convergence where the fate of all living things, and even the earth, had been laid. From the jungles of his dreaming he recognized why the Japanese voices had merged with Laguna voices, with Josiah's voice and Rocky's voice; the lines of cultures and worlds were drawn in flat dark lines on fine light sand, converging in the middle of witchery's final ceremonial sand painting. From that time on, human beings were one clan again, united by the fate the destroyers planned for all of them, for all living things; united by a circle of death that devoured people in cities twelve thousand miles away, victims who had never known these mesas, who had never seen the delicate colors of the rocks which boiled up their slaughter.

He walked to the mine shaft slowly, and the feeling became overwhelming: the pattern of the ceremony was completed there. He knelt and found an ore rock. The gray stone was streaked with powdery yellow uranium, bright and alive as pollen; veins of sooty black formed lines with the yellow, making mountain ranges and rivers across the stone. But they had taken these beautiful rocks from deep within earth and they had laid them in a monstrous design, realizing destruction on a scale only *they* could have dreamed.

He cried the relief he felt at finally seeing the pattern, the way all the stories fit together—the old stories, the war stories, their stories—to become the story that was still being told. He was not crazy; he had never been crazy. He had only seen and heard the world as it always was: no boundaries, only transitions through all distances and time.

He turned. The moon was rising above the last mesa he had crossed from the east. A transition was about to be completed: the sun was crossing the zenith to a winter place in the sky, a place where prayers of long winter nights would call out the long summer days of new growth. Tonight the old priests would be praying for the force to continue the relentless motion of the stars. But there were others who would be working this night, casting loose countermotions to suck in a great spiral, swallowing the universe endlessly into the black mouth, their diagrams in black ash on cave walls outlining the end in motionless dead stars. But he saw the constellation in the north sky, and the fourth star was directly above him; the pattern of the ceremony was in the stars, and the constellation formed a map of the mountains in the directions he had gone for the ceremony. For each star there was a night and a place; this was the last night and the last place, when the darkness of night and the light of day were balanced. His protection was there in the sky, in the position of the sun, in the pattern of the stars. He had only to complete this night, to keep the story out of the reach of the destroyers for a few more hours, and their witchery would turn, upon itself, upon them.

Arrowboy got up after she left.
He followed her into the hills
up where the caves were.
The others were waiting.
They held the hoop
and danced around the fire
four times.
The witchman stepped through the hoop
he called out that he would be a wolf.
His head and upper body became hairy like a wolf
But his lower body was still human.
"Something is wrong," he said.
"Ck'o'yo magic won't work
if someone is watching us."

The headlights appeared suddenly from the northeast, tiny points of light, blinking as

259

the vehicle bounced over the road. The small hairs on his neck bristled, but he reasoned with himself: many land-grant people and white ranchers used that road too. He would know soon if the vehicle kept going west or if it turned south down the sandy road overgrown with weeds, and came toward the mine. Cold moved over him when the headlights turned, bigger now, visibly weaving down the road; he could hear the hum of the engine now. They were coming.

He ran past the shaft to the boulders that had been bulldozed away from the opening. The night was getting colder; he could see the steam from his breath in the moonlight. He climbed up boulders big as box cars and squeezed himself into a hollow space between them. It was warm there, the sandrock still held the sun's heat. He leaned forward and pressed his forehead against the narrow opening so that he could see everything.

He expected Leroy's pickup truck, but as the vehicle rounded the last curve before the mine, he could see it was a car. For an instant he thought it might be land-grant people, and his muscles tensed, ready to jump down and run to flag them down for a ride. But there was something too familiar about the sound the car made, a broken muffler sound he had heard before. Emo.

Someone got out and raised the car hood. The other door opened and two more got out. He could hear voices and the sound of water splashing on the ground. He recognized Pinkie's laugh. He smelled a fire and saw three figures bending over a small fire. It flared up suddenly and he saw their faces: Leroy, Pinkie, and Emo. But Harley was missing. They were feeding dry tumbleweeds to the fire, holding them high over their heads and circling the fire before they let go and the tumbleweeds exploded into fiery balls that lighted up the area around the windmill where the car was parked. They had a bottle they passed between them, and Leroy staggered when he walked down the old barbed-wire fence, gathering tumbleweed tangled in the bottom wire.

Pinkie pounded on the hood of the car, and the metallic booming echoed against the sandstone across the narrow valley.

Tayo's knees and elbows hurt from resting against the rock. He dropped to his belly and pulled his head back, away from the crack between the rocks. The destroyers. They would be there all night, he knew it, working for drought to sear the land, to kill the livestock, to stunt the corn plants and squash in the gardens, leaving the people more and more vulnerable to the lies; and the young people would leave, go to towns like Albuquerque and Gallup where bitterness would overwhelm them, and they would lose their hope and finally themselves in drinking.

The witchery would be at work all night so that the people would see only the losses—the land and the lives lost—since the whites came; the witchery would work so that the people would be fooled into blaming only the whites and not the witchery. It would work to make the people forget the stories of the creation and continuation of the five worlds; the old priests would be afraid too, and cling to ritual without making new ceremonies as they always had before, the way they still made new Buffalo Dance songs each year.

Emo pulled down the collapsed frame of the watchman's shed and threw the boards on the fire. The flames extended the circle of light. Pinkie dropped the tire iron; it clattered down the front fender to the ground. They stood behind the car, passing the bottle, taking long swallows, pointing over to the mine shaft and into the rocks where he was hiding. He wondered if they knew he was there, or if they were only planning something else. He wondered if they had tracked him like a thirsty animal, certain they would find him near the only source of water in that area.

He was hungry, and he felt shaky and weak. He hadn't eaten since Ts'eh had left, and he had vomited all the beer. The warmth from the stone was beginning to fade;

his Levi jacket was thin, and he could feel the cold leaking through worn places at the elbows and under the arms. He had seen them now and he was certain; he could go back to tell the people. He was in no condition to confront them. He watched how slowly the moon was rising, and hunched his shoulders against the cold. He would be lucky just to make it home that night.

He looked down at them. If he had not known about their witchery, they might have fooled him. People had been drinking out in the hills on wood-hauling roads and sheep-camp roads since they first bootlegged liquor to Indians. Standing around the fire, passing cheap wine around; Pinkie smashed the empty bottle against the water trough. There were circles of charcoal, tire tracks off side roads and, since the men came back from the war, broken bottle glass all over the reservation. His throat got tight. He might be wrong about them. Harley had helped him last year; he had come and got him moving again. He was exhausted; the fear and the running from that day and from the night before had left him weak. He needed to rest. This ceremony was draining his endurance. He could not feel anything then, not for Josiah or Rocky and not for the woman. Maybe the other Navajos had been right about old Betonie.

Emo and Pinkie kept him there; Pinkie found the tire iron and was pounding the hood of the car again. The sound set his teeth on edge and angered him in a way he had not felt since the day he had stabbed Emo. It was the sound of witchery: smashing through the night, shrill and cold as black metal. It was the empty sound of his nightmares; even the voices he recognized. He covered his ears with both hands and ground his molars together.

The pounding stopped with the scream. He moved forward suddenly, bruising his knees on the rock. The trunk lid was raised and they were standing around it. The screaming was coming from inside the trunk. He pressed his forehead against the rock until he could feel its print on his skin. He turned his head with his ear between

262

the rocks, frantically trying to catch the sound. Harley. He watched them drag him into the light from the coals. Pinkie dropped something into the coals and the fire sprang up; it was Harley's red-and-white Hawaiian print shirt, but in a moment the fire turned the white print bloody red. Leroy and Emo stripped off his jeans, and Pinkie dropped them into the fire. Harley twisted and rolled on the ground; his hands and feet seemed to be tied. Pinkie dropped his boots into the fire; their soles made thick black smoke, and the light from the fire was temporarily obscured. Harley screamed again, and this time Tayo climbed out from the boulders. He heard laughter and when he looked around the corner of the boulder, his heart went numb in his chest, and he wasn't aware of his own rapid breathing any more. In the moonlight he could see Harley's body hanging from the fence, where they had tangled it upright between strands of barbed wire. Harley's brown skin had gone as pale as the cloudy sandstone in the moonlight, and Tayo could see blood shining on his thighs and his fingertips.

He reached into his hip pocket for the screwdriver. He felt the wooden handle and the sharp edges at the end. Squatting close to the ground, he followed the long shadow cast by the continuous mounds of mining debris. He knew what they were doing; Harley had failed them, and all that had been intended for Tayo had now turned on Harley. There was no way the destroyers could lose: either way they had a victim and a corpse. He was close enough to hear them.

"We told you to watch him. We told you to stay there."

"We told you. We told you, and now you know what you got for yourself."

Pinkie held his leg, and Leroy cut the whorl from the bottom of his big toe. Harley screamed hoarsely; the sound trailed off to a groan.

"Scream!" Emo said. "Scream loud so he can hear you."

The screwdriver was slippery in his hands. It nauseated

him to see Harley's body jerking and twitching in the sagging barbed wire, with hands and knives so greedy for human flesh. He fought back a bitter stomach taste; the sweat was running down from under his arms, following the hollow ridges of his ribs. He had to hug his arms close to his side to hold off the shivering.

They had a paper bag they had emptied of wine bottles. Emo was holding it with the palm of his hand supporting the bottom of the bag because it was soaked with blood and the brown paper was beginning to dissolve around the bleeding chunks of human skin. Emo shifted the bag to his other hand and held the bloody palm up to Harley; but Harley's eyes were closed, and he did not seem to be conscious of anything Emo said.

"Look at this, you half-breed! White son of a bitch! You can't hide from this! Look! Your buddy, Harley."

Emo jumped forward with a bottle of wine; it splashed over the ground at Harley's feet, and unlike the blood, which clotted in shiny lumps on the sand, the wine soaked in thin and quick.

"Have some, buddy!" Emo said as he shoved the bottle into Harley's mouth. The glass against the teeth made a brittle grinding sound, and Tayo heard Harley groan. He closed his fingers around the screwdriver and squeezed it until it was part of his hand. He understood that Harley had bargained for it; he realized that Harley knew how it would end if he failed to get the victim he had named. But Tayo could not endure it any longer. He was certain his own sanity would be destroyed if he did not stop them and all the suffering and dying they caused—the people incinerated and exploded, and little children asleep on streets outside Gallup bars. He was not strong enough to stand by and watch any more. He would rather die himself.

He knew he could get to Emo before Pinkie or Leroy could stop him. They were drunk. Emo's words were thick and slurred. Pinkie had stumbled to his knees beside Leroy, squatting next to the fire.

He visualized the contours of Emo's skull; the GI haircut exposed thin bone at the temples, bone that would flex slightly before it gave way under the thrust of the steel edge.

The wind came suddenly and fanned the coals into yellow flames; Leroy jumped back and stumbled hard against Pinkie. Pinkie pushed him away and Leroy fell. "You fucking little queer!" Leroy kicked sand in his face and Pinkie lunged at him. Emo stood close to them; the fat under his chin was wrinkled with his grinning. The fire's reflection made two flashing yellow eyes on Emo's glasses. The wind was moving clouds rapidly across the sky, and as they crossed over the moon, darkness and light rolled back and forth like the men wrestling on the ground. The sand their feet kicked loose made a swirling trail in the wind.

The wind made his sweat go cold. This was the time. But his fingers were numb, and he fumbled with the screwdriver as he tried to rub warmth back into his hands. There would be no one to help Emo. But Tayo stayed on his knees in the shadows. Leroy had a knee on Pinkie's throat, and he could hear raspy choking sounds. Emo was laughing loudly, pointing at the body hanging stiffly, swaying a little in the gusts of wind, then pointing at Leroy kneeling on Pinkie's throat.

The moon was lost in a cloud bank. He moved back into the boulders. It had been a close call. The witchery had almost ended the story according to its plan; Tayo had almost jammed the screwdriver into Emo's skull the way the witchery had wanted, savoring the yielding bone and membrane as the steel ruptured the brain. Their deadly ritual for the autumn solstice would have been completed by him. He would have been another victim, a drunk Indian war veteran settling an old feud; and the Army doctors would say that the indications of this end has been there all along, since his release from the mental ward at the Veterans' Hospital in Los Angeles. The white people would shake their heads, more proud than sad that it took a white man to survive in their world and that these Indians couldn't seem to make it. At home the people would blame liquor, the Army, and the war, but the blame on the whites would never match the vehemence the people would keep in their own bellies, reserving the greatest bitterness and blame for themselves, for one of themselves they could not save.

He crouched between the boulders and laid his head against the rock to look up at the sky. Big clouds covered the moon, but he could still see the stars. He had arrived at a convergence of patterns; he could see them clearly now. The stars had always been with them, existing beyond memory, and they were all held together there. Under these same stars the people had come down from White House in the north. They had seen mountains shift and rivers change course and even disappear back into the earth; but always there were these stars. Accordingly, the story goes on with these stars of the old war shield; they go on, lasting until the fifth world ends, then maybe beyond. The only thing is: it has never been easy.

They heaved the body into the trunk and slammed the trunk lid and car doors shut. The red taillights shrank into the distance; the chalky ring of ashes merged into the moonlight. The wind gusted across the tire tracks and imprints of human shoulders and hands; and there was nothing left but broken bottles and a black mark on the ground where the fire had been.

He would go back there now, where she had shown him the plant. He would gather the seeds for her and plant them with great care in places near sandy hills. The rainwater would seep down gently and the delicate membranes would not be crushed or broken before the emergence of tiny fingers, roots, and leaves pressing out in all directions. The plants would grow there like the story, strong and translucent as the stars.

His body was lost in exhaustion; he kept moving, his bones and skin staggering behind him. He dreamed with his eyes open that he was wrapped in a blanket in the back of Josiah's wagon, crossing the sandy flat below Paguate Hill. The cholla and juniper shivered in the wind, and the rumps of the two gray mules were twin moons in front of him. Josiah was driving the wagon, old Grandma was holding him, and Rocky whispered "my brother." They were taking him home.

The creosote and tar smell of the railroad tracks woke him from the dreaming. The cinders made hollow crunching noises under his boots. He had come a long way with them; but it was his own two feet that got him there. He stepped high over the steel rails and went down the cinder-bank roadbed toward the river. When he felt the dampness of the river, he started running. The sun was pushing against the gray horizon hills, sending yellow light across the clouds, and the yellow river sand was speckled with the broken shadows of tamaric and river willow. The transition was completed. In the west and in the south too, the clouds with round heavy bellies had gathered for the dawn. It was not necessary, but it was right, and even if the sky had been cloudless the end was the same. The ear for the story and the eye for the pattern were theirs; the feeling was theirs: we came out of this land and we are hers.

In the distance he could hear big diesel trucks rumbling down Highway 66 past Laguna. The leaves of the big cottonwood tree had turned pale yellow; the first sunlight caught the tips of the leaves at the top of the old tree and made them bright gold. They had always been loved. He thought of her then; she had always loved him, she had never left him; she had always been there. He crossed the river at sunrise.

Hummingbird and Fly thanked him.
They took the tobacco to old Buzzard.
"Here it is. We finally got it but it
sure wasn't very easy."
"Okay," Buzzard said
"Go back and tell them
I'll purify the town."

And he did—
first to the east
then to the south
then to the west
and finally to the north.
Everything was set straight again
after all that ck'o'yo' magic.

The storm clouds returned
the grass and plants started growing again.
There was food
and the people were happy again.

So she told them
"Stay out of trouble
from now on.

It isn't very easy
to fix up things again.
Remember that
next time
some ck'o'yo magician
comes to town."

At the center of the kiva, old man Ku'oosh was poking kindling into the potbellied stove. The new adobe floor was still curing and the hairline cracks were not yet filled with plaster. The whitewash was only partially completed, and the kiva murals were veiled under the white clay wash, not yet repainted for the winter ceremonies. The old men nodded at a folding steel chair with ST. JOSEPH MISSION stenciled in white paint on the back. He sat down, wondering how far the chair had gone from the parish hall before it came to the kiva. He looked at them sitting on the wooden benches that went all the way around the long kiva. They nodded at him, and when Ku'oosh was satisfied with the fire he joined them. In the southwest corner there were boxes and trunks with tarps pulled over them to protect them from uninitiated eyes.

It took a long time to tell them the story; they stopped him frequently with questions about the location and the time of day; they asked about the direction she had come from and the color of her eyes. It was while he was sitting there, facing southeast, that he noticed how the four windows along the south wall of the kiva had a particular relationship to this late autumn position of the sun.

A'moo'ooh, you say you have seen her
Last winter
up north

with Mountain Lion
the hunter

All summer
she was south
near Acu

They started crying
the old men started crying
"A'moo'ooh! A'moo'ooh!"
You have seen her
We will be blessed
again.

At noon one of old Grandma's grandnieces brought Ku'oosh two lard pails. The steam from one smelled like red chili stew; the other was full of oven bread and pieces of fried bread. They passed around the pail of stew, using pieces of bread to scoop out the meat and to soak up the chili. When they had finished, he followed them to the back of the kiva where the gourd dipper floated on top of the water pail; he drank last, and after he drank, Ku'oosh poked at the fire and dropped the dipper into the flames.

When the sun was dropping near the center of the west window, they stood up. They were going home to rest and eat supper; they would be back later, after dark, old man Ku'oosh told him. He could have water, but no food; he was not to leave the kiva. Ku'oosh showed him an old enamel chamber pot with a lid. He said to drink the water cupping it in the hands.

They unraveled
the dead skin
Coyote threw
on him.

They cut it up
bundle by bundle.

Every evil
which entangled him
was cut
to pieces.

They found Harley and Le-roy together in the big boulders below the road off Paguate Hill. The old GMC pickup was crushed around them like the shiny metal coffin the Veterans Office bought for each of them. In that way it was not much different than if they had died at Wake Island or Iwo Jima: the bodies were dismembered beyond recognition and the coffins were sealed. The morning of the funeral an honor guard from Albuquerque fired the salute; two big flags covered the coffins completely, and it looked as if the people from the village had gathered only to bury the flags.

Auntie talked to him now the way she had talked to Robert and old Grandma all those years, with an edge of accusation about to surface between her words. But after old man Ku'oosh had come around, her eyes dropped from his face as if there were nothing left to watch for. But she said that now the women at Church came to her privately, after mass or before the bingo games, to ask her how she had managed all those years to face the troubles which had been dropped into her lap. And she remarked to old Grandma, dozing beside her stove with the dial turned all the way to HIGH, and to Tayo who was oiling his hunting boots: "I tell them, 'It isn't easy. It never has been easy,' I say."

She came in from mass that morning with a look of triumph.

"Pinkie finally got killed," she said, without even bothering to remind them she had said it would happen all along, ever since he had lost those sheep of hers while he was at their sheep camp.

"How did it happen?"

"Yes, what happened?" old Grandma said, coming out of a doze to sit up straight in her chair.

"He was washing dishes at Sarracino's sheep camp."

"Aww, that lazy old thing," old Grandma said. "How could he have been washing dishes?"

"Remember how I warned you, Tayo? I told you I didn't want that crowd hanging around our ranch with their drinking and carrying on."

"Was Emo there?" Tayo asked.

"Well, he was the one! He did it! Pinkie was standing there, washing dishes in a pan on top of the stove. The others were sitting around the table drinking. They say here were empty beer cans and wine bottles all over the place. Anyway, they say they got to playing around with that rifle Sarracino keeps there."

Old Grandma scuffed her slippers against the floor in front of her chair and rattled her cane against the chair leg. "Dear, could you give Tayo that money in my pocketbook? I think my stove is getting low on oil." She buttoned the top buttons of her old black sweater and pulled her shawl up around her chin.

"Mama," Auntie said, "I'm *trying* to tell you how poor Pinkie got killed instantly. Shot in the back of the head. Besides, Robert filled it yesterday."

Old Grandma acted as if she didn't hear what Auntie said. "Is he in jail?"

"The FBI called it an accident." Auntie shook her head. "After all the trouble he made for us—that time with Tayo—but I heard they told him to go away. They told him to never come back around here. The old man said that. They told him." Auntie paused. "I heard he went to California," she said.

"California," Tayo repeated softly, "that's a good place for him."

Old Grandma shook her head slowly, and closed her cloudy eyes again. "I guess I must be getting old," she said, "because these goings-on around Laguna don't get me excited any more." She sighed, and laid her head back on the chair. "It seems like I already heard these stories before . . . only thing is, the names sound different."

Whirling darkness
started its journey
with its witchery
and
its witchery
has returned upon it.

Its witchery
has returned
into its belly.

Its own witchery

has returned
all around it.

Whirling darkness
has come back on itself.
It keeps all its witchery
to itself.

It doesn't open its eyes
with its witchery.

It has stiffened
with the effects of its own witchery.

It is dead for now.
It is dead for now.
It is dead for now.
It is dead for now.

Sunrise,
accept this offering,
Sunrise.

About the Author

LESLIE MARMON SILKO was born in Albuquerque in 1948, of mixed ancestry—Laguna Pueblo, Mexican, and white—as she
describes herself. She grew up on the Laguna Pueblo Reservation, where she now
lives with her husband and two children.
Her stories have appeared in many magazines, in the anthology *A Man to Send
Rainclouds*, in Martha Foley's *Best Short
Stories of 1975* and *Two Hundred Years of
Great American Short Stories*. She is also a
widely published poet.

More Bestsellers From SIGNET

(0451)

☐ **THEY SHOULDN'T MAKE YOU PROMISE THAT** by Lois Simmie. (118669—$2.50)

☐ **SLEEPING BEAUTY** by L.L. Greene. (115481—$2.50)*

☐ **MIRIAM AT 34** by Alan Lechuk. (113306—$2.50)

☐ **THANK YOU ALL VERY MUCH** by Margaret Drabble. (096088—$1.75)

☐ **THE WILTONS** by William Bitterworth. (095200—$2.75)*

☐ **MIRRORS** by Kay Klem. (118626—$3.50)*

☐ **THE NIGHT CHASERS** by Jamey Cohen. (120604—$3.50)*

☐ **THE UNHOLY** by Alex Nebrensky. (118634—$2.95)*

☐ **UNHOLY CHILD** by Catherine Breslin. (094778—$3.50)*

☐ **THE MIDWIFE** by Gay Coulter. (115031—$3.95)*

☐ **KISS MOMMY GOODBYE** by Joy Fielding. (115449—$3.50)*

☐ **COMING ATTRACTIONS** by Fannie Flagg. (115074—$2.50)*

*Prices slightly higher in Canada

**Buy them at your local
bookstore or use coupon
on next page for ordering.**

Great Reading from SIGNET

SIGNET Bestsellers

**Buy them at your local
bookstore or use coupon
on next page for ordering.**

Fabulous Fiction From SIGNET